DEATH OF A CORPSE

DEATH OF A CORPSE

KENZIE KIRSCH MEDICAL THRILLER
BOOK SEVEN

P.D. WORKMAN

PD WORKMAN

ISBN: 9781774684245 (KDP Paperback)
ISBN: 9781774684252 (KDP Hardcover)
ISBN: 9781774684269 (Large Print)
ISBN: 9781774684276 (Lulu Paperback)
ISBN: 9781774684283 (Kindle)
ISBN: 9781774684290 (ePub)

ALSO BY P.D. WORKMAN

MYSTERY/SUSPENSE:

Kenzie Kirsch Medical Thrillers

Unlawful Harvest

Doctored Death

Dosed to Death

Gentle Angel

Rushin' Death

Posed for Death

Death of a Corpse

Zachary Goldman Mysteries

Private Investigator

She Wore Mourning

His Hands Were Quiet

She Was Dying Anyway

He Was Walking Alone

They Thought He was Safe

He Was Not There

Her Work Was Everything

She Told a Lie

He Never Forgot

She Was At Risk

He Drowned in Memory

Their Walls Were Empty

They Came for Him

They Sought Vengeance (Coming Soon)

She Was Their Target (Coming Soon)

His Fear Was Real (Coming Soon)

Parks Pat Mysteries

Police Procedural Set in Canada

Out with the Sunset

Long Climb to the Top

Dark Water Under the Bridge

Immersed in the View

Skimming Over the Lake

Hazard of the Hills

Knows the Hills (Coming Soon)

Spanning the Creek (Coming Soon)

Sanctuary in the Stream (Coming Soon)

Stand Alone Suspense Novels

Looking Over Your Shoulder

Lion Within

Pursued by the Past

In the Tick of Time

Loose the Dogs

AND MORE AT PDWORKMAN.COM

For all of those who still
have a tale to tell

1

Y ou sure you're ready to go back to work?" Zachary asked.

Kenzie looked up from her phone to meet his gaze, uncertain whether he was serious. With his anxiety, it was not outside of the realm of possibility that he was worried about whether she was ready to go back to work. He sometimes worried about things she thought trivial or obsessed over some issue that was adjacent to what she would have expected him to worry about, as if he were trying to avoid the real problem.

But when she looked into his face, she saw the humor in his eyes and knew he was teasing. He knew very well how difficult it had been for her to relax and enjoy being away from the Medical Examiner's Office for the past week. Not that it was a vacation that she was supposed to enjoy. It was a suspension, not a reward for doing a great job on the autopsy of Joseph Howard. But she had tried to treat it like it was a break she had planned, taking the opportunity to give the house a deep clean and get to some projects she had been putting off.

Zachary would probably be happy to have her out from underfoot. He was used to being able to work alone during the day. Sometimes he was on the phone or out talking to clients or subjects face to face, but much of the work he did was from the computer, and he didn't like having to move from one place to another because Kenzie

1

was vacuuming or distracting him with some other job. While he was capable of hyperfocusing on a file or task, he had been anxious about Kenzie's suspension and how she was feeling, so he was alert to every movement she made. Even across the house, she could sense him monitoring what she was doing, listening for anything that might indicate that she needed his help.

They had both been on top of each other too much, tiptoeing around in an effort not to bother each other, and then snapping at each other when it got to be too much. Couples stuff. Kenzie knew it wasn't anything serious, and that things would go back to normal once she was back at work, but Zachary had already been through one failed marriage and was constantly worried that Kenzie was going to turn on him like Bridget had, unable to stand his shortcomings any longer.

"I'm pretty sure, yeah," Kenzie agreed dryly.

"Anxious to get back to your patients?"

"Probably more anxious than they are for me to get back."

He chuckled. "I'm sure they'll open up to you once you get started."

Kenzie groaned. That was a new one. "How long have you been saving that?"

He shrugged, suppressing a smile. "I figured I had to get some new material. The old stuff was a little *cold* and *stiff*."

Kenzie shook her head. "Give me some of that coffee. I don't think I can take you uncaffeinated this morning."

He had a mug ready for her. Kenzie sat at the table, putting her phone away so they could visit undistracted. Zachary had made an effort to have breakfast on the table once she was out of the shower and dressed, and a glance did not reveal anything he had missed. That told her that he had put a lot of effort into it because he usually would miss at least one essential element. Kenzie picked up her knife and the jar of marmalade and started to spread the marmalade on her buttered toast.

"What will your day be like today?" she asked him as he unwrapped his granola bar. She noticed he was wincing and tried to figure out what was bothering him.

"After I finish crying over you going back to work? I don't know; the whole day is pretty much a write-off after that. I don't know how I'll be able to focus on anything else."

He was still teasing, though. He might be a little anxious about her returning to work, but if he was, he wasn't letting it seep into their conversation. Once Kenzie was gone, she was sure he would throw himself into his email or another task, and wouldn't have another thought about her until she got home that night. Or maybe at lunch, if his growling stomach reminded him to take a break and eat. Sometimes he called her at lunch to touch base.

"Working on that missing teen?" Kenzie prompted.

"Yeah, that will probably be most of my day. With any luck, I'll be able to get a good lead on her. Maybe get a chance to talk to her and encourage her to go back home."

"Do you think so?"

"On a preliminary review, I think there's a good chance. It's the first time she's run away. It was after a fight. Chances are, she'll wake up and regret it and be looking for a way to return home without losing face. She's probably on a friend's couch."

"That doesn't sound too bad, then. She's not an addict or off with a gang banger boyfriend, or a victim of trafficking?"

"I don't think so. Not this time. There *might* be a boyfriend. That's one thing that I'll be trying to find out. But from what I've found so far, I don't think she's that mature."

"Kids can surprise you."

He nodded and munched on his granola bar. "I know that. I'm not saying the parents don't think she was mature enough for a boyfriend. I've looked at her social media, friends, school stuff, and searched her bedroom. I don't see any sign that she's interested in having a serious boyfriend right now or anyone else romantic. I don't think she'll be able to stay away from school for long, even if she doesn't want to go home. That's where her friends are. She spends most of her free time on team sports. She's going to be missing that connection."

"That's good." Kenzie washed down a bite of toast with a swig of hot coffee. "It should be a happy ending, then."

3

"Always nice to be able to bring a kid home. *And* get paid for it."

Kenzie reached for her phone, then pulled back her hand. They had a pretty strict "no phones at the table" rule to help them focus on each other instead of the constant pull of technology.

"I'm guessing that won't be the case for Elysse Allen," she commented.

Zachary sighed and nodded. "I'm glad I wasn't called on to investigate that one—way too much media attention. I wouldn't be able to make a move without an entourage following me. I think she's almost as popular as Brittany."

Brittany Blake was a social media darling who had been stranded with them in a mountain resort. She had rented one of the other cabins. Kenzie had known how popular Instagrammers and other social media moguls could be. Still, she hadn't really understood the phenomenon until meeting Brittany, and after everything that had happened while they were there. It was astounding. And Zachary was right about Elysse Allen. If she hadn't achieved Brittany-level fame before her disappearance, the report that she was missing had certainly catapulted her into internet fame now.

She was everywhere you looked. Or her face was, anyway. Kenzie could barely turn on her phone or computer without seeing Elysse's face below a news item, on TV, in a social media feed, or in her inbox. Even without turning on a screen, she could see Elysse's face on newspapers, billboards, and flyers everywhere she went. Vermont was a small state, and they had adopted Elysse Allen as *their* cause. Vermonters would not rest until she was found.

"We'll leave that one to the police," Kenzie agreed. "Let them take any flak for her not being found yet."

Zachary was a private investigator and, while he sometimes crossed paths with the police, they preferred that he not have anything to do with any case they were actively investigating. So he ended up with smaller cases like the disappearance of the schoolgirl, which the police might have looked into but hadn't found anything significant on. They would keep their eyes open, but had not found any evidence of foul play or that the girl was in any danger. As Zachary said, she was probably sleeping on a friend's couch and would come home sooner or later. She had left voluntarily and would likely return in a day or two without incident. Not something the police wanted to put a lot of manpower into.

"Well…" Kenzie popped the last corner of toast into her mouth. "I guess I should probably be getting on my way."

Zachary bounced out of his chair, leaving his granola bar half-eaten. "What do you want for lunch? I was going to make you something to take with you."

Kenzie was notoriously bad for wanting to have something good and healthy for lunch, yet not making anything and then relying on the vending machine in the basement of the police station, full of stale sandwiches and unappetizing snacks. She glanced at the time displayed on the microwave.

"I really should be heading out soon."

"We can get you something that's quick." Zachary turned toward the cupboard and fridge, pursing his lips thoughtfully. He had prepared a lunch for Kenzie once before, assembled out of his various packaged snacks. But she didn't think that would do it for her this time. Zachary looked at her and raised one eyebrow. "Chicken and Stars?" he suggested.

It was a childhood favorite he had just recently reintroduced into his diet. But it wasn't Kenzie's favorite. She rolled her eyes. "Not Chicken and Stars."

He put his hand over his heart. "I'm wounded that you don't appreciate my culinary skills."

"It's not your culinary skills; it's just what's in the can." Kenzie waved the issue of lunch aside. "We'll get something for lunch next time. Today I'll just grab something at work."

Zachary wrinkled his nose.

"Not something *at* work," Kenzie clarified. "Something *near* work. A sandwich shop or diner."

"I don't think you want to be eating out of the work refrigerator."

Kenzie shook her head. "No. Not out of the big one," she agreed. She put on her shoes and grabbed her purse. "See you tonight. Have a good day!"

"Okay." He kissed her, held her for an instant longer than

expected, and then released her. "You have a good day too. Don't kill anybody."

"All of my patients are already dead."

"You hope."

"They'd better be!"

2

The only person watching the clock was Kenzie herself. There wasn't anyone at the office making sure that she arrived at exactly the right time. She didn't have to clock in and out. She just showed up and got a start on the work on her computer and desk. She tried to time her arrival so that she got there ahead of Dr. Wiltshire, so that she had time to review the emails, lab work, and any new remains that had been checked in overnight, and have everything organized by the time he got there.

Sometimes he foiled her by being there early, however. Kenzie knew she probably should have expected him to be there ahead of her on her first day back after the suspension. Some kind of procedure to acknowledge that she had been away for disciplinary reasons, but was now back after serving her time.

"Let's have a quick meet," Dr. Wiltshire offered as soon as he saw her walk up to her desk. "We'll grab the boardroom. You'll still be able to see if anyone comes to your desk."

Kenzie's desk was the public face of the morgue. At the reception area, she gave people forms to fill out when they had requests. She answered phones and emails. She redirected people when they took the wrong elevator down and were looking for the cafeteria. Even though she would never recommend that anyone eat at the cafeteria.

As long as she kept all of those things under control, and any other administrative duties, she could also join Dr. Wiltshire in autopsy, sometimes performing postmortems on her own as she grew more experienced and needed to call on him less. She was still supervised, but it wasn't like she would get any complaints from the patients.

Kenzie smiled her acknowledgment and sighed as she put her purse into the desk drawer and locked it. She didn't like going directly into a meeting without having checked her email or phone messages. She liked to know what was going on before she did anything else.

She followed Dr. Wiltshire into the boardroom. A box of donuts and a carafe of coffee were already on the table. Kenzie eyed the donuts. "I just had breakfast…"

"Well, you probably didn't have very much. If you're not hungry, you can wait until later. Have one for lunch."

Kenzie remembered how she had told Zachary that she would get something healthy for lunch today. She really did need to be careful of baking. She liked sweets a little too much.

"Later," she acknowledged. She would see how long she could hold out. Maybe she could get through the day without sampling the tasty pastries.

"Have a seat." Dr. Wiltshire sat down himself. He looked at her over the rims of his rectangular glasses frames for a minute, then took them off. "Glad to have you back. Things just don't run as smoothly here without you."

"Thank you. I'm glad to be back too."

"I'm sure you are. I hope you didn't drive Zachary crazy during your 'break.'"

"Well… yeah, I did."

Dr. Wiltshire chuckled. "We'll have to make sure he gets a break then, won't we?"

"I am not going to say or do anything that will reflect poorly on this office," Kenzie assured him. "I'm sorry for everything that happened, and it won't happen again."

"I'm sure it won't. We have to remember that the eyes of the public are on us. They expect us to act with the proper decorum and not to say or do anything that would worry people or make them distrust our findings."

"Yes."

Dr. Wiltshire nodded. "I'm sure I don't need to belabor the point."

Kenzie put her hand on the table, readying herself to stand up and return to her desk.

"Have you been watching the developments on the Elysse Allen case?" Dr. Wiltshire asked.

"Well… trying not to, actually. But it's everywhere. I wonder what her family thinks of all of the publicity. I suppose they like it, because the more people know what happened to Elysse, the better the chances of finding her."

"Yeah, they don't seem to shun the limelight."

Kenzie nodded her agreement. They definitely did not avoid any opportunities to talk to the media. It seemed like someone in her family was always talking to the reporters, trying to keep everyone not just informed, but engaged, almost frantic. A bunch of people running around like chickens with their heads cut off wouldn't help the investigators much. They needed to be able to do their jobs.

"Well, in case you haven't seen everything that's been on the news lately, they're bringing in dogs to join the search and rescue team today."

"That's a good idea. I'm surprised they haven't had any in earlier."

"They have had several scent dogs in to check out the various places she might have been and to see if they could get a trackable trail on her."

"Oh." Kenzie raised her brows. "What's going on now, then?"

"They're bringing in cadaver dogs."

"To see whether she died and is buried somewhere close by?"

Dr. Wiltshire nodded gravely. "Yes. The search has been ongoing for several days, and the police are not very optimistic about being able to find her alive. If she is in the wilderness, lost, injured, or detained by some third party, she's running out of time. Or has already run out of time. It's time to switch the focus of the search from search and rescue to recovery."

"Oh, dear. Her poor family." Kenzie had known that it would be coming. They couldn't keep a rescue mission going on forever. They needed to be realistic and accept that she was probably gone. It had probably been too late when they started looking for her. By the time her boyfriend had decided that enough time had passed and he needed to file a report with the police. If Kenzie understood the headlines correctly, he had waited until she had been missing for several days before getting the police on to it.

Was it any wonder he was the prime suspect?

"They will have to accept reality sooner or later," Dr. Wiltshire said.

Kenzie nodded and again prepared to stand. Talking about stories in the news was small talk, and she needed to get back to work and make sure everything was whipped back into shape.

"I'm telling you this," Dr. Wiltshire said slowly, "because the prime search area is just a few miles away."

Kenzie's heart beat harder as she processed this. "In Roxboro?"

"Within our jurisdiction."

"So if they find her remains, she might be brought here."

"She will be."

Kenzie tried to think of all the consequences of such a case. Media and politicians calling her. Psychics. Who knew who else? Maybe people trying to sneak in to get a picture of the remains themselves.

They would need to place Elysse's examination at the top of the list. There was no way the public would let anyone else ahead of their darling. Dr. Wiltshire should do the post on it, or at least lead. Kenzie would have to be careful how much information about the postmortem she said to anyone.

"This will be quite the media circus," Dr. Wiltshire said, nodding his agreement with what he read in her face. "We must be very careful every step of the way."

"I won't say anything to the reporters."

"Or to *anyone*. Not someone riding the elevator that you think is a law enforcement officer. Not someone who invites you over for a drink. An old friend who touches base and wants to know what you've been doing lately."

"No. I understand."

"Good. At the moment," Dr. Wiltshire pushed himself up from the table, "we know nothing. We have no statement to make. We are just waiting to see what happens."

"There isn't any guarantee that they'll even find anything."

"No. They could be wrong. She could be absolutely fine."

But it wasn't very likely. More than likely, Elysse Allen was dead.

3

T he morning passed without incident. Kenzie had a donut
for lunch—which she figured was better than having lunch
and a donut—and kept on top of the administrative work
that had piled up while she was gone. Julie had been there at least
part of the time to try to keep up with the filing and phone messages.
But she didn't do everything—and Kenzie wouldn't have wanted
her to.

Dr. Wiltshire stayed around until mid-afternoon, when he had to
attend an administrative meeting. Something to do with the Attorney
General's office, Kenzie thought.

Then the call from Dr. Wiltshire came in. Kenzie looked at the
caller ID and picked up the receiver.

"Doctor?"

"They found something."

"What? Who? What did they find?"

"The cadaver dogs found something. I don't have the full details.
Those will come later. Actually, we'll be the ones making the report."

"Okay...?"

Kenzie knew that it came out as a question, and it was. Why was
Dr. Wiltshire calling Kenzie to tell her about the remains being
found? Did he need her to coordinate transfer?

"It's at a little backwater called Petty Pond. I need to stay where I am," Dr. Wiltshire explained. "There is going to be a lot to coordinate from here. I'd like you to do the site review."

"Oh. Okay." Kenzie tried to readjust her thinking to this. She wasn't just there to tell the transport team where to store the remains. "Can you give me the coordinates, and I'll head out there?"

"You bet." He waited a moment to ensure she was ready before giving her the longitude and latitude. Kenzie wrote them down. She would have to input them into her GPS to find her way there.

"Don't forget your ID," Dr. Wiltshire warned. "No one else will be allowed into the site, even if they've got a really good story."

"Even with the medical examiner's van?"

Dr. Wiltshire chuckled. "Well, you would think that would give it away. But then, anyone could paint 'Medical Examiner's Office' on a white van."

"I suppose," Kenzie admitted. But she didn't think anyone would try that. Nevertheless, she would do as Dr. Wiltshire said and ensure she had all of the proper credentials. It would be highly embarrassing to show up at the crime scene and not be allowed in.

Kenzie and Carlos quickly left the streets of Roxboro behind, first hitting the smoothly paved highways and then branching off onto smaller and smaller roads until they were down to gravel roads and beaten paths through the trees. It was more than just remote. Kenzie wondered why anyone would have been camping in such wilderness. It didn't seem like the type of place that a celebrity would go to take pictures. She could imagine a Brittany look-alike in a city park or some resort area easily accessible from town, taking all her selfies and inspirational shots. And not a park that was accessible from little Roxboro, but from Burlington or Brattleboro, somewhere larger and more sophisticated.

The vegetation was green and lush. Vermont's fabled trees crowded around the car. She crept along the road, hoping it would lead her to the right place. She would not want to make the news by getting lost looking for the crime scene. Or by disappearing alto-gether down some ravine. Sometimes the wilderness swallowed people up and it was years before it revealed its secrets. Carlos sat beside her, busy with his phone, uninterested in their surroundings.

There was a movement in the trees to the right of the road. Kenzie looked over and the figure resolved into the shape of a state trooper, dressed in the familiar tan uniform. He motioned for her to continue on the road, motioning a repeated rolling forward motion to keep her going. She raised a hand to greet him. He nodded and kept motioning.

At least she knew she was going in the right direction. At a bend in the road, she saw yellow crime scene tape and another state trooper, his glasses a mirrored black. He leaned toward her window. Kenzie stopped and rolled the window down.

"Medical Examiner?" the state trooper asked.

Kenzie nodded. "Assistant to the Chief Medical Examiner," she clarified. She needed to make sure that he understood her exact posi-tion. That he didn't think that she was holding herself out to be anything other than what she was.

The trooper nodded impatiently. "Sure. This way. Stick to the right. You'll be there within five minutes."

Kenzie rolled forward again. Following his instructions, she found herself at a small gathering of police cars and unmarked cars with people and dogs milling about. One of them waved her forward. "This way…"

Kenzie followed his directions to the edge of an embankment. She didn't like to go even as far as he directed, worried that the edge would crumble and she would end up in the water. What a fiasco that would be. She didn't relish having to call Dr. Wiltshire to say that she had dumped his van in the water. Or to end up soaked in the muddy water herself.

Once she was as close to the edge as she could stand, she parked the van and climbed out.

"You could get closer," the trooper informed her.

"That's okay."

"The farther you are back, the farther you'll have to carry the body."

Carlos got out of the car as well, walking to the edge to look down on the scene below them.

"We'll manage," Kenzie said curtly. She would prefer carrying the remains a few feet farther to destabilizing the embankment and ending up in the drink. Sometimes calculating the risk/reward ratio was not hard at all.

They suited up, getting on the protective gear necessary to prevent any cross contamination of the evidence. From that point on, it was vital to take every precaution necessary to assure the integrity of the evidence.

"You'll need to go around this way," the trooper led her along the embankment until they reached a sort of cutaway with a path sloping toward the water, winding back and forth. "Just keep following the path. It will take you over there." He motioned to a group of men that Kenzie could barely make out through the trees and vegetation.

It *was* going to be a little way to cart the body but, if that was the best way to get it out, that was what they would do.

Kenzie stepped onto the pathway first, Carlos following. She looked back at him anxiously, wanting to make sure that he wasn't going to trip and fall into her as they went down the slope. But he seemed to be sure-footed.

"I'm with you, boss," Carlos assured her.

"Okay. Let's go have a look."

She led the way, listening to Carlos's steps behind her, hoping she would have enough warning if he did stumble and fall. He was a big guy, and she didn't want to be flattened.

They reached the side of the water without mishap and made their way carefully toward the bystanders.

Kenzie could smell the remains before she could see them. No cadaver dog necessary. She got closer, picking each step carefully. She hadn't worn hip waders and hoped she wouldn't need them.

The body was partially obscured by weeds. Kenzie surveyed it dispassionately. About the size and build she had expected. Only partially immersed in the water. She could see a long hank of hair. It was hard to tell the color while it was wet, but it seemed light. Maybe blond. Maybe a light brown.

"The dogs found her?" Kenzie asked the cops standing around.

"Yeah, part of the search and rescue effort."

Kenzie shook her head. "Cadaver dogs are not for search and rescue."

"Well…" the officer who had answered her colored a little. "I mean, obviously, it isn't a rescue at this point."

"Right," Kenzie agreed. "Recovery, not search and rescue."

"Sure. Same difference."

Kenzie kept her mouth shut and didn't argue. "Has anyone touched the body?"

She looked around at the group. They all shook their heads, indicating that they had not. Considering the state of the body, Kenzie was not surprised. With a fresh body, the responders might try to pull her out of the water or take a pulse but, with it in an advanced state of decomposition, there was no reason to.

Kenzie already had gloves on. She crouched as close as she could and put out her hand, seeing if she could reach without tumbling in. She grasped the wrist and gave it a gentle tug. The body bobbed a little. It did not fall apart at her touch. Maybe it wouldn't be too hard to get out of the water in one piece. Or at least, in a minimal number of pieces.

"Get a pulse?" Carlos joked.

"No pulse," Kenzie returned without a smile. Some decorum was expected when observing and discussing human remains. "I think we'll be able to move her with the stretcher. Doesn't look too bad."

"Are you kidding?" One of the cops gagged audibly. "Doesn't look too bad?"

"Well," Kenzie looked back at the remains. "As a practical matter. It doesn't look like she will be too hard to transport. She is in a fairly advanced stage of decomposition, but just the transportation shouldn't be too bad. Do you have some techs to gather the evidence?" Kenzie pulled out her camera to snap a few pictures of the body in situ.

"They're probably just a couple of minutes behind you. Once you've gotten a good look…"

"Great." Kenzie walked in an arc around the body, getting other viewpoints and pushing back the vegetation to get the best shots she could. She backed up to get a wider view and took some establishing shots. The cop was right, and the techs were there in a couple of minutes.

"Is it her?" one of the techs questioned immediately. "Elysse Allen?"

"We haven't yet identified the remains," Kenzie told him; though, of course, he would know that.

Everybody would want to know that.

"They are consistent with Allen's body size and hair," Kenzie admitted, "but that is not a positive ID. It's going to take a while, with the shape the body is in."

"DNA? Dental evidence? Do we have her dental files yet?"

Kenzie glared at him. "Not yet. Too early in the game. This is going to take time."

"Yeah, yeah, of course. But it's got to be her. How many other women like that have been reported missing recently?"

"More than one, you can be sure. It will take a while for us to verify her identity."

"Can you believe it?" the tech said to his partner. "We are among the first people to see Elysse Allen since she disappeared."

Kenzie rolled her eyes. "Let's get some samples of the water, mud, and vegetation around her. Examine for any trace on her while Carlos and I get our equipment."

They went straight to work, accustomed to the sight and smell of a decomposing body, just as Kenzie and Carlos were. Some of the cops looked a little green, but everyone was being professional about it. If any of them had gone off to throw up earlier, no one was teasing them about it.

"Ripe one," Carlos commented as they walked back to the van. "How long has the Allen girl been missing? A week?"

"A little less than that, I think. Depends on what day you start counting. The last day the boyfriend says he saw her, or the day he reported it."

"Hmm. I'm thinking it will be the last time someone *other than him* saw her. Who's going to take him at his word?"

"Probably no one," Kenzie agreed. They worked together to get the equipment and body bags out of the van, synchronized without having to give each other instructions. It was pretty routine once she had done it a few times. There was no point in trying to get a wheeled gurney over the grass, rocks, and mud, or to get it through the switchbacks in the trail. Just a body bag with sturdy handholds made more sense.

4

On returning to the water's edge, Kenzie and Carlos needed to wait for a few minutes to allow the techs to finish gathering as much evidence as they could find. Then the techs moved back so that Kenzie and Carlos could get as close as possible with the stretcher, then the two of them carefully lifted the body out of the water, hoping it wouldn't tear into too many pieces.

There were some swearing and choking noises from the various cops and other observers as they lifted the remains out of the water and placed them into the first body bag. Kenzie didn't look at the offenders, staying focused on the work of not making a worse mess of the corpse than it was already in. After placing the body into the bag, Kenzie bent down over the water, searching for signs of any pieces that might have become separated from the main body. Any decomposing flesh, bones, hair, or pieces of clothing. She directed the techs toward a few more pieces of evidence to be collected.

She looked once more at the body before sealing it into the first body bag. She might or might not be the person unwrapping it again after they transported it to the morgue. Though the body was dressed in clearly feminine clothing, Kenzie couldn't make out any recognizable facial features. Everything was swollen with water, decomposing rapidly in the warm weather. It was a good thing the dogs had discovered it when they had. Another week or two, and there might have been nothing left of the body but bones. At least with flesh still on the body, Kenzie had a chance of being able to determine the cause of death if she were the one to perform the postmortem. It wasn't like on the TV show *Bones* where they had a forensic anthropologist on staff who could tell them all of the secrets of the victim's bones.

If it was Elysse Allen, Kenzie felt sorry for her family. If it was another woman, she felt equally sorry for whoever was mourning over her.

Carlos helped her pull the outer body bag over the first and to secure it in place.

Once the remains were hidden from view, the observers began to lose interest in the proceedings. The dog handler and other non-cops started to move away, murmuring among themselves. The techs examined the area for any other trace evidence that they might have missed. The other cops began looking around as if there might be another body to discover. Or maybe they were looking for a boat or some other large piece of evidence that might have been overlooked. Kenzie couldn't identify any footprints or drag marks to be photographed. The ground was too spongy and covered with vegetation to make clear tread marks. And who knew how much the cops had trampled everything? For such a remote area, an awful lot of people had found it necessary to go walking right up to the body. Kenzie wondered how many had taken pictures and how many of those shots would end up leaked to the ravenous media.

"I think that's it," she said to Carlos. "Do you see anything else?"

He looked a little surprised she would ask. Kenzie shrugged. She didn't care if he was just muscle, used to transporting bodies rather than interpreting crime scenes. He'd been at enough dump sites that he might have twigged to something that she hadn't.

Carlos looked around, considering. "No, I don't think so, Dr. Kirsch."

"Okay. Let me know if you think of anything later. Let's get her back to the van."

Kenzie was sweating heavily after carrying her end of the body all the way back up the embankment and into the van. She was glad to sit down in the van in front of the vents blowing cold air.

"It's warm."

Carlos wiped sweat from his temples. His short hair was plastered to his face. "A little," he agreed.

They were most of the way back to the morgue before he spoke again.

"Do you think it's Elysse Allen?" he asked. "Seems like that body was pretty far gone to be less than a week old."

Kenzie nodded. "We'll have to see what the evidence says. Bodies do decompose quickly in warm water. But something about that site… didn't seem quite right."

By the time they got back to the morgue and Dr. Wiltshire returned from his afternoon meetings, he deemed it too late to begin the postmortem.

"I know I said we need to put this one at the front of the queue," he said, "and we will, but I don't want to be starting this late in the day. I need to get home to my wife and you need to get home to Zachary. There's no point in doing it when we're tired and may make mistakes or miss important clues. We'll do it when we're both fresh."

"Okay. First thing in the morning?"

"We'll start in the a.m., but go ahead and clear your email and voicemail first. I don't want to miss any important communications. I'm sure there will be plenty of people making inquiries by ten o'clock tomorrow."

So Kenzie cleared what she could in the afternoon before heading for home. Each thing she could get out of the way was one less thing to tackle in the morning.

"You're back in pretty good time." Zachary looked at the clock after kissing Kenzie in greeting. "How was the first day back?"

"It wasn't too bad. Have you been watching the news?"

"No. Something I should have seen?"

"Human remains were found. Possibly a young woman."

"Oh." His brows shot up. "Young? Blond and pretty?"

"Blond. Too decomposed for pretty."

"He killed her right away, then," Zachary deduced. "Maybe even a few days before he said she went missing."

"Possibly. It will be up to the police to investigate the timeline and the alibis he gave. If she was killed before he says she disappeared, then yeah, he might be trying to obscure the actual time and place of death, make sure that he's got a solid alibi for the time in question. But she's a celebrity; people would notice if she stopped posting before the boyfriend said she disappeared, wouldn't they?"

"Yeah, but it's easy enough to keep posting pictures on her Instagram account for several days after her death. Pictures that she took before she died, or that he took afterward. Keep posting for a few days to hide the fact that she was already dead."

"It would be a good ploy," Kenzie admitted.

They worked together to pull together some supper. Zachary got out dishes to set the table.

"It's too bad," he said, "I was hoping that everyone was wrong about the boyfriend. What was his name? Dain."

"Dain Porter."

"Right. Dain Porter. I was really hoping that people were just being too quick to judge. He was the boyfriend and the last one to see her, so it must have been him. There are so many other possibilities. I know that the police have to look hard at him, but that doesn't mean they can't consider other people. Other possibilities. People *do* get kidnapped."

Kenzie swallowed and focused on stirring the sauce she was preparing on the stove. "Yes," she agreed, hoping there was no tell-tale quaver in her voice. "They do."

"So it could have been someone random. Someone who just saw her or was out trolling for girls. Or there could be an ex-boyfriend, or a problem with her family. Dad comes after her to take her away from Dain, who he thinks is a bad influence, and something happens. Or she could have decided to take off, alone or with some guy that she hooked up with."

"But no one has admitted to seeing her with anyone else since the day Porter reported her missing. There have been no confirmed sightings of her alone or with someone else."

Zachary set the cups and dishes out a little more firmly than Kenzie would have liked, making her wince, even though she knew they were sturdy. "But no one would see her if someone else kidnapped or murdered her either. And if she didn't want to be seen, she could stay out of sight or wear a disguise."

"I *don't* think that Elysse Allen is wandering around the northeastern states wearing a disguise."

"No," Zachary admitted, laying the cutlery down more quietly. "I guess she's in your cold room now. I was just hoping that it wasn't the boyfriend."

"And there still isn't any proof that it was. Even if we have found her remains, that isn't proof that Porter was the one who killed her. It could still have been some other random person, stalker, family member, or ex-lover. It will be up to the police to determine that."

5

Their conversation had run the gamut of other topics—how Zachary's day had gone, other news stories, the weather forecast, and their plans for the weekend. But it was only natural that they kept returning to the story of Elysse Allen and the remains now lying in the cold room at the Medical Examiner's Office.

Zachary flipped through a few channels as they were trying to find something to watch on TV and occasionally paused at a station discussing the disappearance, and now, presumed murder, of Elysse Allen.

We found her, they announced, over and over again. It would be at least a day until the Medical Examiner's Office could confirm it, but the media were happy to spread the horrible news, true or not.

"Have you ever noticed," Zachary said, "that it is always the pretty white girls who get the attention of law enforcement and the media? I mean, I've never seen this kind of concern or coverage for a Black woman or a man. Or any other race or color, for that matter. Especially an illegal immigrant. People just assume... what? That if they are Black, it was probably gang or drug-related? That if it was an immigrant, they've just gone back home?"

Kenzie knew he was thinking about Jose, Pat Parker's friend who had disappeared. As it had turned out, he had not been the only illegal immigrant to fall prey to the same serial killer. A man who had been operating for decades but never caught, because he targeted gay immigrant men in particular, men who were disposable or distasteful to the media and written off by the police as having disappeared voluntarily.

And maybe he was also thinking about the runaway he was trying to track down—a girl who was just as important as Elysse Allen but would never make it to the TV. At most, her parents or family members might put up posters or an appeal on their social media channels.

"It's not fair," Kenzie admitted. "Everyone should have the same value and get the same level of concern. But you're right. The media and the public at large want something juicy. A beautiful young woman is considered a greater loss. And the fact that she was a minor celeb makes it all that much juicier. She's beloved by thousands who never even met her."

"They didn't know her."

"No. And what they did know was probably carefully planned and marketed. The person behind the social media accounts... could be anything. She could be a terrible person. I'm not saying that she was, but she could have been. She could be a bully. A racist. Self-centered. Uncaring about anyone else's needs or feelings. But that's not the picture she presented to the public."

Zachary stopped at yet another station showing pictures of Elysse Allen in the type of montage that might be used at a wedding or funeral. Elysse's life in pictures, growing from a spaghetti-sauce-covered toddler into an awkward, leggy teen, and then into a young woman, looking smart and self-possessed and perfectly turned out for any picture that appeared in her social media feeds. They both just watched in silence for a few minutes.

"Think about all of the other people who have gone missing since she did," Zachary said in a low voice. "And they haven't even been a blip on the screen. Not even one picture. All the teen runaways. Overwhelmed or abused adults. People being kidnapped and trafficked. Wives killed by their husbands and children by their mothers."

He shook his head. "And not one of them has made it into the media's consciousness."

Kenzie cuddled up to Zachary, hoping to comfort and distract him from his dark thoughts and the sad story of not only the girl lying in the ME's office cold room, but also all of the others who had been murdered or missing without their stories being told. She didn't want his rumination to start another cycle of depression.

"All we can do is what we're doing. You're looking for the girl that you were hired to find. I'll autopsy the one whose remains were found. All we can do is take them one at a time."

They started watching a movie, a western that would not have been at the top of Kenzie's list of movies to watch, but maybe Zachary felt drawn to a plot where a rugged stranger rolls into town to save the girl, the farm, and the town from evil forces. A sort of a universal fantasy that they both knew would result in the hero being recognized as extraordinarily skilled at what he did, and he would achieve something worthwhile, no matter what dark past he might harbor. People would die but, in the end, the girl would be saved and the gunman would either settle down on the farm with her or kiss her and ride off into the sunset.

So she wasn't really disappointed when Zachary's phone rang and he paused the movie to answer it. He put his phone on the mobile laptop table in front of them and tapped the speaker button.

"Tyrrell! You're on speaker, bro."

"Hey, Zach. And Kenzie?"

Zachary hadn't said he was with Kenzie but, of course, that was why he had put the call on speaker.

"Yes. Hi, Tyrrell. How is it going?"

"Really well." Tyrrell's voice sounded mellow and relaxed. She knew that Zachary would be analyzing it too. Both of them automatically checking for signs that he was stressed or had gone back to drinking. He was a closet drinker, skilled in hiding his addiction, so it wouldn't be easy to tell. But he sounded fine. "I'm getting into things at the foundation. I know it's only been a few days, but I really like it. I think this is going to work out well."

"I'm glad," Kenzie told him sincerely. She had managed to get him a job at her family foundation. Just doing filing and data entry to start with but, hopefully, he would be able to work his way up to a position where he would actually be able to use his degree. After a series of jobs lost when he fell off the wagon and went on a drunken binge for weeks or months at a time, not a lot of avenues remained open to him.

"You're not bored yet?" Zachary teased, hoping to get more information from Tyrrell about how he was enjoying what he was doing and his emotional state.

"No! It's fascinating. And Hillary is going to walk me through reviewing grant applications so that I know what to look for and can prescreen them for her. She says it will be a big help to her, and I'll learn a lot about the business that way, and about all the organizations that apply to them for help."

"Yeah? That sounds good. You're not jumping into anything too fast? You don't want to get overwhelmed."

"No. This is the kind of thing I *want* to do. You don't know how tired I am of day labor, working construction or picking up trash. I love what the foundation is doing and the chance to be a part of it. And to really be able to use my brain. Those casual labor jobs are so mind-numbingly boring."

"I'm really glad you're enjoying it and finding it a good fit," Kenzie told Tyrrell. "That's good to hear. If you have any trouble and need to talk to someone about it… you know how to get me."

Kenzie hoped that if Tyrrell started to get too stressed out by the job or if there was some problem with getting along with Hillary or Kenzie's parents, Tyrrell would be able to give her a heads-up before it became untenable. Before he did what he had done before and escaped with alcohol.

"Sure, of course," Tyrrell said cheerfully, nothing in his voice suggesting that he would take the suggestion seriously and use her as a sounding board or relief valve if there were a problem at the foundation. "I know where to find you."

6

K enzie had known when she left the previous day that there might be a lot of people trying to find out information about the remains that had been recovered at Petty Pond, which might require extra security to control, so she shouldn't have been surprised when she arrived the next morning to find the elevators roped off even in the underground parking level that was reserved for staff and law enforcement officers that worked in the building. Nathaniel, one of the security guards she knew, was acting as the elevator operator rather than letting it run automatically. He nodded to her when he let her past the rope barrier onto the elevator. He inserted his key into the slot in the control panel and pressed the button for the basement.

"Morning, doctor."

"It's Kenzie. I take it things must be pretty crazy here today?"

He nodded. "Already had several security breaches with people trying to get to the morgue. Reporters, concerned citizens…" He rolled his eyes. "Freaks. People who want to look at decomposed bodies."

Kenzie raised an eyebrow.

"Not *you*," Nathaniel clarified quickly. "You need to look at decomposed bodies as part of your job. To help people. You don't just look because… that's how you get your kicks. Because you want to take a selfie with a celebrity even if she's dead. Get some kind of social media cred." He shook his head. "That's totally different from doing your job."

Kenzie smiled and chuckled at his embarrassment. "Well, I'm glad you're here to keep the crazies out of our hair. So who are you allowing through?"

"Your staff. Law enforcement if they can show they are on the Allen case or have another legitimate reason to be down there. For members of the public who have forms to file, we have grabbed a handful of forms and they can be filled out at the security desk on the main floor. No reason for them to come down to your desk."

"Okay, great, thanks. That should keep disruptions to a minimum."

"We aim to please!"

They reached the basement level, and Kenzie nodded to the guard. "Thanks, Nathaniel. See you later."

"I'm sure you will."

Kenzie and Dr. Wiltshire were both ready to go early in the day, knowing that they were going to be inundated with demands for information on whether the remains really were those of Elysse Allen, how she had died, and anything else that could point the way toward the killer—and especially whether she had been killed by Dain Porter. They wanted to get out ahead of it as quickly as they could.

But in autopsy, there was no sense of pressure or hurry. They knew they had to be methodical in their approach, always going slowly and checking every little thing. It was best to be thorough the first time and never have to go back to redo part of the postmortem or have someone exhumed because of questions left by the original autopsy. They had all day to do it, and they would take all day, if necessary, to ensure all questions were answered and there were no open questions that had not been examined.

A couple of detectives sat in the observation room where they could see and hear what was going on and could view what Kenzie or Dr. Wiltshire displayed on the monitors, but they did not have to suit up or be exposed to the smells of the autopsy. They could turn on the microphone if they wanted to talk to Dr. Wiltshire and Kenzie. Knowing that the police detectives would be eager to get answers that they didn't yet have, and not wanting to be constantly interrupted, Dr. Wiltshire gave them a stern lecture before starting.

"I expect to be able to work without interruption, unless you have a burning question to ask about the procedure we are performing at the moment. If it can wait, then please do. Write it down and submit your questions to me at the end of the autopsy. And 'do you know who it is yet?' and 'Is it Elysse Allen?' are not questions I will address until I have a definitive answer. As soon as I know, so will you."

The detectives looked both resigned and grumpy. They knew they would be sitting there for a long time without getting the answers they wanted.

With the big exhaust fans blowing, the smell was better than it would have been in a small, closed room, but it would still take a few minutes to get used to the smell of the decomp and be able to tune it out. Mostly. Kenzie studied the remains, frowning. She and Dr. Wiltshire had worked with decomposed bodies before. There were always people who died in their homes or apartments and were not discovered until days or weeks later. And sometimes, remains that had been out in the wilderness for long periods of time, exposed to the weather and animal predation, were found by hikers or dog walkers. But Dr. Wiltshire had much more expertise in the area than Kenzie.

"This looks far more decomposed than I would have expected after less than a week," Kenzie suggested.

"It isn't an exact science. History has shown us that Mother Nature can be quirky and things that we don't expect or account for can affect the rate at which a body decomposes. But yes, I agree that this body appears to be older than just a few days."

"Do you think it's just because of the summer heat and the water?"

"They definitely have an effect. And we don't know what bacteria were present in the body at the time of death or in the water. Some of them are very efficient at breaking down flesh. Or there might have been another influence that we're unaware of. If it was left in a car in the sun for the first day or two, for example, and then moved."

Kenzie nodded. That made sense.

Dr. Wiltshire tapped the record button on the floor with his foot and announced the date, location, his and Kenzie's names, and the identification number assigned to the remains yet to be identified. He identified the remains as female and gave the height of the body and the weight of the remains, noting that the weight of the remains could not be relied upon as being the weight of the victim before death.

He and Kenzie began with the gross examination, working from head to toe to note any signs of violence on the body, anomalies, identifying features, or anything else that was of interest. Dr. Wiltshire noted the long blond hair that remained on the corpse, and the appearance of the skeletal structure of the face, frowning as he did so.

Kenzie was looking at the hands. She motioned to Dr. Wiltshire. "Why are they so different in appearance? What happened here?"

Dr. Wiltshire scrutinized the left hand and then the right. He looked at Kenzie. "What do you think?"

Kenzie shook her head. "The left hand is very soft, lots of decomposition. Already degloved, maybe from animal predation. But the right hand…" She looked closely at it, picking it up to look at it from various angles. "There is hardly any decomposition. It's… mummified."

"This can happen sometimes," Dr. Wiltshire said. "It's mummified, so you know that…"

"It was dry." Kenzie pictured the scene as it had been when she arrived, before they had removed the remains from the water. "It had to dry out to be preserved like that. When I arrived at the scene, the body was only partially submerged."

Kenzie gave the computer voice commands until the pictures she had taken at the scene were displayed on one of the monitors. The right arm and hand were protruding out of the water.

Dr. Wiltshire nodded. "It was left out of the water, so it stayed dry."

"But that wouldn't have been enough to mummify it, would it? And in just a few days? You would need some kind of desiccant to get all of the moisture out in that short a time."

"Then…"

Kenzie didn't want to be the one to say it. She waffled, trying to decide. "Then… the body has been there longer than just a few days."

"The body is more than just a few days old," Dr. Wiltshire clarified.

"Yes." Kenzie thought about what he had said and how it differed from what she had said. And the part about how maybe the body had been in a hot car for a few days. Would it have become mummified that quickly in a hot car? "You don't think it has been in the water the whole time?"

"What whole time?"

"Since she was killed."

"I don't think that she died on that spot, no. She was transported there from somewhere. By someone."

"So it's homicide."

"Not necessarily. Sometimes people feel it necessary to move the body of an accident victim, or someone who has died of natural causes, if it would look bad for a body to be found in that place."

"Like if it was the home of a politician or celebrity, and it might damage their reputation."

"One possibility."

"So she was transported from somewhere else. And it would have taken more than a few days for her hand to become mummified like that."

Dr. Wiltshire nodded, waiting for more.

"Do you think… that her hand was already mummified when she was dumped there?"

He shrugged. "I don't think that a pond is a likely place for a body to dry out. Even just one limb."

"No. Then she was somewhere else… for long enough for the hand to mummify. And then she was transported to the pond and dumped."

"I expect so, yes. That is what the remains would suggest."

"Why would just one hand mummify? Wouldn't the whole body mummify?"

"Not always. What makes you think that's what happened?"

"Because only one hand is…" Kenzie stopped and looked at the remains on the table. "The rest of the body was rehydrated? It was all mummified, but when the—whoever—dumped the body in the pond, then the rest rehydrated, and the hand didn't, because it wasn't immersed."

"That seems like the most likely scenario. We don't know yet, but we can't rule out the possibility that the entire body was mummified before it was dumped."

"And that suggests… that it was somewhere for long enough for it to become mummified before it was dumped."

"Yes."

"How long does it take to become mummified?"

"There is a range. In the desert, exposed to the sun, a couple of weeks. Here in Vermont, where it is cooler and less arid… longer. The ancient Egyptians developed a process that took 70 days."

"So, longer than two weeks."

"Unless they found a hot, dry environment within Vermont. A greenhouse, maybe, but one kept arid rather than humid. Or if the body became mummified somewhere else and was brought into Vermont. Both less likely. But two weeks is probably as close to a minimum as you are going to get."

"And Elysse has not been missing for two weeks." Kenzie chewed on her lip. "Zachary pointed out that someone else could have been posting pictures to her accounts. Making it look like she died later than she did. Obscuring the timeline."

"It could happen, but killers aren't usually that careful to cover up their misdeeds. That's the stuff of TV dramas."

"But he could. He could plant a false trail, making everyone think it occurred at a different time than it did."

"We will need to get a positive identification before coming to any conclusions."

Kenzie grimaced at the reminder. "Yeah. I guess I'm just as eager as everyone else to know what happened to Elysse Allen."

Dr. Wiltshire nodded. "But that bias is how mistakes are made. We need to consider all of the evidence before us and not try to make it fit into one particular circumstance."

"Right."

The medical examiner tapped the record button again and described the appearance of the mummified hand, in contrast with the rest of the body, and noted their hypothesis that the body had been entirely mummified earlier, then dumped in the water. They continued with their examination, making a few notes as they went. Dr. Wiltshire straightened and stared off into space for a moment. Then he looked back at Kenzie.

"It is our job to note what is missing as well as what is present. Is there anything you would expect to see in this body that you do not?"

Obviously, he had something particular in mind; it wasn't just an academic exercise. Kenzie considered what she knew about bodies found in the water. Determining whether the cause of death was drowning or something else. Clues that the body might have been dumped that they hadn't yet considered. The causes of mummification and if there was something else they should be considering for a victim who might have died in a hot, dry place rather than a pond in the middle of the forest.

"How long has the body been exposed?" Dr. Wiltshire prompted.

"Oh. Well, part of that could be determined by the level of putrefaction..."

"Yes. What else?"

Kenzie considered. Her clothing? Insect activity—which would be less in an immersed body. Predation? "Oh—that's it. Predation? If the body was exposed to the elements for any length of time, there should be predation. Is that true of a body in the water as well as one in the open air?" She considered the remains. "Yes," she answered herself. "Fish, crabs, other water creatures. They can be very active and strip a body pretty quickly."

Dr. Wiltshire nodded. "Yes, predation plays a big part in how *much* of the body we have after it has been exposed to the elements like this."

"And it is still largely intact." Kenzie leaned in to examine the skin and putrefying flesh of the young woman. "I don't see a lot of evidence of predation. Some of the skin, maybe, but not the deeper layers." She looked at him. "How long do you think...?"

"What can you tell me about the body of water she was found in?"

Kenzie recalled what she could and had the computer display the establishing shots, which showed more of the pond.

"Is it just a water catchment?" Dr. Wiltshire asked. "Or is it connected to a source of flowing water?"

"Well..." Kenzie frowned and directed the computer to perform an internet search, where she was able to find an aerial shot of Petty Pond, which was fuzzy, but suggested connections to some of the nearby rivers and lakes. "Why does that matter?"

"If it is just a water catchment, collecting rainwater, there may be no fish. If it is connected to a river or lake, then it is probably populated."

"And if there are fish but no fish predation, then it means that the body was not in the pond for very long."

Dr. Wiltshire gave a nod. "Exactly. If there are fish, the remains can't have been in the water long. Long enough to rehydrate, but not be eaten."

7

W hat other signs do we look for in a drowning victim?"
Dr. Wiltshire asked.

"Well, we don't think that she was a drowning victim, so—"

"Are you sure or are you assuming?"

"Well, if she was mummified and then dumped there a day or two ago, then she didn't drown."

"Then she didn't drown *in that pond recently.*"

Kenzie considered this from several angles. "But she could still have drowned somewhere else."

"Yes. If it was homicide, then maybe the person who dumped the body there was mirroring the original scene of death so that nothing would seem out of place."

"She was drowned, then pulled out of the water, mummified, and then put back into the water?"

"We don't know yet," Dr. Wiltshire responded mildly to Kenzie's note of skepticism.

"No. We don't," she agreed.

"There are different kinds of drowning. Right now, you are just considering whether she drowned in a pond or other outdoor body of water, similar to the circumstances she was discovered in."

"Yes."

"But someone can also drown in her bathtub. She can drown after having liquid forced down her throat. Or accidentally during or after an eggnog drinking contest."

Kenzie laughed and looked at him. "An eggnog drinking contest? That's pretty specific."

"I read a case," he said with a shrug. "The contest winner did not swallow the eggnog; he unintentionally forced it down his windpipe. In that case, he did survive, but only because one of his friends was a doctor and got him to the ER in time to treat."

"Wow. Eggnog. Who knew?"

"Many other substances could be aspirated, including vomit after passing out. Not an uncommon cause of death for a heavy drinker."

"So we need to check the lungs for any foreign liquids."

"Yes. If they are still in condition to do so. Any other signs of drowning that we might see?"

"There are a few... but I don't think they will be available with this level of decomposition."

"Most will not. Fresh bodies pulled from the water are one thing. Bodies in this condition are very different. It will not be as easy to figure out this woman's story."

"Are there any signs we might still be able to see?"

"Two common injuries that go along with an outdoor in situ drowning are scrapes on the forehead or the tops of the feet."

They had already done a head-to-toe examination, and Kenzie hadn't noticed any marks on the woman's forehead or feet, but she dutifully went back to examine them. With Dr. Wiltshire watching, she tried different magnification levels and alternate light sources to visualize any injuries on the head or feet. Eventually, Kenzie couldn't think of anything else to look for.

"I don't see anything. We can swab those areas for any trace, just in case, but I can't see any scrapes or cuts."

"But with the level of decomposition, it would be difficult to find any."

"Yeah."

They made note of these findings.

"One thing we sometimes see in bodies immersed in the water for a significant length of time is saponification."

Kenzie blinked. "Soap making?"

He smiled and nodded. "Very good. Yes, the transformation of lipids or adipose tissue into soap. This is something that can happen naturally when a body is left in the water."

Kenzie looked down. "But not in this case."

"No. I see no signs of saponification. Are we ready to move on from the gross examination?"

Kenzie arched her back and rubbed it, happy to be able to continue. "Yes. Are we ready to cut?"

"I would say so, unless you have anything else you would like to check?"

"No. Let's proceed."

Dr. Wiltshire had Kenzie perform the Y-incision and begin the examination of the internal organs. It was not just the skin and outer flesh that was decaying. Much of the inside of their corpse was little more than a putrefied stew.

"We're not going to be able to identify any foam or pond water or other substances in the lungs," Kenzie said, prodding at the masses inside the body cavity.

"No. But other trace evidence may have survived the decomposition process."

"Like what?" Kenzie couldn't imagine anything but bone that would not be affected by the decomposition she was seeing.

"If someone drowns, what do they take into their lungs?"

"Water."

Wiltshire raised his brows. "Just water?"

Kenzie imagined a struggle under the water. The woman's face or head being held down as she writhed and fought her attacker. The water churning. Unable to hold her breath any longer, she sucked in the water.

"And everything in the water. Sand, silt, fragments of plants, water insects, diatoms..."

"And which of those will not decompose?"

"Anything inorganic. The sand and the silt."

Dr. Wiltshire agreed. Kenzie looked at the mess on the autopsy table. "A sieve, I guess? We can't exactly take slices of this."

"Let's see what we can find."

It took much longer than Kenzie would have expected to make a full examination of what had once been the woman's lungs. And in the end, they were not able to identify any inorganic particles that might have been inhaled if the woman had been drowned.

"That was a useless exercise," Kenzie griped.

The doctor shook his head. "No, it was tedious, but I think we established pretty conclusively that this victim was not drowned in a pond or other natural body of water."

"But we already figured that. And we still don't have cause of death. Whether she was drowned or something else."

"Give it time. We may find something yet."

Kenzie nodded and was determined to push ahead. A post-mortem could not be rushed. And she never knew at the beginning what she might find by the end. They might still find something that pointed definitively to a specific cause of death. Maybe something that would even help to identify the killer, if the woman had died at the hands of another person.

Heads bent, they continued their work on the decomposing body, trying to find any clue in the stinking stew that would tell them how she had died and who might have had a hand in it. Clearly, she hadn't just walked into that pond and died there. Someone else had dumped her. After doing what they could in their examination of the internal organs, Dr. Wiltshire proceeded to open the skull to see what they could find there. The brain, like everything else, was too decomposed to make much of. They drained the skull and looked for any signs of fracture or injury that might have contributed to the woman's death. Dr. Wiltshire extended a fiber optic camera into the skull to closely examine all the surfaces. He pointed to the monitor.

"What do you see?"

"There's a darker area," Kenzie contributed, leaning closer to the screen for a better look. "Staining?"

Dr. Wiltshire nodded. "We'll take some samples, but I have seen this kind of staining before, so I'm pretty confident in what we will find."

"You think it is from blood? A bloodstain wouldn't have been soaked off in the water?"

With the decomposition, the skull had not been sealed off from the pond water.

"The iron in the blood is deposited in the lattices of the bone and, since it is inorganic, it does not rot away like the tissue, but leaves a permanent stain."

Kenzie took a deep breath in. She had been breathing too shallowly, stress and the smell of the room as they continually exposed new fluids to the air keeping her from taking the deeper breaths she should. She let her breath out again slowly.

"So, that's pretty definitive. She had a bleed in her brain."

"Yes. Natural or unnatural?"

"Hmm. There aren't any fractures in the skull around the area. But I don't think that's definitive. She could have been hit on the head hard enough to cause a bleed, but not hard enough to fracture the skull."

"We should do a microscopic examination, see whether there are microfractures that are not visible to the naked eye."

"Right."

"An aneurysm will bleed into the subarachnoid space, but it doesn't leak out into the epidural space unless there is some kind of trauma and the meningeal tissues are compromised. Staining on the skull like this is caused by an epidural hematoma... which is caused by head trauma, not natural processes."

"She was injured, then. It wasn't just a weakness in a blood vessel that she was born with and would eventually leak or burst."

"Yes. This definitely points to a traumatic injury, even though there is not any visible fracture or injury on the outside of the head."

"That still doesn't tell us whether it was an accident or homicide."

"Correct," Dr. Wiltshire nodded in agreement. "We can posit from the fact that she was dumped in the pond rather than discovered at the scene of a motor vehicle accident that it was *more likely* homicide, but we cannot prove homicide just by the nature of the injury."

"We do know why she died. Just not how."

"Perhaps. There may have been other injuries as well. Much will depend on the police investigation. We will provide them with as much information as possible, but they will need to find out what they can about the circumstances surrounding her death."

They both looked toward the observation area, where the police detectives were already on their phones, looking serious and focused.

They proceeded to make a microscopic examination of the stained area of the skull and took a few samples, but the skull did not give up any more secrets. Kenzie was discouraged and getting irritable. Long hours over the autopsy table, the smell of decomposition, and too many hours without anything to eat combined to give her a brutal headache.

"I think we can call it a wrap," Dr. Wiltshire said, stripping off his gloves. "Send off those samples and slides to the lab, have George clean up here, and you and I need to get some lunch."

Kenzie looked toward her desk, though of course it was not visible from autopsy. No doubt she would have a bunch of emails and voicemails to respond to. Most of them would be about Elysse Allen, and they weren't going to have any answers other than "no comment" or "our report is in the process of being written."

"You need a break," Dr. Wiltshire said. "Not lunch at your desk. Why don't I take you out?"

It was not their usual practice, so Kenzie looked at him in surprise.

"I mean it. I'm enforcing a break. No running directly to your emails. That will all wait another hour. Let's sit down, debrief, and take a few minutes to relax. You'll be far more productive if you take the time to rest now than if you try to force yourself through it exhausted."

"It's not that bad. I'll sit down and have something to eat, and I'll be fine."

"Nope. You need a real break."

"I've been off for a week."

"That's not the same thing. You may have come in here well-rested, but now you're mentally worn out and sore. Doctor's orders. And if that doesn't work, boss's orders."

Kenzie laughed. "Okay, fine. I'll wash up and let George know that we're done. Then we can go out to…"

"There's a buffet a couple of blocks down. You ever been there?"

"Yeah, sure," Kenzie agreed. It was one of the places she and Zachary liked to go when they were looking for a date night away from the house. "That's good for me."

"Okay. Be ready to go in ten minutes."

8

Kenzie had to admit that she did feel a lot better after lunch with Dr. Wiltshire. They had run through the autopsy findings and a few other office admin matters that needed to be covered. After eating and sitting down away from the office for a while, she felt re-energized and ready to take on the work waiting for her when she returned to her desk.

As expected, a large number of the inquiries in her inbox were to do with Elysse Allen, from everyone from the Governor's office down to reporters, bloggers, and curiosity-seekers. She pulled them all into a new folder. Initially, they would get a "we don't know anything yet" email from the Medical Examiner's Office. Then when they had something ready, she would go through and see who was actually going to get an official answer from them. Everyone else would hear when the press release went out announcing that the remains were not those of Elysse Allen after all.

Kenzie and Dr. Wiltshire were both pretty sure that it was not. All indications were that this body had had a lot more time to mummify and decompose than Elysse, even if she had been killed a day or two before her boyfriend said she had disappeared. Nature could be tricky sometimes, so it was impossible to be definitive yet, but it wouldn't take long to determine whether it was actually her body or not.

Skimming down her email list, Kenzie found one from a police department domain with an attachment and the subject line Dental Exam.

She opened it, touching the speed dial on her phone at the same time, double-clicking on the attachment while her phone dialed Dr. Wiltshire's extension in speaker mode. When he answered, she snatched up the receiver. "We got the dental records."

"Allen's?"

"Yes."

"Put them up in the boardroom and let's have a look."

Kenzie hung up. She pulled up the x-rays that they had taken of the Jane Doe from Petty Pond that morning. She glanced at them, comparing them to the records from Elysse Allen's dentist for a few seconds before closing both and walking across to the boardroom, where she pulled them up again on the big screen. Dr. Wiltshire was there a minute later.

He looked at the two sets of x-rays on the screen for a few seconds and made his determination quickly, even though they were slightly different views.

"Not even close."

Kenzie shook her head. "Nope." Even a layman could see that. The dental work Elysse had done did not appear on Jane Doe's x-rays, and vice versa. They were clearly two different people.

"The first order of business will be to let the detectives know that we have *not* found the remains for Elysse Allen. She is still a missing person. I'll give him a call. And the second order of business will be…"

"To find out who she is."

Dr. Wiltshire nodded. "Exactly. And that may not be easy."

"There haven't been a lot of missing persons who would match her description. It shouldn't take too long to compare each of them."

"No? How far back are you going to go?"

Kenzie shrugged. "A few months. Everything since the beginning of the year."

Dr. Wiltshire didn't say anything. Kenzie considered. "You don't think that I'll find a match?"

"You might be lucky. Start there. Then we can talk."

Despite Kenzie's optimism, there was no match for Jane Doe in the first few files she looked at. It wasn't like they were in New York. Vermont had a small population, so far fewer missing persons to consider. Kenzie considered her search parameters. She knew Jane Doe's height for sure. She could only guess at weight and age. She knew hair color, though, of course, that could be changed with a dye job. But the strands of hair remaining on the corpse had been evenly colored, no other color showing at the roots. She re-ran the search with sex, height, and hair color only. There were more files to look through but, in a few minutes, she had determined that none of them matched.

Of course, there was no reason that Jane Doe couldn't have gone missing from New York or any other state. Few people ran away from New York to hide in Vermont, but it was still possible. Or that she had been taken from another state and transported to Vermont.

But Vermont's database was what she had to work with, so she would focus on that.

She remembered Dr. Wiltshire's look when he had asked her how far back she was going to look. She had told him she expected to find that the woman matched someone who had disappeared since the beginning of the year. That should give her a large enough pool.

But what if she were wrong? If the woman's body had been mummified, dumped, rehydrated, and decomposed, then it might have been quite a while since she had died. Kenzie might need to look further back to find her.

Much further back.

Kenzie sighed, looked at her system clock, and tried to decide whether to continue the search or put it off until the following day.

9

Kenzie opened the door from the garage and walked into the house. It was quiet. Zachary often had the TV or a feed on his computer playing to provide background noise and help to keep him focused, but the house was silent.

There was a knot in her stomach. Kenzie slipped off her shoes and put them on the mat under the coat hooks.

"Zachary? Are you home?"

There was no answer.

Kenzie could look for herself. It wasn't like there were a lot of places Zachary might be. If he were at home, he would either be working at his mobile station on the couch or in the office where there was better, more ergonomic furniture. He liked to be on the couch when she got home, but she was earlier than usual, and he couldn't have predicted that.

"Zachary?"

She could see as soon as she stepped into the kitchen that he was not on the couch. She walked down the hall to the last bedroom. Zachary's computer sat on the desk, but he wasn't there. She looked down the hall to see if the bathroom door was closed. She might have walked by it without noticing. But she could see from where she stood that the door was ajar.

Kenzie knew better than to jump to conclusions. He was out running an errand, talking to a client, or on surveillance. He didn't stay home all day. There were always things to do. She walked back to the bedroom and peeked inside just to make sure that Zachary wasn't there. He could have lain down for a nap or been in the attached bathroom. Or been changing before or after going out.

It wasn't like she really thought that he would be having a nap. But why panic if he were just in the bedroom?

But he wasn't. Kenzie gazed out the bedroom window at Zachary's car parked in front of the house. He wasn't out running errands if his car was still there. Unless he went with someone else, which he never did.

Her anxiety grew as the list of possibilities narrowed yet again.

Kenzie pulled out her phone and tapped his picture. It only rang a few times before he picked up.

"Hey, Kenzie. Going to be late today?" he guessed in a light tone.

Kenzie laughed. "I'm already home."

"You're home? I was sure you'd be late today when you had those fresh remains to deal with."

"Not-so-fresh-remains."

"Not-so-fresh-remains," he amended. "I thought Dr. Wiltshire would keep you there until late. Or you'd insist on staying until you discovered everything you could about your new patient."

"We got to the postmortem early, so we have done everything we could, other than the lab results coming back in the next few days or weeks. I'm kind of stymied on the search for a missing person report, so I thought I'd come home and try again tomorrow when I'm fresh."

"I'll head home, then. I was just out for a walk. Figured I had plenty of time until you were home for supper!"

"You don't need to rush. I'll make something."

"We can order in. You must be tired."

"No, I went to lunch with Dr. Wiltshire, so I don't want more restaurant food. Something homemade and healthy. Or reasonably healthy. It will help me to relax."

"Are you sure?" Zachary asked doubtfully. He had probably

noticed at some point in the last year that Kenzie wasn't one of those people who unwound by cooking.

"I'll be fine. I'll see you when you get here."

"I won't be long," he promised.

They were both trying to develop some more healthy habits. Not just eating better, which they weren't making much headway on, but also getting out in the fresh air to get some exercise, like Zachary was doing. She was impressed that he had taken the time out of his day to get out. It was easy to say that he was going to take up a new habit. Much harder to actually do it. And especially for someone like Zachary, who liked routine and tended to find himself stuck in one even after they were no longer helpful or productive. Good for him.

It was only ten minutes before he arrived home, so he couldn't have been too far away. His camera hung around his neck. He actually had a tan this year, which was a nice change from the ghostly pallor he had sported since she had met him. He gave her a quick kiss.

"Sorry I wasn't here when you got home."

"That's fine. You didn't know what time I would be home. *I* didn't know what time I would be home!"

"I guess neither one of us expected you to be early."

Kenzie looked at the clock on the microwave. "On time."

"Well, on time is early if you always work late."

"I obviously don't *always* work late, or I wouldn't be out on time today."

He rolled his eyes. "What can I help with?"

Kenzie waved him away. "You can go have a shower. You're sweaty."

"I was just walking, not running."

"It's warm out."

Zachary inspected his shirt and sniffed it. "Are you just trying to get rid of me?"

"Yes."

"Okay. I'll be back in a few minutes. You'll have to think of another way to get rid of me."

"That's a dangerous thing to challenge a medical examiner to do."

Zachary laughed as he walked down the hall to the bathroom.

It wasn't anything fancy for dinner, but Kenzie broke out of her pasta-and-bottled-sauce repertoire, made chicken and rice, and added prepackaged salad to the offerings. Zachary pulled his chair out from the table. Kenzie could smell soap and aftershave, and his hair was spiky and still damp. She touched his cheek before she sat down.

"You shaved."

"I thought if you wanted me to clean up for dinner, I'd go all the way."

"It's nice." She bent down to give him a peck, then sat down and they dished up their food.

"So, it wasn't Elysse Allen," Zachary said, cutting off a bite of chicken with the side of his fork.

"What? How did you know that? Is it on the news already?"

"No. They're still saying it is. All kinds of memorial speeches and social media postings and everything else. Encouraging people to give money to battered women shelters, to support laws against domestic violence, all of that. Which is good, of course, but..."

"But it wasn't her. How did you know, then?"

"You said that you were looking at missing person reports."

"Ah. Yeah, I am. But no luck so far. I still don't know who she is."

"The remains are female?"

"I can't really give you any details."

"But if you thought at first it might be Elysse Allen, it was a woman. Blond. Around her height and build."

Kenzie shrugged. "You can make whatever assumptions you like."

"No obvious missing person matches? So it wasn't someone who disappeared recently."

Kenzie was silent, eating her salad. She didn't like to tell Zachary anything that the public didn't already know. Especially on a high-profile case like Elysse Allen, where he knew precisely what case she was working on and she'd been specifically warned against it. The police didn't release information on active police investigations, and neither did the Medical Examiner's Office.

"You said yesterday that the remains were decomposed. That's what's been leaked on the internet too. 'Reliable sources say...'" He shrugged. "You know how it goes."

"All the memorials for someone they didn't even know," Kenzie said, referring back to Zachary's comment about the social media attention Elysse's case was getting, as well as the fact that people were leaking information all over the internet. "There was stuff at work. They have to keep removing flowers and pictures from the main floor —since no one will let them onto the elevators so that they can put their mementos downstairs. They'd go right into the cold room if we didn't have the elevators guarded and doors locked. Why do they care so much about being with the decomposing remains of someone they don't even know? Is it just mass hysteria?"

Zachary nodded slowly, chewing on his chicken. "They want to be part of something. The center of attention. Some of them might actually be followers of her social media accounts before she die— disappeared. But most of them probably never even heard about her before she went missing and it hit the media. Now everyone is so focused and outraged... they just want to be a part of it."

"Well, I wish they would cut it out. It's annoying to have to deal with swarms of people whenever I leave or come back. And too many of them know what I look like, so I can't just sneak by."

"If you're in your car, at least they can't get to you. If everything is being guarded." He looked at her, clearly concerned about this.

"Yes, everything is guarded. I only come and go in my car, so they can't do anything but get in my way while I'm driving. Even when we went out for lunch, we had to take Dr. Wiltshire's car. I didn't want to be accosted on the street by the Elysse fans."

"Do they have a name?"

"What?"

"The fans. Like Brittany's fans were called the Bambas."

"Oh. I have no idea."

"Do you think it will take long to figure out who the remains really are?"

"I hope not. The police will be looking too. Hopefully, just a day or two to sort through the missing person reports."

"No identifying features? None of those implants with serial numbers on them?"

"No, and no rare pollens or insects have been identified."

"You are woefully behind the TV medical examiners."

"I know." Kenzie grinned and had a bite of chicken and rice. "I'll do my best to get caught up."

"What if she's never been reported missing? Or is from out of the state?"

"I don't know. That would make it pretty difficult. I'm working on the assumption right now that she's from Vermont and has been reported missing. If not... I'm not sure how we would figure out her identity. We'll have to circulate what information we have to other jurisdictions."

"The news that it's not Elysse's remains will spread like wildfire. Maybe you can use that publicity. Get the media to circulate a sketch of what she looked like before she died. And a description."

"The trouble is, we don't have much of either one at this point. Getting a forensic artist to do a facial reconstruction from the skull is pretty expensive. I'm not sure it's in the budget. It isn't like she is a key piece of evidence in solving another crime."

"No, just her own."

They ate in silence for a while.

"Do you have cause of death?" Zachary asked.

"I can't tell you anything about it."

"Was it murder or an accident? You could tell me that much."

"You'll know when it is released to the public. But... yes, we know something."

Zachary's eyes lit up. "You have cause of death!"

"I didn't say that."

"But you do, don't you?"

Kenzie just raised her brows and tried to look mysterious. Zachary chuckled at this. He could read her too well.

10

Kenzie thought that she should probably go for a walk after supper. Stretch her legs, get some fresh air, and follow Zachary's good example. But she didn't want to go out anywhere or take the chance that anyone might know who she was and ask her questions about Elysse and the newly discovered remains.

Her neighbors weren't likely to bother her and no one else should be able to find out where she lived, but she had learned from Zachary and recent experiences that it wasn't actually that hard to find out her address. She could have Elysse mourners camped out on her doorstep any time.

She tried to act like she could be productive for a while, checking her email and then sitting down with a book to read, but she never got past the first page. She looked at the TV, which Zachary was playing at a very low volume. He wasn't really watching it, just looking up every now and then to see what was happening on what-ever show he was watching.

He saw her gaze.

"Do you want me to find you something?" he asked. "Maybe watch a movie together?"

"I should do something other than watch TV. There's so much to do around here. The laundry isn't going to do itself. Or the vacuuming…"

"We can worry about those tomorrow." She knew he wouldn't. "Tonight, you should relax. You'll have all that work to do tomorrow, trying to find that woman's identity. You should pamper yourself tonight. Make sure that you're well-rested and ready to face the day tomorrow."

"You're a bad influence, you know that? You should encourage me to get my work done."

"You knew from the start that I was bad news."

Kenzie laughed. "Well, a magnet for trouble, if nothing else. You know, I never skipped the dusting before you moved in here."

"Just how badly does it need to be done?" Zachary reached over to the side table and drew his finger across its surface. He looked at his finger. "See, nothing. You can leave it another week."

Kenzie couldn't help being drawn to the TV screen, where, once again, she was inundated with mourners and memorials. Zachary turned the volume up.

"We bring you a special report," the announcer said in his gravest tones, "on the story *behind* the story of Elysse Allen's disappearance. What secrets is her boyfriend keeping? Where was he when she disappeared? Why did it take him so long to report her missing?"

"We should turn this off," Kenzie said, unable to tear her gaze away from the screen.

"But he has the story *behind* the story," Zachary pointed out, ultra-serious.

"Well, they do have that," Kenzie agreed. She rested her head on his shoulder and closed her eyes, waiting for the opening credits to finish.

"Elysse Allen and Dain Porter were the perfect couple, friends say. They had everything, and they were deeply in love. It was a fairy-tale story, love at first sight. The two were introduced by friends, and they were joined at the hip from the moment they met."

Kenzie shook her head. "Are they really going to try to tell us that they had the perfect relationship?"

"They always start out like that. Before they get to the part about how they were both having affairs and one of them hired a hit man to kill the other."

"You've watched a few of these."

"Despite all appearances, they harbored a dark secret," Zachary intoned dramatically.

"I'm sure they did."

They were quiet while the reporters talked about how perfect Elysse and Dain had been for each other, how their families had been sure that they would be married, and they fit so well with each other.

But then the reporter's voice changed to an ominous tone, very similar to the one Zachary had used. He started talking about the negative points of their relationship, the things they had hidden from everybody else: arguments, heavy drinking, possible physical abuse, rumors of affairs.

"Those didn't mean anything," Elysse's sister or aunt declared to the camera. "They're both really young, and they weren't *married*. Sometimes people still have a little exploring to do..."

"Were they both seeing other people?" the reporter asked.

"It wasn't serious. They weren't in other relationships. But... they weren't dead, you know? People still have feelings, attractions. Old relationships that they aren't quite over."

"Both Elysse and Dain?"

"Yes, I guess so. But that's just the way that they were. They were both very *passionate* people."

"And what do we know about their final days together?"

"They were on vacation. Traveling, taking pictures. All of these wilderness locations, you know. Showing how they were camping and seeing all of the best parts of America. All of the off-the-beaten-track places that people missed out on when they just did tours of the Grand Canyon or Disneyland or whatever. You wouldn't believe how many *untouched* places there still are in America. They still look just the way they did before America was settled. Elysse posted all of these *gorgeous* pictures."

"She was enjoying her trip?"

"They were having a really good time."

"Both of them?"

The sister or aunt hesitated slightly before answering. "There were some stories that got back to the family. I think... things were good, but it's hard when you're so close together all the time and only have each other to rely on. You know how it is on family vacations when everyone is getting on everyone else's nerves."

"So they were having some problems. What stories did you hear?"

"About the big argument they had at the gas station in... I don't know where it was. Alabama? I can't keep track of all of the places they went. They were having... just a heated argument, okay? Couples sometimes do. That can happen when you're cooped up with each other driving for fifteen hours a day."

"Was there any physical violence?"

"It was just an argument. That's what they told the police."

"The police were called?" the reporter asked with interest. As if they hadn't set up these interview questions ahead of time and he hadn't heard anything about a report being made to the police.

"Nothing happened. That's what they told the police. Both of them."

"Elysse and Dain."

"Right. They both said there wasn't anything between them, so there wasn't, right? Why would they lie to the police? If he'd hit her, she wouldn't have stayed with him. And she would have told the cops. She wouldn't act all lovey-dovey and pretend nothing had happened."

"Domestic violence victims often don't tell what is happening to them," the reporter said gravely.

A 1-800 number scrolled across the top of the screen. A domestic violence hotline. *If you or someone you know needs help...*

"Elysse would have told. And she wouldn't have stayed with him. She's a strong woman. She didn't believe in traditional roles. With the man being the head of the house and all of that, you know?"

"Did they argue about that?"

"No. She just didn't believe in that. Thought that a relationship should be one hundred percent equal. She wouldn't put up with being pushed around."

"And what about Dain? Did he ever make any claims of domestic violence against her?"

The sister or aunt laughed. "Against Elysse? Why would he do that? He didn't have any reason to complain. He was lucky to have her."

"The woman who reported the incident at the gas station said she had hit him."

"That's ridiculous." Eye rolling. "Why would he stand for that? He would have just left her if that was true."

"It can be difficult for men to report domestic violence. Our society doesn't accept them as victims."

The hotline number rolled by again.

"Well, Dain was never a victim. Not by Elysse, especially. She would never have hit him. You can watch the recording of the cops talking to them. They had body cams. You can see that Elysse and Dain are fine. They weren't yelling. They said it was nothing, just an argument someone had overreacted to. They were all loving, arms around each other, all that. No one was being hurt in that relationship. You could tell when you looked at them. They were all starry-eyed."

The sister or aunt choked up a bit at this. The camera zoomed in on her eyes, on the tear squeezing from the corner of her eye.

"What do you think happened?" the reporter inquired in a low, understanding tone.

"That's what I don't understand. I guess… they decided to go in different directions. Dain thought that Elysse would change her mind and rejoin him again. But she never did. And when he called and messaged her, he didn't get any kind of response from her. He even tried to track her phone and to go the places that he thought she might have gone after they split up. But he couldn't find any trace of her. Like she had fallen right off the face of the earth." The woman's eyes were wide with wonder. "She was kidnapped. I don't know who would do something like that, but it was someone she didn't know. Not Dain. Just… like… a random thing."

"Do you think she's still alive? That someone is holding her somewhere?"

"It could happen, you know. Like with Elizabeth Smart. Everyone thought it must be someone in her family at first, but it wasn't. It was that weird guy. And then they said that she was dead, that people like that don't keep their victims alive for more than a day or two, and no one was ever going to find her. And they did. And she was alive. Just showed up on the street one day. The police rescued her from that guy, and she was *fine*. That could be what happened to Elysse. She could be fine too. Just because it's been a week… that doesn't mean she's dead. She could still be alive and well and is just waiting for her chance to get away from him."

The reporter nodded slowly.

"What do you say to the reports that the police have found Elysse's remains?"

The sister or aunt broke down, tears running down her face and her mouth in a wide, ugly grimace. "That's *not* Elysse. I won't believe it is. Not ever. Elysse is still out there somewhere, and if the police don't keep looking for her… then they're being negligent. People who saw those remains; they say there's no way that it was Elysse. Couldn't have been."

She was right, of course, but Kenzie wondered how she could be so certain. Did she know where Elysse or her remains really were? Had there been some family argument when Elysse had gone off with her boyfriend against her family's advice? Had the woman or someone else in the family followed her and tried to talk her into coming home? To talk her into leaving Dain?

"Elysse is still out there somewhere," the woman repeated. "I'll never believe she's dead."

The perspective switched to just the reporter sitting on a stool by himself, talking to the camera. The recorded video with the sister or aunt had been taken at a different time and place. He spoke directly to the camera about the remains that had been found and the high likelihood that they were, in fact, the remains of Elysse Allen, tragically killed before her time by an unknown hand. Or by someone that she knew and loved. It would all depend on what the police could find and what could be proven.

When the credits rolled, Zachary muted the TV and looked at Kenzie.

"What do you think? Did the boyfriend kill her?"

Kenzie shrugged. "Statistics say yes. And with the reports of physical violence between them... that just makes it all the more likely. These remains weren't hers, but who knows what ravine or river he might have thrown *her* body into."

11

E verything should have been fine. Kenzie was home in plenty of time to unwind and had spent the evening relaxing with Zachary, not doing work in her free time. Her brain should have been quiet and ready to sleep so she could be refreshed and energized in the morning.

But she still had a feeling of dread coiled in her belly. She didn't know whether it was due to Zachary not being home as she'd expected him to be when she'd arrived home from work. She had *known* that nothing had happened to him, that he just happened to be out, and she had called him, and he had answered his phone immediately. She hadn't been left wondering where he was or what had happened to him. So that *shouldn't* be what was bothering her.

Or it might have been watching the news special about Elysse on the TV. Even though she knew that the remains in the morgue were not Elysse's, that still left the question open as to what had happened to her and whether her boyfriend had been involved in her disappearance or was just an innocent bystander. If he hadn't had anything to do with it, then she felt bad for the poor guy, because half the world —or at least half of America—thought that he had killed her.

And she was thinking about the woman whose remains they had found. Who was she and what had happened to her? They knew that she hadn't just had an accident. Someone had dumped her body. That spoke of violence and guilt.

So maybe that was why she still had a lump in her stomach and felt like she couldn't relax.

Kenzie got ready for bed as usual, ignoring the feeling. It was just anxiety over something that had nothing to do with her. If she ignored it, it would eventually go away on its own. Best not to give it any more thought than she had to. She tried to read again before bed, but she wasn't having much success and knew it was better to go to bed at the same time each night than to wait until she was overly tired. Especially considering Zachary's sleep issues. Sticking to a regular schedule was the best way for him to train his brain to go to sleep at the right time and not have to take the sleeping aid that he despised.

"You ready for bed?" she asked.

"Yeah, sure."

He didn't look particularly tired. But it was time, and he'd had a walk in the afternoon, which would help too. Kenzie was regretting that she hadn't taken an after-supper walk. That would have settled her down better than watching the news show about Elysse Allen's disappearance.

They both went about their usual bedtime routines, brushing teeth, Zachary taking what night meds he felt he needed, and changing for bed. The bedroom was still warm from the heat of the day, and Kenzie wore a thin t-shirt and shorts rather than the comfy flannels she wore during the winter. She cuddled up with Zachary when he came to bed, despite it being a little too warm to be right against each other. She reached for her phone and turned down the thermostat so the air conditioner would kick in. She didn't like wasting money on air conditioning if she didn't have to, but tonight she needed the extra comfort of being close to Zachary without burning up.

They cuddled and talked, murmuring conversations and drifting in and out of sleep. Kenzie startled out of sleep a couple of times and Zachary rubbed her back in warm, soothing circles, helping her to relax and go back to sleep again.

She was trapped. The room was dark, and she didn't know where she was. Someone was in the same room as she was. Her kidnapper? Or another victim? She didn't know what he was going to do to her. Would he hold her there for days or weeks? Would he hurt and abuse her? Or was he planning to kill her? Why had he done it? Why had he taken her?

Kenzie needed to get out of there. She needed to figure out a way out of the room and out of the house, to run until she was free.

She could hear voices, muted conversations from other rooms in thick Russian accents.

What did they want?

How long were they going to hold her there?

The smell of decomp filled Kenzie's nostrils. What had happened to the other woman? Had she died? Was she already dead and rotting on the bed where they had left her? Kenzie was afraid to move, not sure where she was. Flies buzzed around her and bounced repeatedly against the window. The room was close and fetid. Kenzie felt sick.

She hadn't ever thrown up at the Medical Examiner's Office. Yes, there had been a couple of times when she had been queasy and had needed to take a break or eat a cracker to settle her stomach, but she had never been sick. Now, with the smell all around her, closing in on her, unable to see what was going on like she could when she was doing a postmortem, she was overwhelmed with nausea.

A hand landed against her back. Kenzie shrieked, nearly jumping out of her skin. She fought off the hand, not sure whether it was the hand of a live person or a dead one. She was at the edge of the bed, but didn't dare to put her feet on the floor. Where were the rotting remains? The last thing she wanted to do was to step into a gooey glob of decomposing flesh.

"Kenzie!" The hand grabbed at her and Kenzie pulled away, flailing.

"No! Let me go!"

"Kenzie, it's okay. You had a nightmare. Everything is okay."

Zachary's voice gradually worked its way into her consciousness. His words, though nonsensical at first, started to clarify.

"Where are you?"

"I'm right here. I'm right here with you. Come here."

He didn't grab her again, and Kenzie was glad at that. She opened her eyes and blinked, trying to bring everything in the dimness of the room into focus. Her room. Her house. She was there with Zachary, not a kidnapper or a dead body. Everything was fine.

She turned over and felt for him. He pulled her in and held her close.

"It's okay," he assured her. "It was just a dream."

Kenzie pressed her hot cheek against his bristly one, inhaling deeply to replace the smell of decomp still clinging in her brain with his familiar musk. Zachary rubbed her back in firm circles.

"I thought I was the one who was supposed to have crazy nightmares," he teased. "Usually, I'm the one waking you up."

"Did I wake you up?" Kenzie sniffled. "I'm sorry."

"No, don't be. You owe me a whole bunch of times."

It was true. The multiple traumas that Zachary had been through in his life often broke through in his dreams, and there had been many nights when she'd had to wake him up and comfort him, and convince him that a dream had been just that, only a realistic nightmare. Kenzie's dreams were the more garden-variety kind. Usually benign, her brain just working through what she had done during the day or something she had seen on TV. She wasn't sure why it had turned her work into something so terrifying this time.

The kidnapping was behind her. So brief that it should not still be bothering her. It wasn't like she'd been held for days or tortured. She'd bumped her head. She'd been fed chicken soup. And she'd been rescued. Why that should combine with the thoughts of Elysse Allen and the Petty Pond Jane Doe to create such a horrifying nightmare, she didn't know.

It should just stay in the past.

Zachary stroked her hair, listening to her breathing as it slowed. "Feeling better now?"

Kenzie took another deep breath in and out. "Yes. It's okay. It was just a dream."

"You want to talk about it? What was it about?"

"Nothing." She brushed it off. "I don't even remember now."

"No?" He kissed her on the cheek. "You can talk to me about it."

He didn't go as far as to say that he thought she was lying, but he clearly did. And he was right. But Kenzie didn't want to admit it. Whether she didn't remember or didn't want to talk about it, the result was the same. They weren't going to talk about it.

"I'm fine now," Kenzie assured him. "It was just a dream."

He lay down, pulling her gently down with him. He pulled the sheets over her, even though it was a warm night, tucking them around her and making sure she felt safe. Kenzie snuggled against his chest, breathing in his scent again. Warm and safe. Home. Nothing to worry about. Just transitory images in her head, and they were gone now.

"You're safe," Zachary assured her. "This is a safe place."

"Mmm-hmm," Kenzie agreed.

"We shouldn't have watched that program about Elysse before bed. That's probably what bothered you. It's already in your brain, and you were thinking too much."

He was intuitive. The stuff about Elysse was part of the equation, Kenzie was sure.

Zachary was very supportive, and he was in a good place emotionally. She could open up to him about the kidnapping now, and he would be understanding. He wouldn't freak out that she hadn't told him about it before. He kept things buried too, kept them hidden and didn't bring them up until the time was right and he felt safe sharing them. He would understand that she hadn't been able to tell him at the time. Not while he was in the hospital, trying to recover from his depression and adjust to new medications. He had been too fragile; news like that might have pushed him over the edge. Or might have made him check himself out so he could be home to protect her when he wasn't emotionally ready to leave the hospital.

"It's not just that," Kenzie said.

"Hmm?" He stroked her cheek, waiting for more information.

"It's just that... there's something I..."

If she told him now, neither of them would sleep for the rest of the night. And Kenzie needed to get her sleep. She needed to be fresh for the office tomorrow, to sort through missing person reports and figure out who Jane Doe really was. People would not accept that it was not Elysse Allen until either Elysse had been found or Jane Doe's real identity was established. They would continue to insist that it was Elysse and that the Medical Examiner's Office had made a mistake.

"What is it?" Zachary prompted.

"I don't know. I'll tell you about it tomorrow."

"Are you sure? We can talk tonight. It will help you to sleep if you can get it off your chest."

"No. It will just keep me awake."

"Okay." He started to rub her back again. "Whatever works for you."

12

"How are you doing this morning?" Zachary asked as they worked together to get breakfast on the table.

Kenzie yawned. "A little sleepy still, but I'm fine."

"You'll be okay for work? You won't cut off any fingers."

"Not any of mine."

Zachary guffawed at that. Kenzie smiled and had to chuckle along with him. That was one she would have to remember.

"Do you remember what your dream was about last night? You said you wanted to talk about it some more."

That wasn't *exactly* what she'd said.

"Uh… I'll have to think about it. I remember some, but…" Kenzie made a flicking gesture. "It doesn't really matter now."

He stopped what he was doing and looked at her, assessing this.

Kenzie looked away. "Really. I don't need to talk about it."

"You're sure something isn't bothering you?"

"I'm sure. It's just work and all that, I'm sure. And like you said, the TV report last night about her. It was disturbing… and I shouldn't have been watching it when it is so closely related to what I'm doing at work. I mean, I know now that they aren't Elysse's remains, but I can't help thinking about the story anyway. And like you said before… it's just one person out of the thousands who go missing every day across the country. And how many of those do we ever hear about? Hardly any of them. Just the occasional case that captures the media's attention because she's so pretty. It magnifies the tragedy of the case. 'Look at how young and vibrant and beautiful she was, so full of promise, and now she's gone.'"

"We need those cases... to remind us what's going on in the world. To pass the laws that will provide battered women with more protection and to fund the shelters. But there are so many women— and men, and kids—that no one cares about. They go missing, and they're lucky if anyone notices or bothers to report it."

Kenzie's toast popped. She placed it on a plate and buttered it, then took it over to the table.

What if Jane Doe had never been reported missing? What if there was no report on her? Not in another year, not in another state, just nothing? How would they ever identify her? And would anyone care if they didn't? She wouldn't be the first Doe to be cremated and consigned to Potter's Field without ever being identified.

Zachary unwrapped his granola bar, grimacing. Kenzie shook her head, brows drawing down. "What is that all about?"

"What?" Zachary dropped the wrapper on the table and nibbled the granola bar.

"Every time you unwrap one of those things, you look like you're in pain."

"Oh." Zachary looked down at it, his earlobes reddening. "Yeah. I don't know; it's probably a side effect of one of the meds. Some noises *really* bother me. Stuff that never did before."

"Like unwrapping your granola bar."

He nodded. "It's... painful. Like you said. Not quite the same way as when a really loud noise hurts your ears. More like... finger-nails on a blackboard."

"What else?"

"Hmm?"

"What other noises are a problem, other than unwrapping a granola bar?"

"Uh... I don't know." He didn't look at her, very focused on his meal. "Just random stuff."

"Something I do?" Kenzie guessed.

"No, just stuff. I don't know. I do my best to ignore it. If I make a big deal of it, focus on it… I don't want to get obsessed or to get so anxious that I avoid it." He lifted his granola bar slightly to indicate it. "I like these. They're easy to have for breakfast. I don't have to think too much about it and, even when I was so nauseated, I could still get them down, and it helped to have something in my stomach. So I refuse to start avoiding them because of the noise it makes when I unwrap them."

"Okay. I get that."

He shook his head. "I don't want to focus on those other things, either. I think… that if I ignore them long enough, they'll stop bothering me."

Kenzie shrugged. He understood the way that his brain worked better than anyone else. If he didn't want to tell her what things she was doing that bothered him so she could stop, that was his business. And he was probably right. Exposure was probably the best way for him to desensitize himself.

"What day is it today?" Zachary pulled out his phone and pressed the wake-up button briefly to check the date. "Wednesday. So couple's therapy tomorrow."

Kenzie nodded. "I've got the afternoon off," she confirmed.

"Even with this stuff about Elysse Allen and the new remains?"

"Yeah. If something changes, I'll let you know. But we need to cancel more than twenty-four hours ahead of time if there's a problem, so I would have to do that by this afternoon."

"If you can't go, just let me know. I'll just take it as a regular therapy day." He shrugged. "Then we don't waste any money."

"Deal," Kenzie agreed. "As far as I can tell right now, it won't be a problem. But if something comes up, I'll let you know."

He nodded and turned his attention back to his breakfast. Kenzie had missed one couple's therapy day, ending up getting stuck on a case at work and completely forgetting that it was their day. It had really upset Zachary. He was over it now but continued to make sure she knew which days were their couple's therapy sessions so that she wouldn't miss again. It was irritating, but Kenzie knew it was her fault for having missed. She couldn't blame that on him. He'd missed his individual therapy once recently, too. She'd panicked when she could not reach him by phone for hours after that. So she couldn't fault him for being upset when she had missed either.

It was just that he couldn't let it go, but had to bring it up over and over. No matter how casually or subtly he brought it up, it still irritated her.

"You'll probably be working on those remains most of the day?" Zachary asked.

"Maybe. It depends on how long it takes. It could be quick... or I could get nowhere today."

"I hope you figure out who she is. I hate the idea of her going unidentified."

"Me too. And I hope you manage to track down your missing girl. No luck yet?"

"Well..." Zachary held his hand up and rocked it back and forth in a *sort of* gesture. "I haven't seen her face to face or talked to anyone who has admitted to knowing where she is. But I have a pretty good idea that she's been circulating between a few friends. They're not... their reactions are off. They don't act like their friend is missing and might be in danger. They're either not worried enough, or it's over the top. They know where she is. But they're not going to tell and she isn't ready to go back home yet."

"So what are you going to do? Is that what you're going to tell her parents? That you think she's with one of these friends?"

"I'm going to watch them today. Coming and going... see if I can figure out which one she is with right now."

"You're stalking them?"

He nodded. "Yep."

"What if one of them sees you?"

"They won't."

"But if they do?"

"They know who I am and that I'm looking for her. Someone could call the cops to get me to move on. But the police know I'm looking for her too. All they're going to do is ask me to get on my way because I'm disturbing the girls."

"I don't want you ending up in jail," Kenzie warned. Following teenage girls didn't seem like a very smart thing to do. It could land him in a lot of trouble. Yes, they knew he was looking for the missing girl, but what if one of them decided to spin it like Zachary was the one who had made her disappear and now he was looking for another victim? It could take a long time to sort out an accusation like that.

But Zachary seemed unconcerned with the possibility of jail. It wouldn't be the first time he'd been jailed, Kenzie knew, and none of the charges had ever amounted to anything. Had he ever been in jail for more than a few hours? A few days or weeks? She didn't know. It wasn't something he talked about. And when he did mention jail, it wasn't with the same intensity as when he referred to Bonnie Brown or foster care or group homes he had lived in. Those institutions had damaged him. Jail had apparently not.

"Call me at noon?" Kenzie suggested.

"To let you know that I'm not in jail?"

Kenzie grimaced and shook her head. "No. Just… to talk to someone who doesn't deal with crime and dead bodies every day."

"Sure."

Kenzie stood up and put her dishes in the dishwasher. She bent down to kiss him goodbye. "Don't do anything I wouldn't do."

Zachary got up as well. "That's not really fair, you know. I can't tell *you* not to do anything *I* wouldn't do."

Zachary would not be cutting open dead bodies or examining slides and lab reports. And that was a good thing.

13

M orning, Kenzie," Dr. Wiltshire greeted upon his arrival. There were still guards at all possible entries to the morgue, keeping out people who didn't belong there. It gave Kenzie the weird feeling of being inside a prison rather than protected from all the people who wanted to get in to look at Elysse Allen's alleged remains.

"Morning, Doctor."

"How are things looking this morning?"

"More emails and voicemails asking about Elysse Allen and when we will confirm that the remains are hers."

Dr. Wiltshire shook his head in irritation. "We've already informed the police department that they are not. Why haven't they made an announcement to the public?"

"I don't know. They've had plenty of time. There's all kinds of stuff all over the internet and TV about how we found her. I don't know; maybe they figure that people will be focused on the remains that they found and that will allow them to continue the search without people getting in their way."

"Well, that could be. I don't imagine there are a lot of volunteers out getting into things and messing up potential evidence now. They think we've got her, so there's no point in looking for her elsewhere."

"I hope they make the announcement soon. Then I can start turning people away instead of just saying that there is an investigation underway and we have no comment."

Dr. Wiltshire nodded. "We'll stick to the tactics that the detective lays out, but I would like to be able to get rid of some of the extra security measures."

"You too? I should feel grateful for everything they are doing to make sure that the morgue is protected from these people. But..."

"You feel like you're living in a haunted house?"

"I was thinking prison. But that's... creepy."

The Medical Examiner laughed. "Creepy is what we do best. Shoot me anything that I need to follow up on, but I don't need to be informed of any inquiries into the status of the Petty Pond Jane Doe, even if it is from the governor's office."

Kenzie nodded her understanding. "Do you think we'll see any lab results back today?"

"I doubt it. Even basic tox is a few days delayed right now."

"Do you know what I was thinking about? Do you remember that forensic artist I told you about last year?"

"Sketches from skulls?" Dr. Wiltshire inquired.

"No. Phenotyping. Forensic DNA Profiles."

He squinted at her, thinking about it. "Yes. I do remember something about that. I seem to remember that it's several thousand dollars for her services, and there's no guarantee that what she produces will look like the subject."

"Yes," Kenzie admitted. "But she does multiple sketches, and the results I've seen have been remarkable."

"I don't imagine they show off the ones where the sketches didn't look anything like the subject they were trying to identify."

"Well... probably not. Anyway, I just thought it might be helpful in the case of this Jane Doe. She could get the computer-generated results, and then touch it up based on the actual skeletal structure of the skull. We know the height, hair color, and build of the victim. What she was dressed in. We can give an estimate of age. With all of that, we should get a pretty accurate sketch, I would think."

"Yes, you're probably right. With all that we have, I'm not even sure we need DNA phenotyping. Just the skull should tell us most of what we want to know. However…" He trailed off, looking somewhat uncomfortable.

Kenzie's brows drew down. She shook her head. "What?"

"We need to use our resources wisely. We can't spend too much on tests or sketches for just one subject. Especially when… it's not a case that will garner a lot of political or public attention once they realize she isn't actually Elysse Allen."

"You mean we don't want to put a lot of money into what might turn out to be some backwoods hillbilly or a teen runaway?"

He shrugged his shoulders and blew out a breath. "I wouldn't put it so indelicately, but essentially… yes. We have to be careful where we spend our money. We don't have endless resources."

"Well, we won't know whether it is anybody high-profile until we identify her."

"A catch-22," Dr. Wiltshire agreed. "We'll do the best with what we've got so far and see if we get anywhere before we make any decisions on higher-priced efforts."

Kenzie nodded. "Okay."

"She's obviously been waiting for a while already. There's no point in a big rush except to shut up the Elysse Allen fans."

"Speaking of political and public pressure, maybe we should use that to push through a couple of larger expenses."

"Since we've already proven that it is not Elysse Allen, I don't think that would go very far."

"Too bad."

"Assemble what you can of possible identities from missing person reports. How far back have you gone?"

"Not far enough yet." Kenzie hesitated. "How old do you think the remains are?"

"With the mummification… hard to say. It might have been a while. Modern dress, so we don't need to worry about her being an ancient American. But we might need to go back quite a ways to find her."

"If she came from Vermont," Kenzie clarified.

"Yes."

"And if she was reported missing."

"Right again. To begin with, that's what we have to assume."

"Okay. I'll get on it shortly, once I check through the other reports we got back today."

Even though Dr. Wiltshire said that they might have to go back quite a long time to find the missing person report for their Jane Doe, Kenzie hoped that she wouldn't have to go too far back. While the mummified remains could be pretty old, Jane's resting place had recently been disturbed and her body moved. There was a reason for that. Someone who knew her had moved her. If it was someone who knew her, then she was contemporary, and it couldn't be someone too old and frail to move a body unless he'd had help. He'd had a reason to move her, which meant that either he was trying to get rid of evidence that might point to his guilt in her death, or he had decided that the investigation into her death had cooled down enough that he could move her body. Either one pointed to a death that had occurred in the last few years, not fifty or a hundred years ago.

Dr. Wiltshire had mentioned her clothing being modern, so Kenzie brought the photos that had been logged of her clothing up on her computer screen. He was right, of course. Textile blends, plastic buttons, and zippers that were all modern inventions. Kenzie zoomed in on the tags to make note of the brands and sizes. The clothes were not in the best shape but, since the labels were on double-sewn seams, they were on the sturdiest part of the clothes. Stained and worn though they were, Kenzie could still get the information she needed.

"Thrift store chic," she suggested aloud as she looked at the pieces. Somewhat worn even before they had been stained by bodily fluids. Rips in the jeans, which may be real wear or intentional fashion. Styles that were slightly out of date, but still classic.

The slim cut told her that Jane Doe had a thin build. At the lower weight range for her height. That was another piece of information that might help them as they built a profile.

While mothers and even grandmothers sometimes adopted younger styles, Kenzie thought that the clothes were probably more appropriate for a teen to thirty-something. Dr. Wiltshire would take a closer look at the bones and give Kenzie an age range for Jane Doe. He might be able to narrow it down a little more.

An odd combination of daywear and sleepwear suggested she had died while she had been changing, maybe getting ready for bed at the end of a long day. Had she slipped in the tub and hit her head? Then her boyfriend had freaked out and covered it up, worried that he would be charged?

Kenzie looked through the itemized list of effects that had been checked in with Jane. No purse or wallet with ID in it, unfortunately. That would have made it too easy. She had some jewelry. Nothing expensive. It all looked like stuff that could be picked up at any department store. Nothing precious. Just styles and colors meant to accessorize outfits, not to convince anyone of her wealth.

No watch or phone. No personal electronics of any kind. No implants. Her hair was her own, no wig or extensions. Kenzie brought up the pictures of the woman's hands to look at her nails. Uneven and quite short. A couple of false nails were still glued in place on the mummified hand. Kenzie assumed she'd had all of her nails done, but only two had survived her death and decomposition.

There was little else to look at. One shoe. A few coins and a sodden mash of papers that might have been receipts. One of the techs would be in the process of unraveling and drying out the papers to see if there was anything identifiable on them. Kenzie suspected they wouldn't be much good. But if they could get a date off of a receipt, that would help set the time period for when she had been killed and might have been reported missing. And the location of where she had last been shopping, which might narrow down the location of her home or office to a particular neighborhood.

Kenzie clicked on the coins and zoomed in on them. Regular pocket change. Nothing fancy or collectible. But they might still be helpful… she wrote down the year of each one. Five coins, and not one of them issued more recently than fifteen years.

"Okay, then." Kenzie chewed on her lip, thinking about that, and returned to the clothing. Maybe the clothes hadn't been out of style. Perhaps they had been in style when the woman was killed. They were just out of fashion now. She broadened her search to the year after the last issued coin. Then she started playing with the filters, narrowing and expanding the search, looking for someone who fit her vision of what the woman looked like. Long, blond hair. Skinny. She'd had dental work done. Nothing really fancy, but there was also no major work that had to be done. She hadn't neglected her teeth for twenty or thirty years, hadn't had any knocked out or rotted out due to meth use—no wear due to age or grinding. Dr. Wiltshire would have to confirm her age based on his examination of the bones or a consultation with a forensic anthropologist. Unlike on *Bones,* they did not have someone in the office who could do the kind of work that Temperance Brennan did.

14

Zachary remembered to call at noon, which Kenzie hadn't expected. She figured he would get distracted by his work and forget about it. It would be easy for anyone to do, but especially someone with executive function as severely impaired as Zachary's by ADHD and his other issues.

"How's your day going?" Zachary asked. "You wanted to hear from someone who didn't spend his day cutting up dead bodies, and I didn't cut up even one."

Kenzie laughed appreciatively. "I'm glad to hear that. I might be a little concerned if you said that you had."

"Well, to be honest, I probably wouldn't tell you."

"That *wouldn't* be honest."

"Heh. No. So did you spend *your* morning cutting up bodies?"

"No. Mostly just looking at lab work and the dead person's stuff."

"Any luck in narrowing down the field? Identifying her?"

"Getting closer. I have some possible hits now, so I'll go through them in detail. I did have to go back a lot farther than I thought I would, like Dr. Wiltshire said."

"Guess he must know something about what he's talking about."

"I guess so. He does have a *bit* more experience than I do. How about you? How has your morning gone stalking teenagers?"

76

"I'm pretty sure I know where she is. Just hanging around for a while to see if she shows her face."

"Then what will you do? Tell her parents where to find her?"

"Talk to her. See if she's ready to go back."

"That's not really what they hired you to do, is it?"

"They hired me to find her and make sure that she was safe. If she turns around and tells me that she's not safe at home for one reason or another, I'm not going to tell her parents or make her go back. But from what I've learned, I think she'll be ready to go back. She might just need a little nudge. Someone telling her that it will be okay and that her parents still want her back. That she didn't burn all of her bridges by running away."

"I hope so. That would be a much nicer ending than her ending up on the street or in some shelter."

"Fingers crossed," Zachary agreed. "Hey, I see that the police finally announced that the remains found at Petty Pond have been examined and they are not a match for Elysse Allen."

"Did they? Finally. Maybe now I can start beating off these thrill-seekers who want to be closer to her remains."

"And they'll be back to calling the police again."

"Sounds good to me. That will be their problem."

"No word on them actually finding Allen's remains?"

"No, nothing." Kenzie thought about it, trying to decide whether she was surprised. It wouldn't be surprising to find out that Elysse Allen was dead. After all of the manpower put into finding her, it seemed likely at that point. But where was she? Why hadn't the cadaver dogs picked up anything else? Were they looking in the wrong place? Had Allen been taken far away from where they thought she had been kidnapped or killed? If Dain Porter had killed her and hadn't reported it for two days, he could have driven her remains far away. The place he reported her missing from could be hundreds of miles from where he'd actually disposed of her body. They might never find her. Like Jane Doe, her body might not surface for years, if ever.

"So you'll work the case you've got," Zachary guessed. "Try to identify the remains found at Petty Pond."

"That's exactly what I'm going to do."

And she would. As long as the woman had been reported missing, Kenzie was going to match up her identity and put a name and face to the poor girl.

She had suspected that there would be people who didn't believe that the human remains discovered were not Elysse Allen until they had a face and name to go with the body. But she hadn't realized exactly how resistant they would be. When Kenzie left at the end of the day, the security guard who was guarding the parking level Kenzie was on gave her a heads-up.

"You are going to need to be very careful leaving here today. There are a lot of angry people out there. Try to keep the car moving, but if they won't get out of the way, call the police." He smiled. "It won't take them long to get there."

"Angry people?" Kenzie raised her brows, wondering what was going on now.

"People who are unhappy about the failure to identify Elysse Allen."

"I didn't think they'd be happy about it, but I was hoping they would at least decide to back off a bit."

"No such luck. They have decided to be angry and self-righteous instead. If they can't lynch the boyfriend, maybe they can do something about the law enforcement officers who have failed to find her or bring her killer to justice."

"We can't *make* the remains match Elysse Allen."

He chuckled. "Don't expect people to make sense."

Kenzie shook her head and continued on to her car. When she rolled down the windows and put the top down, the guard hurried over to talk to her again.

"No, don't do that. Leave your windows and top up until you're safely away from here."

"You think there's really going to be trouble? What are they going to do? Climb into my car? Throw tomatoes?"

"I wouldn't put either scenario past them. You don't know how angry these people are. Please trust me."

"Okay, okay." Kenzie pushed the button to put her top back up. "See you tomorrow." She rolled up the windows as well, feeling a little claustrophobic in the warm car. It was only for a few minutes. She would put the top back down once she was far enough away from the protesters or fans around the police station.

She had thought that the guard was overreacting.

But as soon as her car was out of the parking garage, not even past the final barricade arm, she was swarmed. People—angry people, as the guard had told her—started banging on her window and the side of her car, yanking on the door handles to try to get in at her, shouting their accusations and waving their signs at her. They were all red faces and yelling voices, an overwhelming press of people. Kenzie did as the guard had suggested and let her car keep creeping forward, her foot on the brake rather than the gas, hoping that people would continue to step back from the moving car rather than attacking it or forming a human barricade that she couldn't get through. She wouldn't run over anyone. If it looked like she didn't have any way to get out of there without hurting someone, she would call the police, no matter how embarrassing it was to have to be rescued right behind the police station.

"They're just upset," Kenzie told herself aloud, as she watched the angry crowd and read their signs.

Conspiracy to hide Elysse Allen's death
Bring back Elysse Allen
Bring Elysse Allen home
Justice for Elysse
Kill Dain Porter (with graphic representations)

It was hard to believe these were people who would have considered themselves intelligent and well-adjusted. How could they believe that it was a conspiracy or cover-up? Who did they think was paying them off? And why?

A woman pounded on Kenzie's door with something hard, making Kenzie jump. What was she hitting it with? A gun barrel or hammer? She didn't want her window getting broken. Kenzie lifted her foot slightly from the brake pedal, letting the car take a jump forward. Not fast or far, but enough of a change from the previous pace that people jumped back from it, yelling at her and telling her that she was going to kill someone.

Then why didn't they get out of the way? They only withdrew a step and then were yelling threats and banging on the car again.

Kenzie hadn't called the police, but the roar of the crowd was suddenly broken by the whoop of a siren, and blue and red lights flashed around the lane. Several uniformed police officers hurried out of the building and toward the crowd, batons out, yelling at the crowd to get back from Kenzie's car and to let her go. Kenzie thought they would stick to verbal instructions and defensive postures, but they moved into the crowd, pushing them back and warning them that they were in breach of the peace.

The members of the mob yelled and complained, but they moved back, and Kenzie could take her foot off the brake and move forward faster. She waved at the law enforcement officers. She felt like she should stop and talk with them and thank them personally for stepping in to see to her safety, but she didn't want to make things worse by stopping, so she just waved and kept going.

The crowd watched her go, yelling and waving their signs the whole time.

15

Kenzie hadn't remembered that she had set up a dinner appointment with Walter Kirsch, her father. She got home from work and was ready to crash, to relax after a long, busy, and ultimately fruitless day at the office. She would put on her jammies early, have a drink—not alcohol, but something sweet and bubbly that would help her to feel more relaxed at the end of the day—and she and Zachary would have a nice supper and relax together. Maybe they would go for a walk together. Though if they were going to do that, she should hold off on the jammies for a while. Go for an after-dinner stroll and *then* get her pajamas on.

But when she arrived home, Walter was relaxing in her living room, waiting for her.

Kenzie looked at him blankly, then looked at her phone and verified that it was, in fact, the day that she was supposed to meet him. "Oh, I forgot. I'm sorry. I should have at least called to confirm."

"No need," Walter said with a smile. "I'm here. You're here."

"Yeah. I just forgot, even though I looked at my schedule. Went right out of my head."

"You can still go, can't you?"

"Yeah. Of course." Kenzie glanced around for Zachary. "Zach?"

"He said to tell you that he had to go back out. Something about talking to the girl's parents?" His voice ended the statement with a question mark, expecting Kenzie to explain it to him or at least to confirm that the message made sense to her.

"Oh, okay. He's not going to join us today?"

"Said he could be a while and that we should just go ahead without him." Walter gave a benign smile. "I don't think he was that interested in going out with us in the first place."

Kenzie shrugged. She had been trying to do more with her parents the last few months. Sometimes Zachary joined her, and sometimes he had other things to do. She thought he was trying to achieve a good balance of supporting her but not getting in the way of her relationships with her parents. Considering the fact that he probably just wanted to escape from having anything to do with them, he was doing well.

"Okay, I guess it's just you and me," Kenzie said, shrugging. She mentally pushed aside her regrets over not being able to just crash for the evening. Dinner with her father was not a low-stress, relaxing affair. She needed to stay on her best behavior, look good, and always be aware of how she presented herself. Even if Walter weren't judging her, anyone who saw them together would be—watching to see how they got along and making judgments about how that reflected on her and Walter. Deciding whether she "lived up to" her mother's and father's reputations.

And she would be trying to please Walter, even if she told herself that she wasn't. Did kids ever get over wanting to show their parents that they were acceptable, successful, productive, or good? Would Kenzie ever reach the point where she didn't care what her parents thought about her? She *said* that she didn't care, but she knew that she really did, under all of her talk about how she was her own person with her own morals and didn't need to worry about what her parents had to say about it.

"Shall we go in my car?" Walter offered, standing up and jingling his keys in his pocket.

It would be silly to insist that they go in separate cars or that Kenzie had to drive to maintain the illusion that she was in charge of the evening. And after the incident leaving the morgue, Kenzie didn't want her car to be out on the street, visible to anyone who knew it. Sitting in a parking lot, just waiting to have the windows smashed, paintwork keyed, or tires slashed. Until people had calmed down a little about the announcement about the remains not being identified as Elysse Allen's, Kenzie needed to maintain a low profile. It was probably better if she didn't even go out, but she didn't want to back out of the commitment she had made to her father and she didn't want to stay in for pizza or some other casual meal. She wanted him out of her house. It wouldn't be polite to insist that he leave her house when she finished her meal, but he would understand if she said that she needed to get home so she could be prepared for work the next day.

Walter was still looking at her inquiringly, waiting for her answer.

"Umm, yes. Let's take your car," Kenzie agreed.

Walter smiled, his shoulders relaxing a little. Despite his outward appearance of being calm and relaxed, it was probably awkward for him too. He also wanted Kenzie to think well of him and wanted to improve their relationship. He was tiptoeing through the same minefield, trying to have a nice time with her, not to aggravate or put too much pressure on her. Relationships could be complicated. Especially if both of them were masking their own feelings, acting happy, polite, and relaxed when they were not. Dr. B would have had a lot to say about how they were dancing around each other, not being honest about how they felt about everything.

Walter led the way to the front door. Kenzie armed the burglar alarm and the door locked behind her when she shut the door. Walter clicked the remote on his keychain. The Lexus at the curb gave a little chirp and the quiet engine purred to life. Walter managed to stay a couple of steps ahead of Kenzie to hold her door for her, which was *really* not necessary. She felt like he did it for show, an ostentatious display of how much he respected his daughter when in fact, he did not.

But she couldn't tell him not to open the door for her. He wouldn't listen anyway. Kenzie slipped into the front seat and sat frozen for a moment while she waited for him to close the door so it wouldn't hit her elbow. Once the door was closed, she buckled her seatbelt and readjusted the air vents blowing cool air in her direction.

Walter got into the driver's seat and warning bells told him to put on his seatbelt. He looked sideways at her. She knew that he didn't like to wear a belt. Most of the time, he probably quieted the alarm by buckling the seatbelt behind him.

"Do you know how much more likely you are to end up in the morgue if you're not buckled in?" Kenzie asked. "I would have died in that accident on New Year's Eve if I hadn't been wearing my belt. Zachary too."

"Maybe he wouldn't have been injured so badly if he hadn't been wearing one."

"It saved his life," Kenzie told him with certainty. "The car rolled several times, and he would have been thrown out of the car, maybe crushed by it. Your chances of survival are best if you use your belt and any other safety devices built into your car."

"This is a very safe vehicle," he grumbled, pulling the belt across his lap and pushing the tongue firmly into the buckle with a click. "Lots of very advanced safety features built into it to prevent me from ever having an accident in the first place."

"I'm sure there are. But none of those will help if someone else hits you and you're not wearing a seatbelt. The only things that will help you at that point are your belt, airbag, and safety cage."

Walter pulled the car out smoothly onto the road. He was a good driver. The Lexus handled beautifully and felt luxuriously smooth.

He didn't ask where she wanted to go, but instead drove to an upscale restaurant that he'd probably booked a month in advance. He would never agree to "just a burger" or some ethnic place he hadn't checked out ahead of time. He was more than a little classist. He did not choose valet parking, instead taking a space well away from other cars. They walked in together, Walter holding Kenzie's arm as if he were escorting royalty.

"Mr. Kirsch," the maître d' knew him by sight and gave a little bow. "I'm so glad you could join us tonight. If you would follow me?"

They did so. Of course, he hadn't reserved a table in the dining room but had a private room booked, so they were away from prying eyes and ears.

"You didn't need to go to all this trouble," Kenzie protested.

Walter shook his head. "You've had a long day. You deserve to go out somewhere you can relax."

Kenzie was not relaxed. All of the ostentation was not making her feel more like herself. Instead, she felt like she was somebody completely different. A prop in Walter's play. Arm candy. He was pretending she was someone she was not.

They were seated, and Kenzie perused the single-sheet menu in elaborate cursive writing on heavy cream paper. Handwritten, not spit out from an inkjet printer. Walter ordered a bottle of wine, and she didn't object or order a separate drink.

"Do you need some time?" Walter asked, indicating the menu.

Kenzie shook her head, putting it to the side. "The chicken," she said.

Walter raised his brows. "There are oysters. Lobster. You can have chicken any time."

"And that's what I want today."

He shrugged. The maître d' nodded. "And you, sir?"

"Prime rib. Rare."

"Yes, sir." He exited quietly, pulling the door shut behind him.

16

Walter relaxed into the butter-soft, high back leather chair, letting out a sigh. "Thank you for agreeing to join me. I really do appreciate you taking the time."

Kenzie nodded. She had remained aloof from Walter for a lot of years, seeing him when she had to at Christmas or on special occasions, but putting him off when he called to talk or suggested getting together, just the two of them. She preferred to have Lisa there as a buffer. But then she didn't get to know him. The real Walter. Instead, she got the diluted version. The Lisa-mediated version. Now she was trying to get to know him. What he was really like as a person. Not just as her father.

"This will be nice," she said, not really meaning it. Everything about the dinner would be nice, of course, but that didn't mean that the experience itself would be.

"So, how have you been?" Walter asked, though it was not that long since they had last talked, and he already knew what was going on in her life.

"Good. Everything is going well. Things were kind of crazy today, but other than that, it's been pretty routine. Enjoying the nice weather."

"Vermont winters are beautiful, but I do enjoy the summers," Walter agreed.

"Yeah. Me too. Snow is nice when it first falls, when you get those big, sparkly, magical flakes. But when you have to drive in it, slosh through puddles of muddy slush, or shovel the walk... I think it lasts too long. A week or two, that would be nice, and then more summer."

Walter chuckled. "Dream away."

"I know it's not going to happen. It would just be nice if it had been designed with a little more forethought." Kenzie laughed.

"You should go away during the winter. Take a vacation. A cruise or a beach somewhere nice. It makes a big difference."

"And how would you know that?"

Walter looked trapped. "Err..."

"When was the last time you took a vacation?"

"I did have that time off around Christmas."

"Not hiding from assassins. On a beach or a cruise."

"I think the last time I took a cruise must have been with your mother." Walter's eyes were distant as he considered it.

"Was that before Amanda was born?"

"No. There was one when she was well. After the first transplant. When we were sure she was healthy and would not reject it or react to the drugs." He nodded, thinking about it. "That was a nice time."

"That was a long time ago."

"Well... yes."

A waiter knocked and entered, bringing the wine. He uncorked it and poured glasses for them, waiting until Walter tasted his and nodded, dismissing him.

"And they weren't assassins," Walter said.

"Hmm?"

"The Russians... they weren't assassins."

"Some of them were."

He shifted uncomfortably. "Not the ones I was dealing with."

"The one who killed the man I was supposed to meet for lunch was," Kenzie said firmly, looking him in the eye. He couldn't lie to her. He couldn't talk his way out of this one. She knew what she was talking about.

Walter cleared his throat and had another sip of the wine. "Very nice."

Kenzie nodded. She wasn't a connoisseur, but it was pleasant enough to her tastebuds.

"And Zachary? He's well?" Walter asked, changing the subject.

"He's good," Kenzie agreed, allowing herself a genuine smile and flush of pleasure. She was happy with how he had improved on the new med cocktail. Next Christmas was in the distant future, he was getting sunshine and fresh air on his walks, was able to eat better without the nausea the last drugs had caused, and was looking fit and happy. While his ADHD, PTSD, and anxiety still caused some problems, the worst of his issues were under control for the time being. "He's been doing really well lately."

"Has he?" Walter sounded doubtful, which made Kenzie frown and look at him.

"Why do you say it like that? Yes, he's been doing well. A lot better on his current meds."

"Okay." Walter shrugged. "I just thought when I saw him today... he seemed agitated. Not just about me being there before you got home, but... I thought something else was wrong."

Kenzie pondered this. He had been pretty calm lately. But his ADHD might look like agitation to someone who didn't know him. Or something might have happened that he hadn't had a chance to tell her about yet. He didn't call her at work because he didn't want her to be upset, so he waited until she got home. But she was out with Walter, and he was out dealing with the parents of the girl he had been looking for, so it would have to wait.

"Did he say anything about this case that he's on? The parents that he's going to talk to?"

"No. He sounded like you would know what I was talking about."

"I do. And he shouldn't have been stressed about that. Unless he found out something..." If the girl had turned out to be hurt, addicted, or dead, then going to talk to the parents would obviously be a huge stressor. But surely, he would have called her if that had turned out to be the case? He would have told her that he was going to talk to the parents and why, instead of just making a casual comment to Walter about it, not even knowing if Walter would remember to pass it on to Kenzie. Going to talk to the parents without telling her about any of the intervening activity *should* just mean that he knew where the girl was, had talked to her, and was going to fill in the parents. That was good news. Not something he would be upset about.

"What did he say or do that made you think something was wrong?"

"I don't know." Walter tried to just brush it off. "I must have misjudged. Maybe he didn't like me being there or didn't want you going out with me tonight. Relationship stuff..."

"Maybe. But he's been really good about us seeing more of each other. Encouraging me to go."

"Doesn't mean he can't be jealous or worried about how it will go."

"That's true. Oh, well. I guess I'll find out tonight if something is wrong." She thought about his confessing to how much noises were bothering him lately. A symptom that he had been hiding from her until she had pressed him about his obvious discomfort. How much other stuff was going on that he was masking? She didn't like the idea of his hiding things from her.

Though she couldn't very well criticize him for his secrets while she was keeping her own. It was okay for couples not to tell each other everything, Dr. B had told them. It was okay to have private thoughts and feelings. Experiences that they were not ready to share. They would be stronger as a couple if they gave each other the space to be individuals and didn't smother each other.

"So, how is your work?" Kenzie turned the conversation back to Walter. She knew he could talk all day about the causes he was lobbying for. "What great evils are you fighting against these days?"

Walter eagerly launched into a description of the various bills that he was supporting or fighting against in the senate. Of course he was against anything that promoted more government oversight or regulation. The family foundation was supporting a bill on home care regulation, so he stayed out of that one so as not to cause any conflict of interest or bias. Kenzie hoped that even if the bill did not pass, it would at least raise awareness of how elder abuse or neglect could exist in homes where elderly parents were living out their lives under their children's care or the care of a home care nurse rather than in a nursing home. Completely unregulated, untrained carers could cause injury or even death when they were just trying to do what was best for their loved ones. After what she had seen in the morgue, she hoped there could be a little government oversight in homes, even if Walter thought they should just butt out.

17

W e want the Mom and Pop shops to be able to flourish in Vermont," Walter was saying. Kenzie realized she'd zoned out, lost in her thoughts rather than listening to what he had to say. But he didn't appear to have noticed.

Kenzie nodded and tried to refocus on what his current lecture was about.

"The big chains think they can just come in and take over, to bury the little guys," Walter explained. "Their scale means that they can undercut prices, pay higher rents, and steal employees, stores, and customers right out from under the independents. If the little guy can't make it in Vermont, where will he go? Canada? We can't afford to lose these small businesses that make it a real community. If we replace all of these family stores that have been around for generations with big box and big chain stores, we lose our culture and what makes Vermont so special."

Kenzie nodded again. "Pride of ownership, locally owned and operated, stores where people know their customers by name."

"Exactly. We need to ensure that there are protections in place so that the little guys can hold on and run a profitable family business."

"That sounds good," Kenzie agreed. Though she wondered how he thought they could prevent the big companies from buying up everything without increased government oversight. Maybe he had already explained why he felt this cause was more important when she had been distracted.

Walter studied her, and maybe saw that this particular issue wasn't grabbing her interest quite as much as he thought it should.

"Have you read up on the early screening tests that the foundation is supporting?" he asked. "There are so many diseases that, if caught early, would be much more treatable, but the doctors and hospitals won't do it because it costs money to test people who aren't showing any symptoms. They would rather wait until they're *really* sick and treat them then, when they aren't as likely to be able to recover or have a good outcome. But if we can get these tests into the hands of the public—tests that are easy to administer and read—then people can be treated much earlier for a wide variety of diseases that can be slowed down or stopped early if caught quickly enough."

"I was reading the case memo on that," Kenzie acknowledged. She had been interested in the types of testing and how accurate home tests would be. The lab tests were reliable but, when they relied upon people to test themselves at home, there would be many more false positives and negatives because people didn't understand what they were supposed to do. And the companies that commercialized the tests would likely cut some corners, making the tests less reliable. "There are risks in that approach. That people will think that they don't need treatment when they do, or they'll panic about having something they don't."

"But we are raising the bar. Making it easier for everyone to be tested improves treatment possibilities for everyone. Even if you have some incorrect results, they are so much smaller than the number of people who would have been missed and lost out on the chance for treatment."

"Only if the false results are small enough, and I don't think we've established that yet. In a commercially viable product. If not, then the results are meaningless."

"If a loved one was sick, wouldn't you want to know right away? If we had known that Amanda was sick earlier, would her outcome have been better?"

"I don't think it would have been. I doubt it would have made much difference. They did everything they could have."

Walter shrugged, unable to argue with her medical opinion.

Their dinners arrived and they ate for a couple of minutes in silence. Kenzie considered Walter's words and what they were trying to do. She had wondered when she saw him after Christmas whether he had been sick or on a diet, or whether when he said that he had just been in hiding, he had actually been held by the same criminals as had kidnapped her. His weight had been down and he had seemed pale. He had more color now, but she didn't think he had put any of the weight back on. Was it intentional? Was he trying to eat better and get into better shape?

"How are you and Mother doing? Are you guys both okay?"

Walter looked up from his meal, one eyebrow raised.

"I just mean… these questions about early screening and being able to treat these diseases quickly, that's not because one of you is sick, is it? I mean… you've lost weight, and I've wondered about Mother a couple of times. She hasn't really seemed herself…"

"No, we're both fine," Walter assured her. He put his hand over his slimmer stomach. "It's good that I'm losing weight, right? It's better for me."

"Yes. Definitely. You're looking good. It's just one of those things. A sudden weight loss can be a clue to a lot of medical problems…"

"No." He shook his head. "You don't need to worry about that. I'm going to be around for a long time."

"Good."

"And your mother?" Walter gave his head a slight shake. "What's going on with her? I haven't noticed anything off…"

"I don't know. I just get the feeling sometimes when I talk to her that… things have changed. Maybe she's not happy, or has something on her mind. It isn't like when Amanda was sick, but… I've worried whether she is depressed… if she's overdoing it with the foundation work and needs to dial it back… I just worry. I guess that's normal, that as you get older, you start to worry more about your parents."

"No, you shouldn't have to worry about us. Have you talked to her about this? Asked her whether she is depressed or overstressed?"

"No. You know Mother. She would be offended. She'd think that she must have done something wrong to make me think that, and she'd get all defensive, and I wouldn't be able to talk to her again without her bringing it up."

Walter took another bite of his prime rib and chewed slowly, considering it. "I hadn't really thought about it. She's fine. I don't think there's anything to worry about. But maybe she's been a little more anxious since Christmas. That's normal." He shrugged. "After what she went through with Maksim, and not knowing what had happened to me. The stuff that you got involved with. It would make anyone a little more sensitive for a while. I'm sure it will pass."

"It's been six months."

"More or less. But you know how it is with emotional stuff. It takes time." He pointed his fork at her. "How long does it take Zachary to get over his depression?"

"Well… he doesn't really get over it. He goes through cycles."

"And they take months."

Kenzie nodded. "Yes."

But a better comparison might be how he had reacted after his encounter with Archuro. And it had taken him a long time to get over some of the effects of that. And there were still some longer-lasting problems, even though he was doing both individual therapy and couple's counseling. They might never be completely gone. Zachary's experience had been more traumatic physically and emotionally than Lisa's, but there was no arguing that Lisa might still be feeling anxiety brought on by the events around Christmas. Some people suffered for years after a particularly frightening or emotionally taxing situation.

Kenzie needed to give Lisa a break. She would heal in her own time. If she wanted to talk about it, she could call Kenzie anytime. Kenzie didn't need to be digging into her personal business, wondering about her emotional health and why she wasn't "over it" yet.

"The foundation is focusing more on mental health now," Kenzie said. "Maybe Mother will avail herself of some of the resources we have researched."

"Maybe." Walter's lip twitched. "Don't count on it."

Kenzie grinned. Her mother was one of those people who would drive herself into the ground before she admitted that she needed help or was subject to human frailties like everyone else. She might be spearheading all kinds of mental health projects right now, but that didn't mean she'd ever admit to susceptibility to any mental illness herself.

"Tyrrell seems to be enjoying his job at the foundation. Have you heard anything about how he's doing?"

"All reports are positive. Your mother and Hillary both seem to like him, and that's really all that matters. If he's got them both on his side, he can't go wrong."

"Well... you know that he could have a setback at any time."

"We all know that. And we are committed to giving him whatever help he needs, now and if he does fall off the wagon. The foundation is there for him. It isn't just words, MacKenzie."

Kenzie knew that they thought they would be able to be there and be supportive, but how people thought they would react and how they really reacted when faced with a raging drunk or an employee who completely fell off of the landscape could be very different. When the old prejudices and the belief that Tyrrell could just get better if he had the willpower reasserted themselves... then Kenzie would see how much they really understood about addiction and the depth of Tyrrell's problem. She wasn't at all convinced that they would be quite so open and helpful at that point.

"Good," she nodded. "I'm glad to hear that. I just hope it all works out the way that you foresee."

"You think I'm an old man and don't understand these things the way you do. And maybe I don't, but I'm savvier than you give me credit for."

Kenzie's face got hot, and she hoped her flush wasn't too obvious under the dim lights of the private dining room.

18

nd how is your own mental health, while we're on the subject?" Walter asked.

Kenzie opened her mouth and didn't know what to say to that. Her first reaction was to brush him off. To tell him she was "fine" and move the conversation in another direction. But her sessions with Dr. Boyle and Zachary had taught her not to use "fine" to deflect such inquiries, but to find a way to answer them truthfully or to tell him if she didn't want to discuss it. If she expected her father to take mental health issues seriously, and if she believed that mental health should be addressed as openly and naturally as physical health, then she shouldn't be embarrassed to answer his question or brush it off as unimportant or none of his business.

"You've been in the media spotlight a bit lately," Walter went on when she didn't answer immediately. "You've been under a lot of pressure. And I'm not sure that *you've* recovered from what happened after Christmas."

"It's a work in progress," Kenzie agreed, feeling her way through her answer. "Some days, I feel like everything is perfectly okay and everything is the same as before. And other days... I feel like a completely different person. I can't believe that everyone else around me can't see it. Like I'm an impostor, but they have no idea that I've replaced the person I used to be."

"You're seeing a therapist too? The one you have through couples counseling?"

"Uh… no. I've talked about it, but I'm not seeing anyone separate yet…"

"Hmm. That surprises me. I thought that since you're a big proponent of seeking therapy for mental illness… destigmatizing it… I would think you would go to someone as soon as you felt the need."

Here Kenzie was judging her father for saying that he would support Tyrrell in the event of a relapse, suspecting that he would not follow through with the actions he said he would, when he was right, she had not put her money where her mouth was concerning mental health and seeking treatment.

"Yeah. You're right. I'm… resisting it. And I shouldn't. I should be doing what I tell others to do."

He nodded, but he didn't lecture her about it.

"Do you want to talk to *me* about it? You don't have to explain anything to me. The background. Because I already know all of that."

"I'm… a lot more anxious than I ever was before. Certain words or subjects bother me, even out of context. I find myself… thinking about things when someone is talking or I should be focusing on something else."

Walter nodded understandingly and did not interrupt.

"I'm having nightmares. I never used to. I mean, I had normal nightmares. A brief one in the night, especially if I have a fever. But then I wake up and it's fine. And I was never soaked in sweat, out of breath, afraid for my life."

Walter reached across the table and took her hand, holding it warmly in his own for a moment.

"Now… they're very realistic. Very frightening. I wake up or partially awaken, but I'm still dreaming and don't know where I am. And the feeling in my stomach… it stays with me. Even the next morning. Like something terrible is hiding right around the corner."

"How is Zachary handling that?"

"He's good. He's always very supportive. Holds on to me. Tells me it was just a dream. Rubs my back. If he's there. Sometimes when I wake up, he's not. He's already up or he's on surveillance. Maybe that's one of the things that triggers the nightmares. Subconsciously recognizing that he isn't there beside me."

"Can't you ask him not to go on surveillance? Call out to him if you wake up and he's in the other room?"

"No. I don't want to make it a bigger deal than it is."

"Because, like your mother, everything is fine. It's perfectly fine and you're a superwoman. Supporting everyone else's problems and ignoring your own."

"I'm not ignoring it. I'm just... dealing with it."

"Are you?"

Kenzie tried to force down a couple more bites of her chicken, but her mouth and throat were too dry and it hurt going down.

"No. Maybe I'm not. Maybe I'm just hiding and hoping it will go away."

"It won't."

"What about you?" Uncomfortable, Kenzie turned the tables on him. "I don't know all of what happened to you around Christmas, but I think it was just as difficult as what I went through. Probably more so. So what are you doing? Are you getting counseling? Are you having nightmares and trouble focusing?"

"I was not kidnapped. I was not threatened. I was not hurt." Walter shrugged his shoulders. "I was negotiating with a group of businessmen, just like I do all the time. I think you're just trying to put your feelings on me. I did not suffer anything. I resisted pressure. Held out in my negotiations. That's all."

Even if he hadn't been held captive as Kenzie suspected, he had still been through the experience of his daughter being kidnapped and threatened. Knowing that he was the cause of the violence toward her. And that had caused him to buckle in his "negotiations." They had been able to get what they wanted out of him.

That kind of experience had to be just as disturbing and life-altering as Kenzie being snatched off the street and abducted. Kenzie knew Walter loved her, even if he didn't always behave as she expected him to or show it in the ways she would have wanted him to.

His family being threatened—both Kenzie and Lisa—had made Walter change his tune and fall in line with the Russians' demands. He could act like that hadn't had a lasting impact on him emotionally, but Kenzie didn't believe it.

They looked at each other for a moment, each considering the other's refusal to get professional treatment when they knew they should, and grimaced.

"So, this case you are on now," Walter said, moving away from the subject of therapy. "How is that going? I've heard so much about this Elysse Allen that I feel like I know her."

Kenzie dabbed her mouth with her napkin. "Everybody seems to think that her boyfriend killed her. And we know that's the pattern we're used to seeing. A woman is far more likely to be murdered at the hands of her boyfriend or husband than to be kidnapped by a stranger. Stranger abductions are extremely rare."

"That's what the statistics say. But there isn't any evidence, as far as I'm aware, that shows that Dain Porter did anything to hurt Elysse, or that he had anything to do with her disappearance other than being the one to report her missing—which you have to admit would be a stupid thing to do if he was the one who 'disappeared' her."

"Not really." Kenzie shook her head. "If he didn't report her missing, someone else would have, and it would have looked really suspicious that he hadn't. He didn't really have any choice; they would suspect him either way."

"The boy doesn't have any chance of *not* being suspected. A hundred years ago, maybe he'd be able to say that his wife just left him or wandered off into the wilderness and got eaten by a bear, and people would have believed him, but in today's culture… you know that everyone will believe he had something to do with it."

"What is suspicious is that he didn't report her missing right away. He didn't just wait a few hours to see if she would cool off and come back to him. He waited a few days. I can't think of many cases where I wouldn't be panicking over my significant other disappearing the first night he didn't come back."

"Everyone knows from TV that you can't report someone missing for forty-eight hours, though. If he'd gone to the police before that, they wouldn't have taken him seriously. They would have just told him to go home and wait for her."

"No, they wouldn't. That's just a TV thing; it isn't true. You don't have to wait twenty-four or forty-eight hours to report someone missing. If you believe something has happened to them, you go to the police immediately. They're not going to tell you you're just being silly."

"Ever?" Walter challenged.

"Well... okay, maybe there would be some circumstances under which they would tell you to wait to see if he came back. Someone who had disappeared several times before. Someone who was supposed to be away. Maybe someone with a drug problem. An illegal immigrant. But *normally*, if you're concerned that someone has been kidnapped or something horrible happened to them, the police aren't going to tell you to go home."

"You've had good experiences with the police."

"Yes. I've always found them to be friendly and helpful."

"Not everyone has had that same experience."

"Okay. True. But he still should have reported her missing right away."

"They'd had a fight. He thought she would come back when she'd cooled down."

"If he's telling the truth. If he didn't kill her, then he might have just been waiting for her to cool off and come back," Kenzie admitted.

"So you think he did it too."

"I don't know. I think it's a possibility. But I do know one thing for sure, and that is that Elysse Allen's remains are not in the cold room at the Medical Examiner's Office."

Walter smiled. "I hear that the Medical Examiner's Office is actually part of the official conspiracy to prevent Elysse Allen's murder from being solved. That somebody like Dain Porter has paid them off."

19

Once she finished her initial review and organization the next morning, Kenzie picked up where she had left off with the missing person reports, going through them one at a time to see whether they were potential matches or something excluded them. A number of them were missing critical pieces of information in the computer database and file system. Hopefully, the information she needed would be in the paper files, but it would be up to somebody else to check that out. The police would have to go through their own files to track down any file updates, missing dental x-rays or DNA analysis, or other bits that she needed to check before she could exclude a file.

The stack of reports that could be matches for Jane Doe was getting smaller, and she didn't know whether to be excited or worried about that. Would she find Jane's information in one of the remaining files, or would she get to the bottom of the pile and, having excluded everyone, have to admit that she had hit a dead end?

She knew that Jane Doe could be from New Hampshire, New York, or even Canada. There was no telling how far a kidnapper might have taken her from her home or how far a killer might have driven with her stuffed in the trunk of the car. Or she might have fallen through the cracks in another way, never even identified as missing. An illegal immigrant, a child who had aged out of foster care, a homeless person or drifter who didn't have any ties anchoring her to a family or good friend to report that she had dropped out of view.

Eventually, Kenzie was left with three files that seemed to be good matches to Jane Doe and included dental x-rays. Kenzie opened the x-rays from the first and viewed them on her screen. There wasn't anything that excluded them from being a match to Jane Doe immediately. She had looked at Jane's x-rays enough times to know roughly what they looked like. She opened the comparison x-rays up and positioned them side by side, holding her breath as she looked at them.

They were close, but not close enough. Some fillings were in the wrong teeth. A root canal didn't show up on Jane's x-ray. She closed the first set of x-rays and pulled up the next one. Quite different, unless Jane Doe had been in a serious accident and had her whole mouth rebuilt. And if she had, Kenzie would have expected to see a lot of screws and hardware, which were not present.

Kenzie sighed. She wasn't going to be able to identify Jane. Maybe the files that the police pulled would solve the riddle. She pulled up the third set of x-rays and glanced back and forth between the missing person and Jane Doe.

She caught her breath and held it again. She looked at the tops of the x-rays for the filenames to ensure she hadn't opened the same x-rays twice. But she had not. The missing person's x-rays and Jane's were almost identical. Jane Doe had had a couple more procedures done since seeing that dentist last. Maybe it had been her family dentist and she had moved out and found another closer to where she lived. Or maybe the dentist hadn't taken new x-rays after the last round of work had been completed.

Kenzie punched the button on her phone. Dr. Wiltshire picked it up almost immediately. "Kenzie?"

"I think I've found her."

Dr. Wiltshire could undoubtedly hear the excitement in her voice and didn't bother asking who she had found. "You want me to come out there?"

"I'll put them up in the boardroom."

"See you in a minute, then."

Kenzie launched herself from her desk to the boardroom and was still a little out of breath when Dr. Wiltshire got there a minute later to look at the x-rays up on the big screen. He looked slowly back and forth between them, taking way more time than he needed to to verify that they were the same jaw and teeth. Kenzie saw his eyes go up to the filenames as well.

"Sharon Briggs."

Kenzie felt a rush of warmth, as if naming her made the match even more certain. She nodded and also invoked the name. "Sharon Briggs."

Kenzie didn't know for sure if she believed in an afterlife, but she had to wonder if part of the thrill that she felt was due to Sharon Briggs's consciousness, somewhere out there in the universe in some form, knowing that her body had finally been found and someone knew what had happened to her.

"Good work, Dr. Kirsch. How long has Ms. Briggs been missing?"

Kenzie swallowed. "Thirteen years."

Dr. Wiltshire nodded, as if he had expected this. Kenzie had assumed that the remains were much newer than that. But Dr. Wiltshire's instincts had been more accurate.

"Advise the boys upstairs. Maybe now they'll be able to calm people down about it being Elysse Allen's remains."

"They won't think this is just part of the conspiracy?" Kenzie asked, chuckling.

"Oh, I'm sure they will. But we can only do the best we can. If the public gets a few details, enough to build a picture of this woman and what happened to her, hopefully they will find her story just as interesting as Elysse Allen's disappearance. Tell me what we know about her."

"Twenty-two at the time of her disappearance. A history of running away and addiction since she was a teen."

"So the police didn't put a lot of resources into finding her."

"The file is pretty thin. They checked all of the boxes. Inquired at her work and last known residence. Canvassed the area she was last seen. Did a media release. Other than that... they just said they had exhausted all resources and let the file go cold."

"Who reported her missing?"

Kenzie pulled up the missing person report and skimmed it. "Someone she worked with, it looks like. She had missed a few shifts at work and wasn't answering her phone."

"Where did she work?"

"Retail, I think." Kenzie looked down the columns of text. "Yeah. Associate, salesperson, whatever they called her. Part-time."

"If she was an addict, I assume she also had another source of income."

Kenzie grimaced. "Yeah, probably. Or someone else was putting her up. She wouldn't have been able to afford rent anywhere decent on part-time sales associate wages."

"No. You're right about that."

"Now that we've identified her... what's next? Aside from informing the police department, I mean. As part of our investigation, we can call the people on the file to ask further questions."

"Let the police do the police work," Dr. Wiltshire warned. "Our investigation is confined to the circumstances of her death. Where she lived and where she was last seen may be relevant, but you can't be knocking on doors asking people if they knew if she had any enemies or ever heard any rumors that she had been bashed over the head and was dead."

Kenzie nodded. Her inquiries into previous cases had taught her that she needed to be more careful. Not to step on anyone's toes. Let the police make the police inquiries and stick to the morgue and the death report. And that was exactly what she would do with Sharon Briggs's death.

20

Kenzie remembered about it being Thursday afternoon, her couple's therapy appointment with Zachary and Dr. Boyle. She gave herself plenty of time to get there so that she and Zachary would both be relaxed and in a good place mentally for their appointment. Some sessions could be tough, with lots of mental and emotional digging, and it was best to be in a good frame of mind before it began.

Zachary put away his phone when Kenzie walked in. She sat down beside him. "How was your morning?"

"Good. Pretty quiet, getting caught up on some billings and background checks."

"I never did hear how things went with your missing girl. Walter said that you were going over there, so that sounds like good news."

Kenzie had been tired on her return home after dinner with Walter, and she and Zachary had spent some time unwinding before bed, not discussing anything important. Kenzie wasn't even sure when she had fallen asleep. She might actually have passed out on the couch while they were watching TV, moving to the bed when she woke up in the night. It felt like her sleep had been disrupted, but she couldn't remember much about it.

"Yes," Zachary confirmed. "I did a bit of mediating between the girl and her parents. She wanted to go back, but needed someone to test the waters first, make sure it was okay. Figure out how they could get back on track again."

"So, is she back home with them today?"

He smiled, his eyes lighting up. "Yes. All safely settled with them last night, and no messages this morning to say that she'd taken off again or things hadn't gone well. I think she'll be able to move forward without any major bumps in the road. There aren't any addiction or abuse issues as far as I can tell. Just hormones and a kid trying to please her parents and become more independent."

"Being a teenager is tough," Kenzie said sympathetically. "I'm glad I don't have to go through that again."

He rolled his eyes. "Me too."

Kenzie felt a little guilty. She didn't have anything to complain about as far as her adolescence had gone. She hadn't been a rebel. She hadn't been smoking, drinking, and partying. She'd been responsible, helping to look after Amanda when she was home and sometimes while she was in the hospital too. As soon as she turned eighteen, she had consented to the donation of her kidney to her sister. That was her rebellion, donating a vital organ when her parents had said that she was too young to make such a decision, and saving her sister's life. Yes, she'd had her share of mood swings and temper tantrums, but most were confined to her bedroom where no one could see or hear her. She'd known her parents didn't need the extra worry.

Zachary's teen years, on the other hand, had been spent pinballing from foster family to group home to residential care and back again, never settled in the same place more than a few months at a time. She sometimes thought he was lucky to have survived those years. He nearly hadn't, with more than one suicide attempt. And who knew how bad the abuse had been; he'd only ever hinted about it, never describing anything in detail.

Elizabeth, the nurse receptionist called to Kenzie and Zachary. "Dr. Boyle will see you now."

They stood and made their way to Dr. Boyle's office, where she usually met with them. There were the usual greetings and casual comments. Zachary and Kenzie sat down and looked at each other and Dr. B, wondering where their therapy would take them today.

Dr. B asked them each how they had been doing the last two weeks. Zachary nodded and smiled and said that he'd been doing well. He looked it, within a healthy weight range, tanned, and appearing relaxed. Kenzie's time had been a little more stressful, with her suspension the previous week and the drama with Elysse Allen and the unidentified remains taking up most of her time since returning to the Medical Examiner's Office. She gave a brief summary and shrugged, as if none of it was that important.

Dr. B nodded, taking her at her word. But Zachary looked at her sidelong.

"I think there's more going on than that."

Kenzie glanced at him, surprised that he would challenge her statement. Then she looked at Dr. B, expecting her to say that if Kenzie didn't want to share anything more, that was up to her. But Dr. B's lips were pressed together as she looked at Kenzie.

"I think Zachary is right. I get the feeling that you're glossing over it. Is there anything in particular that's bothering you this week?"

"No... I'm not sure what you mean. That's what I've been dealing with at work. It's been a bit stressful with all of the media attention and people getting everything wrong, but that's not my responsibility. I just do my job and let the police public relations deal with the media."

"You haven't felt threatened by these 'fans'?"

"No, not really. For a few minutes yesterday, but the police arrived to help disperse them so I could get out of there, and then I was fine."

Zachary was looking at her, a worried frown creasing his forehead. "What happened? The police had to be there for what?"

Kenzie shifted uncomfortably. Zachary not being home when she arrived, and being too tired and wrung out to talk after the dinner with Walter, Kenzie hadn't shared the details of her day with Zachary, just as she hadn't taken the time to find out how his missing girl investigation had gone. Then they hadn't discussed much more than "how was your sleep?", the weather, and the schedule for the day at breakfast. She hadn't meant to keep the details of the difficulties with Elysse Allen fans from him. It had just worked out that way.

"We just haven't really talked since then," she told him apologetically. "It wasn't anything really, just that… when we determined that the remains were not those of Elysse Allen, the fans decided that it was because of some conspiracy and, instead of going away because there wasn't any point in trying to get closer to the remains anymore, they went a little bonkers."

"And…?"

"The security staff has been really good at keeping them out of the morgue and the parking garage. Top-notch security. But when I drove out of the parking into the alley, the fans swarmed the car. I guess they knew me or my car, and they were banging on it, yelling, not letting me through."

She watched the alarm grow in Zachary's eyes and forced a smile.

"It's not as bad as it sounds. I didn't run over anyone. They didn't damage the car or threaten me directly. Within a minute or two, the police were there to push them back so I could get out. And that's all. I just drove out of there and made it home without incident. There might be a few fingerprints smudging the paintwork, but I'll have her detailed and she'll be as good as new." She said the last in a teasing tone, hoping he would be reassured there was nothing to be concerned about. If all she was worried about was fingerprints then, obviously, it had not been anything.

"Why weren't the police out there ahead of you if they knew there was trouble? They should have had that area taped off or guarded so you could get through. What if someone had thrown something through the window? Fired a gun?"

"It wasn't like that. It was just some upset fans. They weren't going to hurt me."

Even as she said it, she knew that wouldn't be good enough. He would remember Brittany's fans and how quickly and thoroughly they had removed the threat to her life when they had arrived on the scene. Upset fans were not harmless.

"The guard told me not to put the top down or roll down my windows. And the police were there right away. It was just a minute."

Zachary shook his head. And he was right; if one of those fans had pulled a gun on her and shot through the window, the police would have been too late to do anything but clean up afterward.

But they had not been that threatening. There hadn't been any real danger.

Kenzie's heart started to race. Not because of what had happened coming out of the parking garage, but because of what had happened after Christmas. It was totally different. Not the same kind of situation at all. But just the thought of *real danger* brought it all back. The fear—the terror of being overwhelmed, of the physical violence that had immediately immobilized her, the memory of a hood being pulled over her head and sitting there in the cell-like room she had been held in, terrified of what they were going to do to her. Trying to be a good hostage so that they wouldn't kill her.

21

K enzie?"

Kenzie covered her face, pretending that she was just rubbing the bony ridges over her eyes. That she was just tired and fighting a headache. Behind her hands, she tried to compose her face into a mask that would not show what she was thinking and feeling and to collect herself. She wasn't in any danger. What had happened months ago was over and the Russians were no longer a threat.

"Sorry. I guess I needed a bit more sleep last night."

She lowered her hands, giving them both a tired smile. Just fatigue. That was all.

Both Zachary and Dr. B were watching her, and Kenzie could see that neither believed her. They had seen something of her true feelings; both were concerned and wanted to know what was happening.

"What's going on?" Zachary asked. "If there was more to it than that... it's okay to talk about it. This is a safe setting. I'm not going to repeat anything to Dr. Wiltshire or the police. Or anyone."

"No, really, that's all that happened," Kenzie assured him. "It was just a minute, a mild scare, and then it was over."

Neither of them said anything.

"It's just that..." Kenzie started. She could talk about the kidnapping. She could tell them now what had happened. Zachary had been stable on the new med protocol for several months, even if he was having some symptoms that he hadn't told her about. He was in a good place emotionally and Dr. B was there if he freaked out and needed someone other than Kenzie to talk him down.

She shook her head quickly. "Nothing. It's nothing. Just one of those things that is unexpected. So it gave me a bit of a turn. But I'm fine now. I was fine when I got home afterward. I was disappointed that you were out and I'd forgotten about Walter making a dinner date. But I didn't even remember to tell you about it when I got home later." She gave a short laugh. "So how traumatic could it have been?"

"Then something else is going on," Zachary pressed gently.

"No…"

Neither one believed her. That was clear. Kenzie cleared her throat and tried to think of how to explain what had happened without it sounding like a big deal. It had only been a few hours. Not even overnight. She hadn't been hurt, other than a bump on the head, which was due to her own clumsiness, not an intentional injury. But no matter how she tried to approach it, it sounded bad. And when she tried, her throat closed and her mouth dried out.

"I'm not ready to talk about it," she said finally.

That was the protocol they had settled on to keep things honest but still maintain privacy and give them time to process things and wait until they were ready. She couldn't say she was fine. She couldn't lie and say that there wasn't anything bothering her. But she could say that she didn't want to talk about it. The rule was really meant for Zachary, but it had to go both ways. If she was going to let him have his privacy over things he wasn't willing to share, the same privilege had to extend to her.

"Okay," Dr. B said, when Zachary didn't accept this immediately, but kept looking at Kenzie, hoping his silent stare would persuade her to share with him. "If Kenzie isn't ready to talk about it, then we need to move on to other things. Right, Zachary?"

"But…" He tried to come up with a reason she had to share, but he didn't.

"Maybe we could talk about your med cocktail," Kenzie suggested. "You've been having side effects but not telling anyone about it."

Zachary drew back, sucking in air suddenly and glancing over at Dr. B to see her reaction to this revelation.

Dr. B just raised her brows. She didn't look accusatory or jump all over him.

"Minor symptoms," Zachary said. "They're much better than the previous meds. Nothing I'm worried about."

Dr. B nodded. "If they're minor, then there's no need to suggest any changes at this point. But sometimes, what seems like a minor symptom can actually be a dangerous sign. You haven't talked to me about any side effects. I assume you discussed them with Dr. Mike while you were still in the hospital."

Zachary nodded, but it was clear from how he tilted his head and looked away that it wasn't actually a "yes."

"*Have* you talked to a medical professional about the side effects?" Dr. B asked.

"No."

"Will you?"

Kenzie wanted to insist that Zachary spill the beans right there. He knew what symptoms he was having. Kenzie and Dr. B were both medical professionals who could help analyze whether the "minor" symptoms were something they needed to be concerned about. While the misophonia that Zachary had described when unwrapping his granola bars didn't sound like anything to be worried about, there might be other effects that he was hiding. Hearing voices, having suicidal thoughts, increased compulsions—something they had been hoping to cut down on with the new prescription—heartburn, angina, or headaches. There were many things he might be trying to ignore, and he didn't want Kenzie to worry about.

But she couldn't force him to tell her about them. She wasn't his treating physician and, as a family member, should not have anything to do with his treatment. If he promised to go to one of his medical team about it, Dr. B would let it go, maybe follow up with him on it privately at his next session.

Zachary licked his lips and looked back and forth at them, not happy that he was now the one in the hot seat.

"Fine," he agreed. "I'll talk to someone about them."

"Before our next session?" Dr. Boyle asked.

He looked away, wanting to find a way out of it. His fingers tapped the arms of his chair. "Okay."

Dr. B nodded, indicating that she was done. They could move on to other topics.

Kenzie was going to need more ice cream than usual after this session.

22

Things had been awkward between Kenzie and Zachary when they returned home after the therapy session. Usually, even though Kenzie felt emotionally raw after a session, she felt like things had been resolved and that they had moved forward in their relationship. This time, she felt unsettled by both her inability to talk about the kidnapping and Zachary knowing that something was wrong, and by Zachary not wanting to talk to her or Dr. B about his med side effects. The two things being left unresolved gnawed at her.

She considered telling him that she had to return to the office to complete some more work before going home to avoid the festering issues between them.

But lying to him and trying to avoid the awkwardness wasn't going to make anything any better. So they went home and tiptoed around each other, pretending everything was fine. Respecting each other's need for privacy, both of them probably resenting it.

Kenzie was glad to get to the morgue in the morning. There was plenty to do, lots of things for her to keep her mind off the kidnapping and any relationship problems. She had already seen that the fact that they had identified Sharon Briggs's remains had made it to the news, although they hadn't included Sharon's name. Her immediate family would have to be informed before they spread her name all over the internet.

In a lull, Kenzie pulled up the Sharon Briggs file and skimmed through it, looking for the address of her last known residence. There wasn't much she could do from the Medical Examiner's Office, but she could at least start forming a picture in her mind of what the woman's life had been like. She knew a little, but being able to place her in a specific neighborhood or building would help. Kenzie knew most of the neighborhoods around Roxboro more or less, and a map search might give her a picture of the front of the building.

She typed the address into her search engine and clicked on the resulting link. And there it was, the house that Sharon Briggs had lived in before she died. It was not, as Kenzie had feared, a flophouse, some condemned building that junkies gathered at to shoot up or sleep it off. Maybe to turn tricks for enough cash to score the next hit. Instead, it was a bungalow in an older area of town. The yard looked a little neglected, but there weren't carcasses of old cars with no wheels up on blocks or boarded-up windows. Somebody did their best to look after the place, even if the paint was starting to flake and the grass in the yard had burned to brown in the summer sun.

She navigated to the city's municipal tax database and typed in the address again, which gave her the name on the tax roll. She had known that it wouldn't be in Sharon Briggs's name. Even if she had once owned it—which, from reading Sharon's background, Kenzie didn't think was likely. She had been gone for thirteen years and, if she had stopped paying taxes, the city would have seized it.

Titon, Charles

Kenzie wrote it down in her notes. Chances were the house had probably gone through several owners since Sharon's disappearance. But she could start tracing the title back to find out who had owned it at the time she had disappeared. No doubt she would be duplicating police efforts, but she could at least fill in a few more of the blanks in Sharon's history. The more they knew about her, the better their chance of understanding what had happened to her.

Kenzie checked for new emails to be handled or filed. There were a couple of lab test results. One was tox screens on Jane Doe, now identified as Sharon Briggs. Kenzie opened it and skimmed through the results. The woman's long hair had come in helpful in tracking how much she had been drinking and doping in the years before her death. Her alcohol, amphetamines, opiates, and cannabis levels were all consistently high. She'd been using pretty heavily.

The blow to her head might have resulted from a fall while she'd been drunk or high. She might not even have realized that she'd hurt herself, and walked away from the accident. Or she might have been knocked unconscious and bled out where she fell.

And then what? One of her drinking buddies, afraid of being discovered, had hidden her body somewhere out of sight. But why would he take that long to dispose of it properly? Or why had he decided to do so now? Was the place her body had been hidden being demolished? Renovated? Whoever had hidden it had anticipated her body being found and had decided to move it. And why not in the wilderness, where the media hype said that Elysse Allen had disappeared? Kenzie had heard more than one talking head say that it could be years before someone discovered Elysse's remains. The woods were thick and, if it was an area that there wasn't a lot of foot traffic through, a body could decompose to practically nothing, predators scattering the remaining bones over several square miles.

She felt sorry for Sharon Briggs. She didn't know what had triggered Sharon's drinking, but she had heard a lot of sad stories about how people had been trapped by addiction. There was usually more to it than just getting a taste for alcohol or drugs through partying or experimenting. The young people who used the most, who went through several years of such heavy use, were frequently abused, homeless, or mentally ill. Or all three. Look at Tyrrell. Though on the surface, it looked like he'd had a fairly normal upbringing in a middle-class family and had been privileged enough to go to college and gain a degree, the first six years of his life had been hell. So bad that he had been unable to bond with his new family and had started drinking some time before his teen years. He had worked hard to earn the money to go to school and to get that degree, but it was the only two-year period since he was nine or ten that he'd been dry.

What was Sharon's story? Why had she started drinking and what pain had she been trying to anesthetize?

Titon, Charles.

Why did that name sound so familiar?

Kenzie looked down at the piece of paper she had written it on. She was sure that she knew the name from somewhere else. Had it been on Sharon's file already? She didn't think so. She opened the missing person file again and skimmed it for the name Titon. She pressed Control-F and searched for it. It did not occur anywhere in the file.

So, where did she know it from?

23

D r. Wiltshire was walking by on his way to the kitchen and raised an eyebrow at Kenzie. "You look troubled. Is something wrong?"

"No…" Kenzie tapped her pen on the desk, trying to figure out where she knew the name from. A minor celebrity? Someone on the police force? She was sure she had seen it just recently. "It's just that… this name…"

She opened the ME's database and tapped Charles Titon into the search field. If someone by that name had any association with a file, he should show up.

"What name?" Dr. Wiltshire asked as the search results popped up on Kenzie's screen.

"Charles Titon," Kenzie said faintly, staring at the results on her screen.

Dr. Wiltshire nodded agreeably. "Postmortem I did two or three weeks ago."

"Three and a half."

"So why are you wondering about him? That case is finished, off of our desks."

"It was natural causes?" Kenzie asked.

She could see the report right in front of her. But she was trying to wrap her mind around it and reconcile it with what she now knew.

"Yes. Heart attack on the bus in the morning. Much more common than people would like to think. They tell you to get up early in the morning to be healthy. To walk and take the bus. It's healthy and economical, but Titon isn't the only one to die of a heart attack on one this year —" Dr. Wiltshire cut himself off, frowning at Kenzie's expression or the fact that she didn't appear to be following his lecture. "What? Do you think there was a mistake? Something else has shown up in a lab test?"

Sometimes that happened. They thought they knew what was going on, but then a test came back weeks or months later, turning everything upside-down.

"Umm... no. His name showed up on another file."

"Really." Dr. Wiltshire scratched the back of his neck. "What file?"

"He owns the house that Sharon Briggs was living in when she disappeared. Or rather, he did own it. I guess someone else does now."

"Sharon Briggs's residence?"

"Yes."

"Well, how did that happen?" Dr. Wiltshire's brows drew down, and he looked just as puzzled as Kenzie felt.

"He must have known... maybe his doctor told him that he had a heart condition and didn't have long to live. He knew he had to dispose of her body so that no one would discover it after he died." Kenzie shook her head. "Does that make any sense at all?"

"That body had not been in the water for a month," Dr. Wiltshire said with certainty.

"It was very decomposed. We both recognized that it had to have been decomposing for longer than the time that Elysse Allen has been missing."

"But it couldn't have been that old. With how warm it has been, and the body being in the water, and the fish, there would have been practically nothing left of her after a month."

"Maybe it took her longer than you think to rehydrate. She was mummified, and she didn't start to putrefy until the body had been completely rehydrated..."

"No. It wouldn't have taken that long to rehydrate. And being so old, the decomposition processes would have proceeded very quickly. It would likely have been faster, not slower, than a fresh body dump."

"Well then... you're saying that someone else dumped her body. And it just happened to be a few weeks after Charles Titon died. You think it's a coincidence?"

"By no means. I think the police need to talk to whoever took possession of his house after his death."

The police had expressed considerable astonishment at the connection between the remains discovered at Petty Pond and the man who had dropped dead on the bus three and a half weeks earlier. It didn't take them long to contact Mr. Ryder Phelps, Charles Titon's next of kin, and to ask him to come to the police station for an interview.

According to Detective Edwards, the homicide officer who called Ryder Phelps, he had protested at first. Still, when Edwards had threatened instead to show up at his workplace or his home, he had quickly agreed that his attendance at the police station would be preferred. People tended not to like their coworkers or neighbors to know when they had any involvement with the police.

Phelps must have known that the police were on to him for something but, instead of running, he decided to try to play it cool, pretend ignorance of whatever they asked him and hope that they would believe he was innocent of any wrongdoing and leave him alone after an initial interview.

"You don't mind me listening in, do you?" Kenzie asked as Edwards led her to an observation room where she could see and hear the interview with Ryder Phelps via the AV equipment installed in the interview room.

"Usually, we're the ones who are coming down to watch you work," Edwards pointed out. "I guess I can't complain about you coming up to watch me."

"Good. I'd really like to hear what he says about all of this. It's very bizarre."

"I doubt if he'll have much to say about it, although you never know, he could break down and confess. Some people do. But the hope is that we can get a warrant to search his house while he's still here, maybe even get a head start on the search before he decides to go home."

"What do you think you'll find?"

"I'm sure you've heard as many stories about these ghouls as anybody else. The rocking chair Titon kept her in until his death? Maybe even his bed? A shrine in the basement? Who knows which kind of sicko he is, but it's obvious he was some kind of sick. And so is this guy," Edwards jerked a thumb in the direction of Phelps's interview room. "The kind of guy who decides to dispose of a body he finds in the house he inherited instead of calling the police and asking them to deal with it? There's something wrong with him, too. Maybe he was involved in her death somehow. Maybe he had argued with Titon before, tried to talk him into disposing of the body, but Titon was blackmailing him. 'Pay up or I'll tell the cops about your shriveled little friend.'"

Kenzie shrugged, shaking her head. "It sounds like a stretch, but that's out of my wheelhouse. It does seem strange that he would dispose of the body like he did if he wasn't involved in some way. He and Charles Titon were obviously related or good friends, for Titon to leave him the house. Maybe Phelps agreed before Titon's death that if anything happened to him, he'd get rid of the evidence."

"Another possibility," Edwards agreed with a nod. "Not a bad thought."

He made sure that Kenzie was comfortable and had everything she needed—a chair and a cup of coffee in front of the screen was all she required—and left her there to interview Ryder Phelps.

24

Ryder Phelps was not a happy man. Watching him on the camera feed, Kenzie tried not to judge by appearances, but he looked like the stereotype of a guy still living in his mother's basement in his thirties. Sloppy in a t-shirt and sweats, slightly overweight, with a full beard and hair sticking up as if they had just pulled him from bed. He certainly didn't take much pride in his appearance.

The t-shirt wasn't even anything interesting like his favorite band or anime, a clever or sarcastic saying. It was between gray and the olive drab of an army uniform in color. Like it had started as something else, but the color had been washed out of it, leaving the dingy, drab gray. Phelps looked around the room nervously, not happy sitting there by himself waiting for something to happen. How much did he think the police knew? He clearly wouldn't be there if he thought that they had anything on him or would be able to prove that he had killed Sharon Briggs or had anything to do with her death. He thought that he could bluff his way through the interview and they wouldn't be able to pin anything on him. And, as far as Kenzie was concerned, he was right. The police didn't have anything yet to connect him with the young woman's disappearance and murder. They didn't even know if he had been in town at the time or knew Sharon or Charles Titon. He might have made Titon's acquaintance some time after that. He might have never met Sharon.

The door opened, making Phelps jump, and Edwards entered. Phelps sat up straight, but then leaned back in the uncomfortable-looking plastic chair, attempting to look casual and unconcerned. Nice and relaxed about a random interview with the police about a dead girl. Kenzie didn't imagine she would ever be comfortable in such a situation.

"Mr. Phelps, I appreciate you coming in," Edwards said politely, and sat down across the table from Phelps. He sat at an angle, with the table mostly beside him, not facing Phelps in a confrontational way, but attempting to look, as Phelps was, as if this were simply a routine interview and there was nothing to worry about. Edwards held a stack of papers, somewhat messy, and made a half-hearted attempt to square the edges to neaten them up. He put the papers down casually on the table.

Phelps's eyes went to the papers, and Kenzie imagined he was probably trying to read whatever he could on the top page to see whether it was anything he needed to be worried about. He shifted his position, trying to get a bit closer and to look at them from a better angle. Edwards didn't appear to notice this.

"I'm not sure what this is about," Phelps said. "You said it was about Charlie's house. I've only been in there for a couple of weeks, so I can't really tell you anything. You know that he died, right?"

"I did hear that, yes."

"I don't know anything that Charlie might have been involved in. We didn't have very much to do with each other. I inherited the house, hadn't ever even been in it before. It was a bit of a surprise to me. But in a good way. Who wouldn't want a house? A lot of people are having trouble getting a leg up right now, starting out on their own. Most people would be happy with a house."

He was talking too much, nervous, the words just falling out. Trying to get ahead of any questions Edwards might have, yet pretending to be relaxed and calm. Just a normal day at the police station. Something about his friend Charlie, not about him.

"The title hasn't even been transferred into your hands yet," Edwards said agreeably.

"No. But it is in the works. But I'm not responsible for anything that happened on the property before I inherited it. You can't get me for anything that Charlie did on the property. I wasn't living there until three weeks ago. Nothing that happened before then has anything to do with me."

Edwards nodded and wrote something deliberately into the notebook on the desk in front of him. "What kind of condition is it in?"

Phelps hesitated. "What do you mean?"

"I mean… had it been kept up well? Clean and properly maintained? Electrical, plumbing, not a hoarder or anything like that?"

"Oh. Yeah. I mean he had a lot of junk, a lot of stuff that I won't keep, stuff stashed away, but it wasn't a public health risk."

He would be better off claiming that Charlie had been a hoarder, right down to keeping the corpse of the dead girl. Saying that he had found the mummified body buried beneath a stack of newspapers. Distance himself more. Didn't he understand that the police had already connected the remains to him? Why did he think they had called him in?

"What's it like?" Edwards paged through the papers on the table in front of him, pulling out a black and white printout that Kenzie could see was the exterior of a house. The house that she had looked up on the internet. "Looks like a nice little place. Two or three bedrooms?"

"Three," Phelps agreed. "I can use one as an office and one as a guest room. And my own room, of course." He gave a little laugh.

He didn't say that he had started using one as an office and one as a guest room, even though he had been in there for three weeks. Just that he could. What had he been doing in that time? Cleaning out junk and ordering furniture? Watching TV and planning to do it sometime in the future? Finding a body and being too creeped out by the discovery to ever use the room for its planned purpose?

"And what did you find there?"

"Find there? I don't know what you mean. A house, three

bedrooms. All of Charles's stuff. I mean... it was his house. What would you expect to find there?"

What any of them would have expected to find there and what had apparently been there were two very different things.

"You've been cleaning out Charles's possessions? And excuse me, I didn't ask, exactly what is your relationship with Charles? The two of you were related? Old friends?"

"He's a cousin. Second cousin or something, I never understood all the babble about who is what kind of cousin. I'll leave the genealogy to someone else."

"But you were his closest living relative?"

"As far as I know. But I never expected to inherit anything from him, that's for sure."

"Who did you think he would leave it to?"

"No idea. I don't know his friends. I would think that he'd have at least one friend that he would have wanted to leave something to. And something like a house, that's a pretty big possession."

"But he didn't leave it to someone else; he left it to you."

"Not on purpose, I don't think," Phelps said with a shrug. "He didn't bother writing a will. It's what they call *intestate*. He didn't leave it to anyone, so the government has to decide who inherits it. He didn't have parents or siblings, so they had to go through any other remaining relatives. Neither one of us has siblings."

"How did they find you?"

"When he died, they needed someone to claim the body. So I guess they pulled his birth certificate to get his parents' names, searched for them and searched for him online. Between his parents' obituaries and social media connections, I guess they got to me. Called me out of the blue. Explained that he had died and they needed someone to claim the body and take care of arrangements."

It had probably been Kenzie who had made that call. She didn't remember doing it, but she did them fairly regularly and there wasn't any reason that particular notification would have stood out above the rest. She enjoyed doing internet research to track down people's relatives. Someone who could take care of arrangements and care for the body instead of just cremating the remains and sprinkling them in a potter's field. Zachary had given her a few tips for tracing family members, and she always felt like a private investigator when she did it. Finding a connection and reaching out to them was very satisfying. Even if it was a shock that estranged cousin Charles had died and left no one who could take care of him, most people could be talked into claiming the remains and interring the person with some small private ceremony. Kenzie did what she could to point them toward affordable funeral arrangements. Cremation and an urn. Something inexpensive that still honored their connection with a person they probably hadn't seen in years.

"That was very good of you to take that on," Edwards told Phelps.

Phelps puffed up a bit at this, his chest expanding and his hunched shoulders rising and straightening. "Yes. It wasn't something that I'd been planning on, that's for sure. Even if Charlie had made arrangements ahead of time, I don't think anyone was expecting him to die when he did."

"The Medical Examiner ruled it a natural death?" Edwards shuffled some more papers to check on this detail. "No sign of foul play?"

"No, of course not. The guy died on the bus on his morning commute. Why would it be anything else?"

"Sometimes strange things happen." Edwards looked at Phelps. "Unexpected things."

There was an awkward silence. Kenzie wondered for a moment whether he would be bold enough to speak up about other unexpected things he had discovered when he entered Charlie Titon's house. Kenzie or someone at the office would have passed Charles Titon's wallet and keys and any other possessions he had been carrying with him on his morning commute. Phelps would take the keys and go find the house, if he hadn't been there before, open it up, and decide what to do with it. Move in? Turn around and sell it and buy a house closer to where he lived or worked? Knock the place down and have a developer build two skinny houses on the wide lot and make twice as much on the sale? There were a lot of options. Phelps would not have expected to open the house and find a mummified body waiting for him.

Or had he?

25

Phelps was not ready to give it up yet. He looked away from Edwards, unable to meet his eyes, but did not start babbling about the strange thing he had discovered when he took possession of cousin Charlie's house.

"Why don't you tell me about your cousin?" Edwards suggested.

"What about him?"

"I know that you said you're not close. You weren't best buds; you didn't hang out together. But had you met him before?"

"Yeah." Phelps nodded jerkily. "Sure, we'd met before—family reunions, when our parents would force us all to play together. Or when we got to be older, we'd take off together to have a smoke or drink. But we didn't see each other a lot. Just now and then, as kids."

"You haven't seen him recently?"

"No. Been ten years or more." Phelps gave a shrug and an exaggerated searching look as he stared off into space, trying to remember something that would make the cop happy. "Maybe fifteen. So I can't be of much help to you. I don't know of anything that he might have been involved with. So unless it's something that means I can't keep the house... I'll just go on living my life and you can ask around somewhere else. People who actually knew him."

"What about Sharon Briggs?"

Phelps flinched and tried to cover it up, rubbing his nose and cheekbones as if he were tired or felt a headache coming on. "Who?"

"Sharon Briggs. Titon's girlfriend."

"I wouldn't know anything about that. I don't think I ever met anyone by that name."

"He wasn't dating when you'd see him at family reunions?"

"No, I don't think so. Neither of us was that social. And you wouldn't bring a girl to one of those things. Not unless you were really committed to each other. Engaged or close to it. Because of all of the questions you have to answer from the relatives, the number of times you have to explain yourself... introduce her... answer awkward questions or put up with the older uncles putting the moves on her right in front of you. No, you don't take a girlfriend to a family reunion. Not unless you're serious."

"And you didn't think that Titon was serious about Sharon Briggs? Their relationship didn't seem to be that close? They were living together, weren't they?"

"Were they?" Phelps made a wide, helpless gesture. "You see, I don't know anything. I didn't know he was serious with someone or living together. We didn't keep in close touch. I don't know when the last time I talked with him was, even a casual conversation or some social media exchange. Neither of us sends out Christmas cards. Or if he did, I wasn't on his list." Phelps gave a little laugh.

Edwards gave Phelps a hard stare. If it had been Kenzie, she would be quaking in her boots. Any time she dealt with law enforcement, she had been on the right side of the desk, not a suspect. Even if she had done something that might have caused them trouble in an investigation—accidentally, of course—then it had just been out of overzealousness. She hadn't been trying to hide nefarious misdeeds. Phelps swallowed and looked around for an escape. He didn't have to stay there. Maybe he was trying to decide whether it would look better or worse if he left in the middle of the interview. Stay and keep trying to bluff, or walk out and confirm that he had something to hide, but avoid giving anything away accidentally? Phelps's hands pressed to the table, ready to rise to his feet.

"Let's stop playing games, Mr. Phelps," Edwards said coldly. "You and I both know what is going on here. So why don't you drop the act and tell me what happened from the beginning?"

Phelps shook his head, eyes wide. "No, I don't know..."

"Do you know the penalties for indignity to a dead body? For obstructing a murder investigation? Do you have any idea the crapload of trouble you are in?"

Phelps's Adam's apple bobbed as he swallowed hard. Kenzie wondered if he were going to cry. He looked very close to it.

"What are you talking about?" he squeaked out.

"I'm talking about Sharon Briggs. Her body didn't just get up and walk away by itself."

"I told you, I don't know her. I don't know what you're talking about. Murder?"

"Apparently, a murder that you are mixed up in. I don't know yet what your role was in the whole thing, but you can bet I'm going to turn your life upside down to find out."

"I didn't kill anyone. I wasn't involved in anything."

"Then stop obstructing this investigation and tell me what you know."

"I don't know anything. Just that... just that..." His throat worked, but he didn't seem to be able to get the words out.

"You know things that could help us. You are preventing us from finding that girl's killer. And maybe that's because it was you."

"No! I didn't kill anyone. I've never killed anyone. I wouldn't do anything like that. I've never even been in a fistfight. I'm not that kind of person."

"You're just the kind of person who drags a body around the county to find a good place to get rid of it. To prevent us from getting justice for that girl."

"No, no, it wasn't like that. I didn't think there was any investigation. It's been years, so... I didn't think there was any harm..."

"You thought it would be okay to move a dead body," he said with heavy sarcasm. "That we just let people do that whenever they like. That it wouldn't matter what had happened to her and that her family had never had any closure and that no one had ever been put behind bars for it. That it had been long enough that nobody cared anymore, so you might as well just *dump* her like a bag of manure."

"I didn't mean anything by it. I honestly didn't think that anyone would… still be looking for her. That no one would care about it. I just found her a place…" He trailed off, trying to figure out a way to make his actions sound logical, even altruistic. Just giving poor Sharon a final resting place. He'd only had the best of intentions.

"You think we dump people in the pond to inter them? Is that what you did with your cousin when you claimed his body?"

"Of course not. The crematorium, they took him and gave me his ashes. I didn't have to do anything. But I couldn't exactly call them to pick up… that *thing* from the house."

"Oh, no?" Edwards leaned forward, feigning interest in Phelps's explanation. "And why is that?"

"Because…" Phelps stammered, trying to answer what was clearly a rhetorical question. "She hadn't… there wasn't any paperwork… she'd been there for so long, there's no way they would… they would report it…"

"Of course they would. And that's exactly what you should have done. What kind of a moron do you have to be to decide to dump a body in the pond instead of *calling the police to inform them that you have a dead woman in your house?*"

"I didn't want any trouble. I didn't want them poking around, and I didn't want to have to answer a bunch of questions." Phelps used his hands to indicate his surroundings. "I just wanted… for it not to be there, and for me to be able to live in that house without being creeped out by it. I mean… living in a house with a dead body?" He made a gagging sound. "I don't understand how Charlie could have done it. *Why* he did it. Who does that kind of thing?"

"You're the one who knew the sicko, not me."

"I don't know why he did it," Phelps reiterated. "I would never do something like that. He *was* sick. That's obvious. A normal person doesn't do something like that."

"No, he doesn't. But a well person doesn't grab a mummified corpse from his house and take it out on a joyride either! So what if you didn't want to have to answer questions? You haven't exactly avoided that, have you? You call the police. They come over. They have a look around, and they take care of it for you. You don't have to manhandle a shriveled-up body into your car, find a place to dump her, carry her out there and…" Edwards made a tossing motion with his hands, "dump her somewhere. That's just as sick as living with her in the house!"

"No, I was getting rid of it. I just wanted to get her out of my house and find her a final resting place."

"You think she's at peace now? You think she's resting after you dumped her in the water, then she was found by those dogs, and there was a three-ring circus to pick her up? Now she's had to go through an autopsy and still doesn't have a place to rest. You're an idiot! Do you always do things the hard way?"

Phelps's eyes dropped to the table, hiding his reaction. Clearly, this was someone used to being criticized for doing stupid things. He hadn't gotten this far in life without being reamed out before for some stupid infractions.

"It's time to start talking!" Edwards slammed his fist down on the table, the noise echoing around the bare room.

Phelps jumped back from him. "I'm sorry. I'm sorry, I don't know what I was thinking. I know that you're not supposed to interfere with a dead body. I know that. I just didn't want any trouble. I was trying to avoid getting into trouble."

"Well, you didn't do a very good job of it, did you? Because now you're here. And you need to explain the whole thing, start to finish, to my satisfaction. Or you're not leaving here, except to go to jail. You may be looking at hard time in prison. Normal people don't do things like that, Ryder. Normal people don't decide to haul around dead bodies on their own."

"It was just like you said. When I got to the house and opened it up… I found the body. And I didn't know what to do about it. I just wanted it out of there. I panicked and, before I knew it, I was looking for a place where there was no one around, to get it as far away from me as possible. And I just left it there… I don't know how you could even identify who it was. She was so shriveled up. Was it DNA? I know you can do that now. But I didn't think you'd have anything to compare it to. Not from that long ago."

26

nd how do you know how long ago it was?" Edwards asked, sitting back in his chair.

He let the question hang in the air, not asking Phelps anything else. Phelps looked trapped. He got to his feet.

"You're not going anywhere," Edwards told him.

"I'm just… I can't sit still." Phelps ran his fingers through his hair, both hands at the same time. "I don't know what to do. What am I supposed to do in a case like this? I swear I didn't have anything to do with her death. I was just cleaning up."

"I said, 'how do you know how long ago it was?'"

"I didn't. I don't. It was just old… you could tell looking at it that it was really old. It had been there for years. It wasn't something that just happened. Something like that… it must take years to dry out and look like that."

"You're an expert on mummification? Have you done something like this before? Maybe done some experimenting? Maybe cats instead of people? Lots of people start that way, you know. With cats or other dumb creatures. And by the time anyone knows what's going on…"

"No, I told you, I didn't have anything to do with that. I would never do anything like that. It was disgusting. It was freaky. I threw up. I had cold chills every time I walked into the room. I had to get rid of it. I just did."

He started to pace back and forth across the small room. Kenzie watched him, feeling bad for him. He was obviously very distressed. She'd seen Zachary pace like that when he was trying to keep himself from having a complete meltdown. Panicking, trying to think his way out of whatever situation he was in, trying to keep moving to bleed off the anxiety before he became overwhelmed. If it had been Zachary instead of Phelps, she would have suggested it was time to take one of his anxiety pills. A rescue dose to calm him down.

"You know more than you're telling me. You're still trying to keep me from finding out the whole story. You want to portray yourself as the victim. Poor Ryder. Finding a dead body in his new house. Of course he had to dump her in the nearest pond. Poor fellow."

Phelps sniffled and snorted down the mucus and tears he was trying to suppress. Kenzie couldn't help grimacing and barely controlled her gag reflex. But Edwards did a masterful job, his expression unaltered.

"Quit playing the victim, Mr. Phelps. *You* are not the victim here."

"I didn't say that," Phelps protested, swiping at the corners of his eyes. "I'm not pretending anything. It's just... it's been hard, and I did what I thought..."

"You didn't do what you thought was best. You did what you thought was the most convenient for you. But it didn't end up being that way. It's come back to bite you in the butt now, so you feel sorry for yourself. But *I* don't feel sorry for you, moron. Why should I feel sorry for you, the way that you treated that young woman? And screwed up my crime scene? Why should I feel sorry that you did something so stupid?"

"What do you want me to say?" Phelps burst out in frustration. "That I'm sorry? Yes, I'm sorry for what I did. I know it wasn't the right thing to do. But it seemed best at the time. I didn't know that anyone was looking for her. That anyone cared what happened to her. I just wanted that stinking, sickening thing out of my house!"

"That *thing* was a girl—a young lady who had barely gotten a start on life. Struck down—murdered—before she could get married, have kids, pursue a career, even just find herself. And you don't think that anyone cares? You don't think it matters?"

"It matters. Okay. I know. Everybody matters. But I don't know what you expect me to do about it now. It's done. I did what I did, and I guess it was the wrong thing."

"What do I want you to do? Why don't you sit down here and talk to me, and I'll tell you exactly what I want you to do."

"I can't sit." Phelps continued to pace frantically. Kenzie thought he was doing pretty well to still be keeping it all together. He looked ready to have a nervous breakdown. But he hadn't left, collapsed, or attacked the man tormenting him. "I can't do anything to change what happened. If you're going to fine me or something, then do it. I can't do anything about it now."

"You can tell me what happened."

"No! I don't know what happened. You already know everything I know. She was there when I opened up the house. What else am I supposed to know? I didn't live there. I didn't have anything to do with her."

"Is that what the neighbors will say when we question them? That you've never been there before? That they never once saw you visit cousin Charlie? Or living there when your mom kicked you out for being such a deadbeat? Don't try to snow me. What will your relatives say when I ask them just how close you and Charlie really were? Are they going to say that you hardly ever saw each other for the past fifteen years? Or are they going to tell me how the two of you were thick as thieves that last time they saw the two of you together? That you were two of a kind. Two peas in a pod. Whatever Charles Titon was into, you were probably in on as well."

"No!" Phelps's face was as white as a sheet. He held up his hands, covering his face. "No, I swear, I didn't have anything to do with what happened to Sharon."

Edwards was quiet. Kenzie analyzed Phelps's response. It was the first time he had referred to her by name instead of pretending not to have heard it before. It was the first time he'd identified her as another human being instead of a thing, an *it* to be disposed of. And he clearly knew that something had happened to Sharon. She hadn't just died in her sleep. It hadn't just been a heart attack, like Charles Titon. Something had *happened to* her.

He rocked forward and back on his feet, knees bending slightly, moaning. He was still covering his face. Kenzie was afraid he was going to go down soon. Pass out or clutch his chest in a full-blown panic attack. She'd seen that happen to Zachary and it wasn't pretty. She felt sorry that no one was there to help Phelps, to comfort him and talk him down. No one there to take his hand and try to anchor him in time and place, to run him through a relaxation exercise to help him release the overwhelming anxiety.

But she was only an observer, not even in the same room. She assumed that the interview room was probably somewhere down the hall from the room she was in. It hadn't taken Edwards long to walk into the interview room door after he had left Kenzie.

But even if he was close by, Kenzie couldn't just walk into a secure interrogation room without an escort. And Phelps wouldn't calm down for her, wouldn't be reassured by her presence, no matter what she said to him.

"Where were you when it happened?" Edwards asked.

"I don't know. I don't know when she was killed. How would I know? I didn't have anything to do with either one of them."

"You know. You knew before you ever went into that house what you would find. Anyone else walking in there, not knowing what to expect, they would have called 9-1-1. You didn't panic and run out of the house screaming and calling for help because you knew before you went there what you were going to find."

Phelps scowled stubbornly and shook his head.

"No, no."

"Well then, if I find out in my investigation that you have lied to me here today..." He left the threat hanging. Phelps could think of a terrible consequence he didn't want to suffer. The truth was, there wasn't much that the detective could do to him for lying. If they found evidence to convict him of something, that would be the consequence. There wouldn't be any added sentence for having lied when he was asked a direct question. Or obfuscating and trying to avoid others.

Phelps looked rather green.

"Maybe I should just leave you to think about that for a bit," Edwards said. "I'm going to go have a coffee and, while I'm gone, you're going to think. And you're going to realize that you're only hurting yourself by lying. When I come back, you're going to tell me exactly what happened so that I can get on with my investigation."

Phelps was a picture of misery. He watched Edwards walk out of the room and shut the door behind him. He paced, moaned, covered his face, talked to himself, and tried to figure out what to tell Edwards so that he would leave him alone. There must be something that he could do to get out of it. To convince them that he really didn't know what had happened to Sharon, that he hadn't been there when it had happened, and he didn't have any foreknowledge of what he would find in the house.

But Kenzie had a pretty good idea that there wasn't anything he could say to convince Edwards of that fact.

27

The door to the observation room opened, and Edwards walked in. He looked at the screen for a moment, watching to see how agitated Phelps was, then sat partway onto the table, facing Kenzie, casual and relaxed.

"Well, what do you think?"

"You were pretty hard on him."

"That was nothing. He's going to crack. Just look at him pacing. He can't hold on much longer."

"What if he really didn't know about Sharon Briggs ahead of time?"

"Then he's a pretty cool cucumber, to just shove her mummy into his car and drive off to dump her somewhere unconnected to him. He didn't call 9-1-1. I've checked the records. Not even a hangup. He just decided he didn't want some dead chick in his house and moved her."

"And that's proof that he knew she was there already."

"Of course it's not proof. But it feels right. I think he was a lot closer to Titon than he admits. I think he knew what was going on and what he would find when he went in that door."

"Maybe." Kenzie shrugged. "It would be interesting to have the whole story."

"Most of these stories are just sad and sick. Not the dramatic moments you would see on TV, the complex plots and motives and trying to put a big cover-up into motion. Someone killed her, and both men covered it up. One was a sicko for keeping her, and the other was a sicko for getting rid of her. They both should have talked to the police. Tried to get it sorted out."

He shifted his position.

"I've seen the girl's history. She probably fell and hit her head. Maybe with some help, maybe not. But they clearly did not have a perfect relationship. If he'd gone to the police, talked about what happened, shown them how it was accidental or the result of a trip or shove that wasn't ever intended to hurt her, he could have gotten off with a suspended sentence, maybe some community service. But the moment they cover it up... then you're looking at murder. That's consciousness of guilt."

They both watched Phelps on the screen.

"You think he will talk to you?"

"I'll give him a few minutes. He'll be climbing the walls, ready to spill everything."

"He could just go home."

"Sure. But he's caught by his own brain. He thinks he has to stay there. That it's his only chance to explain his innocence and make everything right. If he just stays and convinces me that he wasn't the one who killed her, or that if he did, it was accidental, then it will all be over. He can go back to his own house and live out his life undisturbed by the cops. Everything will be right with the world once more."

He was probably right. He knew his suspect psychology. He was far more experienced at the human side of crime fighting than Kenzie was. She was a science person. That was her lens and she followed the clues that she got from looking at a body and the other attendant evidence. She didn't have to think much about the psychological aspects of it. As Edwards had said, TV shows made it look complicated, but most murders *were* actually committed by the most likely suspect and were solved within forty-eight hours. The spouse, the last person to see her alive, the person who had reported her missing—

those were the people most likely to have killed her. And if it was the same person, that was all the more reason to believe that he had done it.

Edwards and Kenzie talked for a little while, then Edwards stood back up, squared his shoulders, and shook out his hands. Prepared himself to go back to face the witness.

Kenzie watched him walk back into the interview room. Phelps was not looking good; very pale and sweaty. Kenzie hoped he didn't take after his cousin and have a heart attack.

"So…" Edwards sat down. He motioned for Phelps to sit, but he clearly wasn't able to sit back down again. "Tell me what happened when you went to your cousin's house for the first time."

At Phelps's questioning look, he clarified. "When you discovered that he had died and you had inherited everything. You went to the Medical Examiner's Office to gather his effects, including his house keys. You drove over to his house, and you let yourself in."

Phelps nodded. Edwards's narrative seemed to help him. Putting everything back into a normal, non-threatening perspective. This was just something that had happened to him, not something that he was being accused of.

"Tell me what you saw when you went into the house."

"Nothing to start with. Just… everything looked normal. Bachelor pad. Kind of messy, but not over-the-top hoarder central. Some things left out. Easy chair in front of the TV. Like normal."

Normal for Charlie? Or normal for a bachelor? Had he been there before?

"Go on."

"It was… kind of musty smelling. But… I mean… could have been laundry. Gym bag. Just Charlie's odor." Phelps waved his hand in front of his face as if wafting the smell away. "Nothing worrisome."

"Uh-huh."

They waited for the punchline. Walking into another room and discovering the mummified body. Phelps just stood there, not sure where to go next.

"And then you found her," Edwards prompted. "Where was she?"

"In… in the bedroom," Phelps finally admitted. "It was on the bed." He made a face as if trying to block it out or suppress a gag. "I don't know… it wasn't the bed Charles slept in. He used the bed in one of the other rooms, it looked like. But it was in the master bedroom." He shook his head in disgust. "How could he do that? Keep her there in the house with him, looking and smelling like that?"

"I thought they stopped smelling bad after a little while."

"Well, it wasn't like rotting meat. Something dead rotting inside the walls. It wasn't like that. But there was a smell. And even if there wasn't, just looking at it… it wasn't like the door was closed and she was covered up. He would see it every time he walked by that room. Why would he do that? How could he stand it in the house?"

Kenzie noted his attempts to depersonalize Sharon Briggs, to never refer to her as "her" or by name. She wasn't a person to him— just a thing. A piece of garbage to be disposed of.

"So you saw her on the bed in the master bedroom. Then what did you do?"

Edwards pulled out his phone and tapped a message to someone while he waited for Phelps to answer. As if this were just a casual, everyday inquiry. *What did you do when you found a body in the house, sir?*

"I shut the door."

28

K enzie chuckled. She could understand that reaction. He saw something horrific, so he shut the door. Hid it away so he didn't have to look at it or think about it. To pretend that it wasn't there. But he had found, presumably, that it wasn't so easy not to think about the body on the bed in the master bedroom.

"How long did that work?" Edwards asked in a dry tone.

"Well, it didn't really. I kept thinking about it, seeing it in my mind. I finally had to go back and look to convince myself that I hadn't imagined it. Or seen something else, something innocent, and just imagined that it was... a body. Maybe a rolled-up blanket, or a doll, or a sculpture. I don't know. Just something other than *that*."

"And when you saw that it was, in fact, a body, did it ever occur to you to call the police?"

"I thought about it!" Phelps protested. "I did, but... I just thought it had been so long, you wouldn't be able to do anything, and it would be a pain in the neck. So what if I just got rid of the body myself? I didn't think it would be that hard."

"Did you try to dig a grave?" Edwards suggested.

Phelps looks surprised at this suggestion. "Well, yeah. I did. You know, you always see it on TV. Someone digs a grave, and it takes like ten minutes and they've got a hole big enough. They put the body in and cover it up. It didn't seem like it should be too hard. I'm not in the best shape anymore," he looked down at his soft body, "but I can dig a hole."

"But it isn't as easy as it looks on TV, is it? That's why when the police find remains, you'll often find the words 'shallow grave.' Because it is very hard work, especially for someone who isn't used to doing that kind of thing. It's much better if you have a backhoe or other heavy equipment to do the work. If you go to a cemetery, you won't see them digging graves by hand anymore."

"I can see why." Phelps rubbed his thumb across his palm as if it might still be sore or blistered.

"How long did you try to do that?"

"I don't know. Seemed like hours. But I wasn't getting anywhere. It's such hard work."

"So this was all the day you found her?"

"Yeah."

"Then you had the brilliant idea to dump her somewhere if you couldn't dig a hole large enough to bury the body."

"I guess it wasn't the smartest idea," Phelps said, looking ashamed for the first time of what he had done. "I wanted to bury her. I wanted to make it right. Lay her at peace and go on with my life. Why should I have to pay for what Charlie did?"

"Pay for what he did?" Edwards repeated. "If you didn't have anything to do with her death, you weren't worrying about going to prison for it. You were concerned about being inconvenienced. Having people inside your home, having to answer questions. All just because you happened to find a dead body in the house. Much better if you could rid yourself of it, pretend it had never happened."

Phelps didn't say anything. He ran his fingers through his hair again, agitated.

"Was it the same day?"

"What?"

"That you decided to dump the body. The same day you took possession of the house and found it?"

"Yes."

143

"And where else did you look? Or did you just have the perfect place to dump a body in your mind already?"

"I drove around a little. I thought at first that I might leave her somewhere in town. A... a dumpster that would be emptied without anyone noticing, or in the foundations of a building..."

"But it isn't that easy. There aren't many places where you can dump a body where it wouldn't be found almost immediately. And someone might see you carrying her. Taking a body from your car and leaving it somewhere else. You didn't want anyone to see you. You wanted to be anonymous. Take her somewhere no one would see what you were doing."

Phelps shrugged. "I didn't want to go to prison. I didn't want someone to think that I had killed her. Even though she was.... like that."

"And did you know about Petty Pond? Had you been there before, or were you just driving around taking random turns?"

"It was pretty random. I thought that if I didn't know where it was, I wouldn't ever have to see it again. And if I didn't know where it was, no one else would either."

"And you figured that dumping her in the water was a better way to get rid of her than digging a grave."

"It just seemed easier... and they bury bodies at sea. It's not disrespectful."

Kenzie thought about the site she had been called do, Sharon's remains in the pond, one arm sticking partially out of the water. Not shrouded or weighed down. Just dumped without any dignity or ceremony. Because he just saw her as a thing. A problem to be dealt with. A piece of junk he didn't want in the house, so he drove around until he found a good place to dump her. And it hadn't even been a good choice for a dump site. He'd done a terrible job.

"It *is* disrespectful. And against the law," Edwards said sternly. "Now sit down so we can discuss this."

Phelps looked around. Kenzie thought for a minute that he was going to leave. He'd gotten it off his chest and just wanted to get out of there now. Did Edwards have his warrant? Were his men searching the house while he tried to get Phelps to give him more information? Was it just a stall to keep him out of the way? Kenzie was sure there wasn't much more that Phelps could give them now that would lead to answers about what had happened to Sharon Briggs.

29

Phelps walked back over to his chair and put his hand on the table for a minute, trying to decide. Now that he had admitted to what he had done with the body, he seemed to be slightly less agitated. A burden lifted. Even though he didn't act like he cared about Sharon Briggs as a person, he had still carried a lot of guilt around for what he had done.

"I don't really have anything else to tell you about it."

"Sit."

Phelps hesitated again, then finally fell into the seat.

"I want to know where you were when Sharon Briggs died."

"I don't know. At home, I guess. I didn't live in Roxboro."

"Where did you live?"

"Montpelier. I lived in Montpelier until Charlie died."

"How long?"

"A long time. Since… college. Fifteen, seventeen years."

"Which is it? Fifteen or seventeen?"

"I don't know. I'd have to think about it, figure it out."

"Well, do it. Could it have been thirteen? Ten? Come on, Phelps. People know when they move to a new city."

"No. Not ten or thirteen. Not less than fifteen," Phelps insisted immediately, his face reddening. "Fifteen at least. Maybe longer. I have to look at my records. I really don't remember."

"But you know it was longer than thirteen."

He swallowed, nodding. He was very sure that he had not been living in Roxboro at the time that Sharon Briggs had died. Kenzie was suspicious of his answer, as she was sure that Edwards was. Was Phelps delaying because he wanted to see if he could get an alibi? Someone to confirm that he had been living in Montpelier when Sharon died rather than in Roxboro?

Not that it mattered that much. Even if he'd been living in Montpelier thirteen years ago, there was no reason he couldn't have come to Roxboro for a visit. To see his cousin. Maybe for a conference or something else, and he'd stopped in to see Charlie. And found what? Had he known Sharon while she had been alive? Had he arrived to find Sharon newly dead? Or had he been involved in an argument with her that had turned violent?

"Tell me how you knew Sharon Briggs," Edwards told Phelps.

"I didn't know her," Phelps shot back quickly. "I told you that. I never met her."

"You never met her."

"No."

"Before you found her on the bed."

"That's not meeting her. But no, I never saw her before that. It was the first time I'd ever laid eyes on her. And as you can imagine… it wasn't a fun experience."

"You don't seem to have suffered from it. There was no call to 9-1-1. No heart attack. No panic attack. You just decided to get rid of her." Edwards leaned forward. "And that tells me it was personal. You knew her. You were somehow involved in her death."

"I didn't have anything to do with her death. I don't even know how she died. Was she shot? Was it drugs? I don't know anything about it."

"It's interesting that those are the two possibilities you went to."

"Why? What do you mean?"

Edwards stared at him steadily.

Kenzie wasn't sure what he was getting at. That Phelps had deliberately not mentioned how Sharon Briggs had actually been killed because it might be suspicious? That he assumed it was violence? That he knew that Sharon was a junkie?

"You never met Sharon Briggs?" Edwards asked.

"No."

"Did you talk to Charles about her?"

There was a hesitation. Phelps trying to see all of the consequences of answering that question? Trying to remember what he had already told Edwards. He clearly wasn't going directly for the truth.

"I didn't talk to Charlie much."

"You didn't talk to him much, or you didn't talk to him at all?"

Again, a hesitation. What could Edwards check? What could be proven? If they had talked on the phone, there would be records of the fact. Even if they only connected via social media, that would also be easy for the police to check. Handwritten letters were a different story, but were highly unlikely. No one wrote letters anymore. Not thirty-something men.

"I didn't talk to him much," Phelps said cautiously.

"But if you talked to him at all, he must have mentioned Sharon at some point. She was clearly important to him. They lived together. He kept her with him after she died. You can't tell me that he never mentioned her."

"He might have." An uncomfortable shrug. "I don't remember. It would only have been in passing. I don't remember if he ever talked about a woman he went out with or was living with."

"Did he have other women home? Shut the master bedroom door and entertain them in another bedroom or on the couch?"

Phelps looked revolted. "I have no idea. I hope not." He rubbed at his nose as if he could still smell the musty old body. "I don't think Charles saw much of anyone. I think he was… reclusive."

"So you talked to him enough to know that, at least."

Phelps shifted in his chair and looked around the room. "We hardly ever talked. I just know… he was home a lot. I mean, you can tell, looking at the house, that he pretty much managed everything from there. He had a car, but it wasn't very well-maintained. I have a mechanic looking at it to see if it is worth fixing it up to use or sell it, but I think it's a write-off. If he used it at all, it was just for emergencies or to run to the grocery store once a month."

"He didn't work from home. Or at least, I assume he didn't, since he died during the morning commute. Was he on his way to work or to something else?"

"He worked, but a lot of that was remote. He only had to go into the office now and then for meetings or to do things that he couldn't do at home."

Edwards stared at Phelps, his question unasked.

Phelps scratched his head, blocking Edwards's gaze. "I've got his phone, his schedule, all that kind of thing. I didn't need to be in constant contact with him to know that."

"No one said that you were in constant contact. But you were obviously in contact."

Phelps shook his head. "Maybe." He pressed his lips together. "But only sometimes. Occasionally."

"And he never mentioned a girlfriend. He never mentioned Sharon Briggs or any other girl he was going out with, living with, or thinking about."

"N-no."

"What exactly did you guys talk about?"

"I don't know. Family. Gaming. We didn't have a lot in common. That's why we didn't talk much," he said exasperatedly.

"Well, we'll see about that, won't we?"

Phelps swallowed. "What do you mean?"

"You realize you're now at the center of a murder investigation. Do you think that's going to be comfortable? Do you think we're just going to take your word for it, believe everything you say? Because we're not."

"You're not going to find anything. I'm telling you the truth."

"Just like you were telling the truth when you said you didn't know what we were talking about. You didn't know why you were here and didn't know anything about any body."

Phelps scratched the table, head bowed while he stared down at it.

"I'm telling you the truth now."

"Like I said. We'll see about that."

30

Edwards popped in to talk to Kenzie again after seeing Phelps on his way. Kenzie shook her head.

"Is he going to be okay driving himself home?"

Edwards raised his brows. "I… assume so. Why? He's not drunk."

"That's not the only thing that can make you a menace on the road. Someone who is so distressed, his world crashing down around him… you don't think he's going to be driving distracted? Or run himself off the road on purpose, in an attempt to harm himself?"

The detective sat on the corner of the table, looking down at Kenzie. "I honestly never thought of it. We deal with people all day long who are distressed and distracted. We can't be expected to drive them all home or make sure they have someone else to drive them."

"I just think… sometimes it would make sense to check. To give him a taxi voucher or have someone drop him off. Then he can come back for his car when he's feeling more stable or send someone else to pick it up for him."

"I'll take it under advisement." Edwards looked at the face of his phone. "What did you think? Find that interview enlightening?"

"It was intense. I've never seen something like that in real life before. Watching it on TV doesn't really capture the… emotion and intensity, does it?"

"No. Even watching true crime, where you actually see the cops talking to suspects and hear them confess, it's just not like being in the same room with them. Talking someone into telling you something they swore they would never reveal. Or being down the hall watching it as it happens," he added, shrugging with one shoulder.

"Yeah."

"I've got a crew over at the house, turning it over."

"That was quick. I knew you were trying to get a warrant."

"It's not too hard when you identify it as the place where someone likely lived with a body for over a dozen years. Sharon Briggs may not be as famous as Elysse Allen, but people know her name now that we told them the identity of the remains that were discovered. And a name like that is good for opening doors. It's quite the story, and people want to know how it could happen. How someone could get away with that, even during the missing person investigation."

"How *did* he hide the body during the missing person investigation?"

"That's something we'll have to find out. Talk to the detective on the case and find out whether he went into the house. If so, did he go into every room? Did he go into the basement? Did he suspect anything or try to get a warrant to search the entire house? Sometimes… a missing person investigation isn't that thorough. When it is an adult who appears to be voluntarily missing or has been reported missing before… I'll admit that the force doesn't put much effort into it. And why would they? Why waste resources on someone who is a repeat missing and will show up again in a day or a week?"

"But she didn't show up again in a day or a week."

Edwards nodded his agreement. He looked at his phone again. "So my question for you is, what should we be looking for at the house? Obviously, we've investigated missing persons and homicide scenes before. That's nothing new. But in *this* case… is there anything less obvious we should be looking for? Whatever happened, it happened thirteen years ago. What evidence may still be there to help us figure out what happened all those years ago?"

"Hmm." Kenzie thought about that. "You know what room she was left in and where her body was, so that will have to be your starting point. He may have cleaned everything up already. But if he hasn't gotten around it… collect the bedding so we can examine it for bodily fluids, remnants of the decomposition process, bugs and castings, and blood. We know that she had a closed head injury; she wouldn't have been bleeding from that blow, but if there is other blood, that will tell a bigger story. Maybe she was stabbed or shot as well as hit over the head. Maybe some CSF leaked onto the bedding."

Edwards was nodding, jotting down some notes in his small spiral field book.

"If there is blood elsewhere in the house. Check under the carpet. If she was stabbed or shot, she might have bled out on the floor and been placed on the bed after she was dead. Just because that's where Phelps found her, that doesn't mean that's where she died. We need to be open to other options. Get the car too. She might have died or been injured somewhere else and he brought her back to the house in his car. If he hasn't used it much over the years, maybe it's the same car and there is still some evidence in it."

"Yeah. I've already got someone on the way to the mechanic for the car. We thought it would also be at the house, but now we know better. And it is the same car as he had back then. It's been registered to him for fifteen years."

"We don't know enough about how she died to be sure of anywhere else there might be evidence. You guys know the psychology stuff better than I do. If he's set up a shrine for her. If he had some kind of psychosis. Whether he kept a journal. If he talked to anyone." Kenzie nodded toward the computer screen she had watched the interview with Phelps on. "Not just him. It sounds like they weren't close, but maybe there's someone else Titon was close to, someone he might have talked to about it or hinted at."

"Great." Edwards nodded his agreement and put his notebook away. "Well, doctor, it's been nice having you up here, but I need to head over to the house now. Hopefully, we'll have some trace to be analyzed. I'll let you know if we discover any more remains."

31

Kenzie was back down at the morgue when a call came through from Zachary. She looked at the phone for a moment before deciding to answer it. She had been away from her desk for some time and was just settling back in. She needed to clear some things off her desk before getting too far behind.

But Zachary rarely called her during the work day other than over what should be her lunch hour, so she picked it up. Lunch was long past. Maybe he was calling to see what she wanted for supper.

"Zachary. How's your day going?"

"You're not going to believe this!" He sounded out of breath. Something good on one of his cases?

"What?"

"She's back."

"Who's back? Your missing girl?"

"Well... yes, she's already back with her family. I'm talking about Elysse Allen."

"Elysse Allen." The words didn't compute. "What do you mean Elysse Allen is back? How is she back? They found her remains?"

"No, they found *her*."

"Was she kidnapped? Is she okay? Are you sure this isn't some hoax or another mistake?"

"She wasn't kidnapped. Nothing happened to her. She just took off on her own. When Dain Porter reported her missing and there was so much publicity, I think she was too chicken to come forward and say that no, she was still alive and well. But she was spotted in the Grand Canyon, and—"

"Spotted in the Grand Canyon? That doesn't sound like a likely story. Are you sure this isn't just some internet gossip that got out of control?"

"I've seen her on TV. Not just people saying that she's been found, but an actual press conference with her speaking to her fans and the public. That she's alive and well and will be returning home to get her things and move them to wherever she plans to live now that she and Dain have broken up."

"They have broken up? Officially?"

"I don't know if he had any say in it, but she's apparently not going back to him. She intended the break when she abandoned him at the gas station to be permanent."

"Where did she go? Why couldn't anyone find her?"

"I don't know. They still have to figure out all those details. I think she hitched a ride or called a friend. I don't know whether she told Dain that she was leaving and he didn't bother to tell the police that part or if she took off and left him there without a word. Either way... let's just say that her fans are not too impressed right now."

"At least the ones who don't believe it's a conspiracy theory."

He chuckled. "You guessed it. Lots of people are saying that it's not really her or that they forced her to say that. People can make anything into a conspiracy."

"If you're willing to ignore all logic and evidence, you can believe anything you like."

"Exactly. Anyway, I thought you should know. I didn't want to interrupt your work but, in case you hadn't heard, you might want to know that the whole country is melting down over it."

"Thanks. I'll be interested in watching some of the coverage when I get home. I want to hear what she has to say. Especially after all of the trouble she caused me."

"That's probably the least of her worries right now."

"Well, if her world can revolve around herself, my world can revolve around my trouble. She didn't have to deal with being swarmed by angry fans."

"She probably will now."

There was plenty of coverage still going on when Kenzie got home from the Medical Examiner's Office. Kenzie sat down in front of the TV and helped herself to a slice of the pizza that Zachary had ordered. They usually ate at the table, with no screens to distract their focus on each other, but this was a special circumstance. It wasn't every day that one of Kenzie's bodies made an appearance on TV, alive and well. When Kenzie had first seen the body in the pond, she had assumed, like everyone else, that it was Elysse. It was strange to see her on TV, not in taped interviews or clips, but actually live, talking in a slightly embarrassed way about how the story had taken on a life of its own.

"I never tried to make anyone think that I was dead or that something had happened to me," Elysse said with a little laugh. "I never told anyone I was dead or being held hostage."

She and the host laughed over that.

"I just broke up with Dain. I didn't expect him to report to anyone that I was missing. I thought that we would just go on and do our separate things. And eventually, I'd go home, and we'd split our stuff up and I'd get a new place…"

"So there wasn't any reason for him to think that you were missing?"

There was a beat, a hesitation before Elysse answered. "No, of course not."

"You told him that you were breaking up with him?" the host pressed.

"Well… yes. We fought. I told him I'd had enough. We went our separate ways."

"You told him you'd had enough."

"Right." Elysse shrugged. "It was over."

"Had you ever told him that you'd had enough before?"

"Maybe, I don't know."

"Had you ever told him that you were breaking up before? Told him to get out? Told him you were leaving?" The host's voice was no longer teasing and amused, but tough and hard-hitting. Elysse looked trapped, wondering how she had ended up in this situation on live TV.

"Yes, some of that. I mean… we had a passionate relationship. When two people are passionate, you have arguments. You have breaks. Stop and reevaluate. And then you go on. Stronger."

"That's what had always happened before."

"Yes."

"But this time, you didn't stay and make up. You didn't go on together, stronger."

"I haven't talked to Dain. I will. But I think… this time it was for good. I just don't think we're good for each other. We love each other… but I don't know if that is enough. We want different things out of life."

"So if you had always stayed and worked things out before, and this time you left and didn't contact him, how was he supposed to know that it was just a breakup and that something hadn't happened to you?"

"I told him we were done. I told him. He knew that."

"Did you call him after that at any point?"

"No."

"Did he call you?"

"Yes. But I didn't want to talk to him. A clean break, you know? I just wanted to make a clean break and go on and do my own thing. I can't help it if he thought that meant that something had happened to me. I didn't mean to upset anyone."

"You knew he called you, but you didn't respond."

"No," she repeated firmly, sounding frustrated. "I told him it was over. I didn't want to talk to him again. He would just beg and try to talk me back into it, and I didn't want to go there again. I just wanted to be by myself… to think things over. To find myself and where it is I want to be."

"You must have listened to his messages. Read his texts. You must have known that he was frantic with worry. You couldn't be bothered just to text him back and tell him you were okay?"

She shrugged helplessly. She tossed her head to throw her long blond hair back over her shoulder. "I told you. I just wanted a clean break. He would say anything to get me back again, and I wasn't going to give in this time. I wasn't going to go back and start over again. I was done with that."

"When did you become aware that the police were looking for you?"

"I was camping, hiking, doing my own thing exploring the backroads and enjoying a solitary experience. I wasn't watching TV. I wasn't in contact with anyone, including the police. My phone died after the first day or two, so I was completely unconnected, and that's how I wanted to be. I just wanted to think."

"Why weren't you posting on your social networks anymore?"

"My phone was dead—"

"Not that first day or two. But you didn't post on any of your social networks."

"I was on vacation," she said with a shrug.

"A vacation that had been highly publicized and blogged about until then. You were posting dozens of times a day, and then you just stopped."

"I told you. I just wanted to disconnect. Not to be a part of the rat race anymore. It's hard, you know, trying to keep your fans happy. Having to think of new things to post every hour or two. Living your life… out in the open, where everyone can see you."

"You had a phone when the police found you."

"The police didn't *find* me," Elysse argued with a huff. "I wasn't lost. And a couple of fans identified me and brought them into it."

"And did you have a phone at that point?"

"Well… yes. You really can't get along without one these days. So I picked up a burner. I used it a few times when I needed to make a call. I wanted it for emergencies, really. So once I got back to civilization, I picked one up, and yes, I had it with me when my fans noticed me in the Grand Canyon. I was not hiding out. I was not trying to stay under the radar. I was just on vacation. Seeing the sites, like anyone else. That great big hole in the ground... what trip across America would have been complete without it?"

"Didn't you already go through the Grand Canyon earlier on your vacation with Dain?"

"Well... yes. But I wanted to see it again. I didn't get to see everything I wanted to when I was there with him. That was the thing, you see, we could never agree on what to look at. We both wanted to see different things, do different things. Half of the vacation was taken up by arguing, instead of getting to see things."

The interviewer looked directly at the camera. "So you didn't tell Dain directly that you were broken up. When he tried to check in with you, you didn't answer. You didn't post anything for your fans from the day you split up with Dain. Your phone mysteriously dies, and you replace it with a new one, but you don't try to contact anyone to let them know where you are or that you're okay. You doubled back on your trip, returning to the Grand Canyon, where you had been before, and no one would be expecting to find you. And once you were spotted, you refused to talk to the police and instead sought out interviews on network television." The host made a motion to encompass the two of them and the set.

He waited a few seconds, while the camera zoomed in on Elysse's wide, innocent eyes.

"But you weren't trying to worry anyone."

32

Wow, that was brutal," Kenzie marveled. "I think he was a tougher interrogator than Detective Edwards."

Zachary's arm was behind Kenzie's shoulders, and he gave her a brief squeeze. "Detective Edwards? Was this on your unidentified remains?"

"Identified," Kenzie corrected. "We know who she was."

"You do." Apparently, he had been too caught up in the news of Elysse's return to hear about the identification of Jane Doe. And Detective Edwards was already questioning someone about her?

"Yeah, they can move fast when they want to."

"Does that mean you know who killed her? Or how she died?"

"Not for sure. We know that she suffered from a brain bleed due to a blow to the head. We don't know if that was her only injury or if she had a soft tissue injury without any bones being damaged. The body was too decomposed to be able to see any injuries like that, so unless we found the bullet, we wouldn't know that she'd been shot as well. As far as who did it… it could have been her boyfriend or room-mate. We don't really know their relationship yet. But he's dead as of a few weeks ago."

"The boyfriend is dead?"

"Yeah. Natural causes. And that leaves us with a lot of questions about what happened to the dead girlfriend."

"He's the one who moved her body from wherever it had been? He knew that he was sick?"

"No. That would be his cousin who took possession of the house."

Zachary looked at Kenzie, frowning, trying to work it out. "Because... she was still there."

Kenzie nodded. "She was still there. In the bed in the master bedroom."

Zachary made a face, then grinned. "You get all the interesting cases."

"You wanted the one with the reappearing corpse?"

"My missing girl is home safe and sound with Mom and Dad. You can't get much more boring than that. But your missing girl, you've got romance and intrigue..."

"There's nothing romantic about a corpse in your bed."

He gave a choking laugh. "Is that what the next of kin said?"

"More or less. For some reason, he was creeped out by it and decided to dispose of her quietly. Since he found he wasn't much good at digging holes, he drove her around until he came to a nice, isolated pond and dumped her in."

"Do-it-yourselfers. They cause everybody problems, you know. They should leave it to the experts."

"He says he didn't want to have to answer a bunch of questions."

"I'll bet Detective Edwards had a lot of them."

"You would be right."

At that moment, the news show segued to a report on the remains previously found by the cadaver dogs, which had been mistakenly assumed to be Elysse Allen. Kenzie and Zachary both switched their attention to the program to see how much information the press had been given on the latest developments.

"Those remains have been identified as being those of Sharon Briggs, reported missing thirteen years ago."

Someone had managed to dig up a picture of Sharon Briggs, a skinny young woman with long, blond hair. It was sad to think that she had disappeared thirteen years earlier with hardly any concern or investigation, especially when contrasted with the hysteria of Elysse Allen's faked disappearance.

After giving a brief biography of Sharon and a description of the circumstances of her disappearance, the reporter leaned toward the camera and used a low, dramatic tone to tell the audience her secret.

"The shocking thing about the discovery of these remains is not that they went undiscovered for thirteen years. A preliminary investigation shows that they were not there for the entire time that she was missing, but were, in fact, dumped there just days before they were found. It would appear that Charles Titon, Sharon Briggs's roommate at the time she disappeared, kept her remains in his house for the past thirteen years."

There was a dramatic flare of the music while the pretty blonde reporter stared into the lens of the camera, letting everyone process just how shocking this news was.

"No, folks, it's not Halloween. It's not April Fool's Day. This man —who recently passed away—kept the corpse of his girlfriend in his home for thirteen years, as he continued to do all of the normal, routine things. Brushing his teeth, making his breakfast, going to sleep, all with the corpse of Sharon Briggs in his bed. Or maybe he moved her around the house sometimes, so that she could do all of those things with him." She shrugged. "Who's to know?"

When the news show broke to commercial, Zachary looked at Kenzie. "That's a lot more detail than I would have expected the police to release."

"Yeah. Me too. All of this..." She motioned to the TV. "It's bizarre that they would release so much information about her. And I'm not even sure about the girlfriend part. They slept in separate rooms. Or Titon slept in a different room than the corpse was left in. I don't know if they were romantically involved or if she had been paying him rent. I don't know if anyone knows that at this point."

"What nobody knows, they are free to invent."

"Except you can't. They're forming people's opinions. Contaminating the jury pool if it turns out she was murdered and it wasn't Titon."

"Maybe there's a leak."

"Yeah. They're not going to be happy to find that out." Edwards would be ticked off if the media screwed up his case. A lump formed in Kenzie's belly. There was one person outside of the police department who knew the details that had been presented on the news show. Or at least most of them. She patted her pockets and found the business card that Detective Edwards had given her earlier in the day.

Zachary watched her dial the phone, raising an eyebrow curiously. He looked ready to get up and walk away. Wondering whether she needed privacy for the call, Kenzie realized. She motioned him to stay.

The phone rang quite a few times, and Kenzie decided it was going to forward to voicemail. She had been hoping to reach Edwards immediately to head off any problems. She tried to compose a script in her head. What she would recite once his voicemail message had played.

"Hello?" Edwards barked in her ear.

"Oh, Detective Edwards. It's Dr. Kenzie Kirsch. I was just watching TV and wanted to give you a heads-up…"

"I just heard about it," Edwards growled. "A whole crapload of trouble has landed on my desk. Who did you talk to?"

"I didn't talk to anyone about it. I went back to the Medical Examiner's Office and finished my day there, then came home. I didn't talk to anyone, especially not a reporter. I don't want this case screwed up any more than you do, and I know how loose lips can do that. Believe me, I'm not your leak. If I was, I wouldn't be calling to warn you it was about to hit the fan."

"Well, it sure has. We don't need all the gory details of the case being played up in the media. Having to deal with the Elysse Allen fans was trouble enough. Is this case cursed? Sheesh, I can't believe it!"

The mummy's curse.

Kenzie pushed the thought out of her mind. Detective Edwards did not need her making any silly or sarcastic comments about his choice of words.

"I'm sorry. I don't know who has access to those details and passed it on to that reporter, but it certainly wasn't me. Or Dr. Wiltshire. We know better."

"Whoever leaked it probably knew better too. It just doesn't stop them. They like the attention. The publicity. The whole freak show just gets them all wound up." He blew out his breath noisily. "Okay. Thanks for the call. The heads-up and the confirmation that it wasn't you. Is there anyone in your office who would have had access to the information that was released?"

Kenzie thought about the people who worked in the Medical Examiner's Office. Other than Kenzie and Dr. Wiltshire, most of the staff were on part-time contracts, also working in other aspects of law enforcement. Or, if they couldn't find work in other departments, they might have retail jobs, drive ride shares, or have some other supplemental income.

Like selling information to the media?

Who would have had access not only to the identity of the remains *and* the fact that Charles Titon had kept her in his bed for thirteen years?

No one. Just Kenzie. That information had only come up in the interrogation that afternoon, and Kenzie had not communicated it to anyone else or recorded it in any form.

"I don't think it could have come from my office. I didn't write down anything about Sharon being in the bed. I didn't tell that to anyone."

"Only someone with access to the police department records would know that, then," Edwards said, his tone angry. Did he still think that it might be her? He'd apparently accepted her explanation, but was he one hundred percent sure or did he still harbor doubts? "Someone who was there this afternoon or had access to the office after that." He swore angrily.

Kenzie didn't say anything. What was she going to do? Tell him that it wasn't a leak at the police department? That he was imagining things? That everything would turn out and he shouldn't worry about it?

"Make sure you stay absolutely silent on any other aspects of this case," Edwards warned Kenzie. "The media is going to be hungry for details, and you have to put them off. Make sure that you don't say anything to anyone. Even within your office—tell them to talk to me. I'll control the flow of information."

"Okay. I will."

"Okay." He sighed again. "Thank you, Dr. Kirsch. I appreciate your call."

He ended the call. Kenzie turned to look at Zachary.

"You heard that?"

He mimed zipping his lips shut, locking them, and throwing away the key.

"It's important," Kenzie emphasized. "I don't want anyone accusing me of giving away anything confidential during pillow talk."

He put his arm around her shoulders again. "For that, we first need to have some pillow talk."

Kenzie laughed. "I didn't mean—"

He tightened his grip, pulling her closer. "Don't you think we'd better go check and make sure that no one left any corpses on our bed?"

"Well, I usually just assume, but…"

She allowed him to pull her to her feet, and they walked down the hall to the bedroom, just to be sure.

33

Kenzie was surprised to be stopped at the entrance of the parking garage by Pratt, one of the security guards.

"Sorry, Doctor," Pratt told her. "We're hand-checking everyone through today."

"What's going on?"

"More fan freaks," he grumbled. "Police had to remove some of them from the premises earlier. They got shrines, they got signs, they're trying to get past every locked door in the place."

"But they know Elysse isn't here. That she's been found."

"These ones aren't for Elysse. They're for the new girl."

"The new girl?" Kenzie repeated. A strange thing for him to be calling Sharon Briggs, assuming that was who he meant.

"Yeah, you know, dead girl the boyfriend kept around. 'A love that survives death,'" he said in a falsetto voice, making air quotes with his fingers.

"Oh, dear."

He nodded morosely.

Kenzie held her security card out to Pratt, and he dutifully looked at her picture on the badge, looked at her face, and swiped the badge to raise the gate before handing it back to her.

"Have a nice day, doc."

"Thanks."

Because of the increased security, Kenzie didn't need to worry about any hysterical fans making an appearance in the parking garage. Since it was a Saturday, there were very few cars there. Kenzie's steps echoed as she walked through the garage, but she didn't see anyone else. She swiped her card to get through the inner door.

There wasn't anyone around the Medical Examiner's Office either. The security lights were on in the hallway, but Kenzie had to turn the main lights on. They flickered to life, washing the surfaces with sterile bluish light.

Before she started on the work she had come in to do, she checked her internet feeds to see what was going on in the outside world. There were pictures of the police station, with mourners/fans/protesters gathered around, some wailing or letting silent tears drip down their faces and others screaming about justice and conspiracies. Still others gathered in little knots to gossip with each other about what they knew or had made up, their eyes wide in mock horror as they enjoyed the drama of the whole thing. There were shrines and signs, as Pratt had said. Some signs featured the one released picture of Sharon Briggs's face; others were verbose protests about the injustices suffered by the girl or the love that survives death. Ugh. There were piles of flowers and teddy bears with candles and cards arranged in front of them. All of the freaks gathered together for a vigil.

Kenzie shook her head and closed the tab. She had work to do. The mourners couldn't do anything to bring justice to Sharon, but maybe Kenzie could. She was going to do everything she could to help the police crack the case.

The woman who had reported Sharon missing in the first place was a good place to start. Her name and contact information were recorded on the missing person report, and Kenzie hoped they were still right or that there was enough information to track her down at her new coordinates.

She had expected Hilda Ingersson to be an older woman with a thick Scandinavian accent, but was completely wrong. The young woman's voice dispelled the picture Kenzie had in her head of a heavyset blond woman. Her voice was light and crisp and thoroughly American.

"Hello?"

"Is this Hilda Ingersson?"

"Yes. Who's calling, please?"

"My name is Dr. Kenzie Kirsch, and I'm with the Medical Examiner's Office."

"The medical examiner." She swore. "You mean where Sharon is?"

"Yes, her remains are still here with us."

"Why are you calling me?"

"I just wanted to get a little bit of information from you as we conduct our investigation into what happened to Sharon."

"I thought you just did the autopsy. Doesn't that tell you everything you need to know?"

"No, unfortunately. A lot of the time, we need to know other things. About the scene where the death occurred, the people in the victim's life. Known medical conditions, allergies, particular stressors in her life before she died, that sort of thing. A lot of different things can affect someone's health. For instance, it can be very difficult to determine whether someone suffocated due to anaphylaxis or by a heart attack or positional asphyxia. If we know more, we can make a better determination."

"Well, Sharon wasn't allergic to anything, if that's what you're asking. Not that I ever heard about. Are you saying that she was smothered?"

"No, that was just an example. Why we need to get as much information as we can about the person's health and what was going on—"

"Right. I got the rest of that. So... what do you want to know? You haven't figured out how he killed her?"

"We don't know yet who killed her, if anyone. We haven't determined the cause and manner of death."

"Well, it had to be Charlie Titon, didn't it? Who else would it be? They say it's always the husband or boyfriend."

"A lot of the time it is, that's true. *Were* Charlie and Sharon intimate partners? I wasn't sure whether they were together or whether she was just renting a room from him?"

"I don't know what *he* thought they were. But I can tell you, Sharon wasn't ready to settle down to one man."

"She had multiple partners?"

"Yeah. That's a nice way to put it." Hilda wasn't being sarcastic. She really did seem to appreciate the turn of phrase. "I don't know how much you've been told about Sharon. She was a bit of a wild child, to tell the truth. I know she'd been through some tough times, so maybe that explains why she lived the way she did and why she made the choices she did. But she was... I don't know. A party girl. She used... alcohol and drugs. I know she was trying to stop, and she'd been through a program, but when it came right down to it, down to when someone was offering her drugs, or she was stressed out and needed something to calm her down, she couldn't say no. I'd talked to her about it before, tried to help her to see it differently and to figure out how to make better choices, but I'm not a professional. She'd talked to professionals already and they hadn't helped her."

"It's a hard thing to overcome," Kenzie said sympathetically. She was lucky not to have had friends who went down that path. Some of them might drink a bit too much when they went out for girls' night out, but they weren't addicts, just immoderate. She'd had a small taste of the experience with Tyrrell. First his closet drinking, then his disappearance, and then the way he had behaved while staying with them waiting to get into a program. Kenzie knew it was an illness but couldn't help being impatient with someone making all the wrong choices. He knew that he was ruining his health and chances for a relationship with his family, but he still chose drinking over a better life. It wasn't easy to watch someone destroying themselves. And Hilda must have known that she was going to lose Sharon. Had probably known when she called to report her missing that it was the end. That Sharon would not be coming back.

"Hard to watch, too," Hilda agreed. "I wish she'd been able to... well, there's no point in crying about it, is there? She made her choices a long time ago and we can't change any of that now."

"Do you know what drugs she used?"

"Pretty much anything she could get her hands on, I think. She probably preferred coke or heroin. But she wasn't opposed to ecstasy, or weed, or just drinking herself blotto. They talk about people who drink to forget? I think that was her. She'd just had such a tough life and such bad childhood experiences that she just wanted to forget it all and not feel the pain anymore."

"What happened to her?"

"Oh, I don't know all of the details. And even if I did, I don't know how much of it was true. She would tell you one thing today and something completely different tomorrow. I never knew what was true and what was just made up. But I believe she had it tough. Her body was... worn. Scars, callouses, track marks, burns, whatever you can think of, she'd had it at some point. She'd been to hell and back. Or maybe not all the way back."

"Was Charles... a friend? Someone who wanted to help her? Or to take advantage of her?"

"Who knows? Some guys come on nice and decent, but when it comes to using you... they're just the same as anyone else. There for the fun. Users. Get what they want and don't care what happens to you after."

"And that's how you saw Charlie? Someone who was there to use Sharon?"

"I can't say that. I thought he was a decent enough guy. But she's dead, isn't she? And he's gotta be the one who did it."

"If she had multiple partners, then all of them would have to be equally as suspect at Charlie."

"Except that she was killed in his house."

"Killed there... or brought there afterward. I don't know which. The police were processing the house yesterday. I don't know what they found yet."

"I suppose."

"So you thought he was decent, but maybe he wasn't. Did you ever meet his cousin? A guy called Ryder Phelps?"

"Phelps... oh, that loser guy? I know you shouldn't judge by looks, but if there was a picture in the dictionary next to 'loser,' that would be him, am I right?"

Kenzie made an indeterminate noise.

"Yeah, I met him once or twice, over there at the house. We'd go there sometimes to drink. When we didn't want to go out somewhere."

"When you say 'the house,' do you mean Charlie's house? Or somewhere else?"

"Charlie and Ryder's. Yeah."

"Wait—Ryder was part owner of the house? He acted like he'd never been there before. And he said he'd hardly ever seen Charlie. Maybe a few times over the years, that was it."

"The house belonged to Charlie. Legally, I mean. But Ryder helped out. He helped pay the mortgage, utilities, stuff like that. It was too much for just Charlie, or even Charlie and Sharon. Sharon didn't make very much money, and it was sporadic. When she could clean herself up enough to work."

34

Kenzie gathered her thoughts. "Did Ryder live there?"

"Some of the time, yeah. Does he live on his own now? I always wondered if he had what it took to live on his own, or if the only reason he wanted a woman was that he didn't know how to take care of himself."

"I'm not sure what his arrangement was in Montpelier. That's where he's been living the past few years. He said he's lived there for fifteen years. Since before Sharon's death. He said he didn't know Sharon."

Hilda laughed. "Well, I hope you didn't believe him. Didn't know Sharon? He was always trying to get together with her. Didn't matter if it was right in front of Charlie. He had no sense of... propriety. If you're going to try to steal another guy's girl, you don't do it right in front of him."

"Classy."

"And I'm not just talking about making eyes at her or asking her if she'd like to go somewhere. I mean his hands all over her, acting like he already owned her."

Kenzie made a face which, of course, Hilda couldn't see. "Nice guy." No wonder he had been so agitated when Edwards had said that he could go to neighbors and friends to find out whether Phelps had

171

ever been at the house. He had good reason to be worried that someone would out him and that everything Hilda was telling Kenzie would become known.

"So the three of them... did they all get along well together? Was Charlie cool about Ryder trying to get together with Sharon?"

"They were usually pretty good, got along better than you would expect in a situation like that. I think that Charlie figured Sharon would never give Ryder the time of day, so he was safe on that score. So he was just best buds with Ryder and together with Sharon, and he thought everything was cool."

"And did Ryder and Sharon ever get together? Or was Ryder just dreaming that he had a chance with her?"

"I told you, she didn't hold herself to any kind of standard with Charlie." Kenzie could almost hear Hilda's shrug at the situation. "So, yeah. I'm sure they did. Sharon never said so, but... that was Sharon."

A love triangle that had ended in death. *That* had never happened before. Kenzie sighed.

"When Sharon disappeared, you were the one who called the police. Neither of them reported her missing."

"Yeah, that's right. I asked Charlie where she had gone, what had happened. He said they had a fight. That she took off. He said she'd come back home when she'd cooled down. But we're not talking about a few hours here. It had already been days since I had seen her. Time missed from work. They said she couldn't come back, if she ever showed up again."

"Did he say what they'd fought about?"

"No... and I don't think I asked. They were always fighting about something. It wasn't unusual. But her disappearing like that and not coming back... I was sure something had happened to her."

"You suspected foul play?"

"Foul play, an accident, an overdose, I don't know. I just knew something wasn't right. Sharon wasn't the most stable person, but she'd never disappeared like that. I knew something must have happened."

"I'm sorry that it turned out you were right."

"Thanks." There was a catch in Hilda's voice. "That's really nice of you. I guess you must say that to a lot of people. With your job."

"I do end up talking with grieving family and friends," Kenzie admitted. "I try to... help them find peace. Some closure on what happened to their loved one. It's not always easy."

Especially with victims of violence. It was one thing telling people that Grandma had died of a stroke. People expected death as the person aged. But someone like Sharon, who had been so young and had never really had a chance to make her place in the world, especially when cut down by violence... it was one of the more challenging parts of Kenzie's job. The part that she could never get really good at, because when the day came that it wasn't hard to tell someone how their loved one had died, that was the day she would have to quit.

"I talked to that cop," Hilda offered. "Told him everything I could."

"Which cop? When you reported it? Or did someone call you today?"

"Late last night. He said he didn't want to wake me up, but that was after the news about Sharon had broken, and there was no way I was going to sleep. Not for a long time."

"Was that Detective Edwards? He's very good."

"Edwards, yeah. That sounds right. I didn't write it down. I wasn't exactly thinking straight. He said to call him back if I thought of anything else, and I didn't even take his number. Don't know how I would have reached him if there was something I wanted to tell him."

"I imagine you would just call the police department and tell them you wanted to talk to a detective on the Sharon Briggs case."

"Yeah, I guess so."

"You told him everything you've told me?"

"More or less. Answered all of his questions. That's all right, isn't it? For me to talk to both of you?"

"Absolutely. There's no question of jurisdiction or us fighting over the case or something. We're both just trying to find out the truth through our investigations."

"Okay. I didn't even know that the medical examiner called

people. I mean, to have them pick up a body for the funeral, maybe, but I didn't know you asked people questions like that."

"You told Edwards about Sharon and Charlie and Ryder all being involved? That Ryder and Sharon knew each other?"

"Yeah, he asked that. If Ryder had ever been at the house and met Sharon. But I didn't tell him... you know."

"About them hooking up?"

"I guess I should have, though, huh? I just answered his questions. I wasn't really in a good place to figure it out on my own."

"I'll let him know, if you like. He might call you back for more details."

"Sure."

"The day Sharon disappeared—or around the time you noticed she was missing—was Ryder around? At the house or in town?"

"Yeah. He'd been around. I don't know what day. I don't know if... you know... he knew that Sharon was dead. He never said anything to me about it. But... he could have been covering for his cousin. They were close. I guess he'd cover for him even if something did happen to Sharon. That's who he would be loyal to."

"And now he's pretending he wasn't even in town."

"What a jerk. What does it matter if he tells what Charlie did now? It isn't like they can do anything to Charlie. He's dead. Does Ryder think they're going to try to put *him* in prison for it instead? Makes no sense. He should just tell them what he knows."

"That sounds like a good idea to me," Kenzie agreed. "How about anyone else? Charlie and Ryder were around the house. I guess you were there regularly if you knew about all of this stuff going on between the three of them and saw the way Ryder was behaving toward Sharon. Was there anyone else around? Or anyone who had something against Sharon? An old ex she didn't want anything to do with?"

Hilda snorted. "There was her brother."

"Sharon had a brother?"

"Yeah. A half-brother or stepbrother, I don't know. But I know she did not like him, didn't want anything to do with him when he showed up."

"What did he say when she disappeared?"

"Said she'd probably OD'd or killed herself. Like he didn't even care. He didn't want to talk to the cops about it, that's for sure. Didn't want anything to do with them. Everybody was being so stupid about the cops. Like they were going to arrest everyone who knew Sharon."

"Do you think her brother knew she was dead? It sounds like he might have."

"I don't think he knew anything. I think he was just being a class-A jerk. Like always."

"Do you know why there was bad blood between them? Why Sharon wouldn't have anything to do with him?"

"I didn't ask." There was a pause while Hilda considered. "I knew she'd grown up in an abusive family, so I didn't ask. I just assumed… that he abused her, like everyone else. I didn't need any details. Didn't feel like putting her through explaining it all. If she didn't want anything to do with him, I could respect that. I didn't need a reason."

"And where was he around the time when she disappeared? Did he know where she was living?"

"I don't know. It wasn't exactly a secret."

"So Charlie, Ryder, and this brother—what's his name?—any of them could have had something to do with her death, or known about it."

"Cody."

"Hmm?"

"Her brother's name. Cody. I don't know his last name."

"Is he her next of kin? Or are her parents still around? I assume the police will be contacting them, but I should put it on our file here too. We'll need to deal with them sooner or later."

"Mom is still alive, as far as I know. Though I haven't seen her on TV yet, and I always thought she was a drama queen, trying to get all of the attention she could. I can't see her passing up this chance to be in the spotlight, showing everyone how much she's missed her little girl and been grieving her these thirteen years. Or fifteen, or however long it's been since she actually saw Sharon."

"They were estranged? Was Sharon a runaway?"

"Multiple times, from what I understand. The cops said they

weren't going to be involved with a chronic runaway, especially since she was an adult now. They wouldn't do anything about it. Made a couple of phone calls. I don't think they ever even went to the house. They told me she'd show up sooner or later."

"And you knew her from work, right? You both worked the same place?"

"I got her that job. Stuck my neck out for her. I was pretty ticked off the first day she didn't show up for work. Didn't want to look bad in front of the boss after I'd recommended her. But after the second day... and then the third... I knew something was wrong and it wasn't just because she'd slept in after partying or was strung out somewhere. By then... three days in... They say that if you don't find them in the first forty-eight hours, you might as well not even try."

Kenzie happened to know that wasn't true. And it wouldn't have stopped her even if it were. Nothing would have prevented her from looking for her father, just like nothing could stop Zachary from looking for Tyrrell when he'd already been missing for weeks. She just couldn't rest until she knew she'd done everything she could. But then, Hilda *had* done everything she could. Tried to help her friend with her addiction, kept track of her, reported her missing when she disappeared. What else could she have done to find Sharon? By the time she had reported Sharon missing, it was probably already too late. That hematoma probably killed her the first day.

"You did everything you could," she assured Hilda.

"I did. But it wasn't enough."

35

Kenzie had been hesitant to attend family dinner at Lorne Peterson's and Pat Parker's on Sunday. Not because she didn't enjoy dinner with Zachary's old foster father and Lorne's partner. She always enjoyed herself there and Pat was an excellent cook, always earning top points on everything he made for them. Even when Zachary had trouble with nausea from his medications, Pat could find something to tempt him to eat a little.

She couldn't explain the anxiety that she felt this time. Maybe she was just overwhelmed by the busy week and wanted to stay home and chill out for a while. But it didn't feel like fatigue. It felt like dread. Like if she went there, something bad was going to happen.

Kenzie was not superstitious and brushed this fear away. What she was feeling was generalized anxiety, most likely brought on by the stress of the week, and she was looking for a way to explain it in a logical way. But anxiety was not rational and did not need a logical trigger.

The best way to deal with it was to face it and do the thing she was anxious about.

She was lucky not to have a more crippling form of anxiety like Zachary did when he was off his meds or they weren't working for him. Her anxiety was more run-of-the-mill and she had never been hospitalized for it or considered medication. Everybody was anxious sometimes. It wasn't pathological.

"Are you okay?" Zachary asked, glancing aside at her.

She was probably too quiet, making him think she was upset or worried about something, or maybe not feeling well.

Maybe because, for once, she hadn't argued about whose turn it was to drive to the Petersons', letting Zachary have his way and take his car instead of taking Kenzie's baby and driving with the top down.

"Yeah, I'm fine. Just tired, I think. It was a busy week."

"A strange week," Zachary commented. "Maybe we should have stayed home. Let you just rest."

If she had suggested it, he would have thought there was something really wrong. And he didn't make the suggestion until they were well on their way, so she couldn't exactly accept and go back home for a nap or to veg out in front of the TV.

"No, it's been a few weeks since we've seen Lorne and Pat. I don't want to neglect them."

He often responded to similar comments that she needed to spend more time with her parents too, but Kenzie had seen her father that week, so he couldn't exactly say that she had been neglecting those relationships.

"Yeah. But if you need a rest sometime, you have to tell me. I don't know if you don't say anything."

Like many women, Kenzie probably expected Zachary to be able to read her mind far better than he could. To know what she was thinking or needed rather than having to be told. The old "if you loved me, you would know" fallacy. She knew it wasn't true, knew that Zachary loved her deeply and would have done anything for her if she asked. But sometimes, she didn't want to ask. She just wanted him to know.

"Sure," she agreed.

He went back to staring at the long highway ahead of them. Still driving a bit too fast, but Kenzie let him, not wanting to be a nag about it. She was irritable enough and didn't want to end up in an argument before going to the Petersons', showing up in a grumpy mood instead of a good one. Lorne and Pat always went out of their way to make things welcoming for Zachary and Kenzie. She didn't want to take any stress there with them. The more quickly they got there, the longer their visit could be.

Kenzie tried to occupy herself, looking at her phone or planning her week rather than just staring into space. If Zachary could see that she was busy, he wouldn't be as concerned.

———

Lorne and Pat were both in good spirits, as usual. Lorne Peterson's round face, fringed with white hair, was wreathed with smiles as he greeted them and gave them both hugs. Pat Parker, younger, bigger, and more muscular, a towel draped over his shoulder, doled out firm hugs and friendly slaps on the back as well, then hurried back to his pots and pans to put the final touches on everything. An early dinner, followed by a long visit, and then the return trip to Roxboro.

"Can I help with anything in the kitchen?" Kenzie offered.

"You should know better than that," Pat told her with a laugh. "You stay here and keep Lorne entertained and out of my hair."

Lorne chuckled. Kenzie had never actually seen him underfoot in the kitchen. He helped with preparations at breakfast and lunch, which were casual meals, but when Pat was working on dinner, Lorne knew to stay out of the way.

It wasn't long before they were all gathering around the dining room table as Pat laid everything out for them.

"It smells great," Kenzie told him. "Chicken?"

"Chicken a la King," Pat agreed, giving the pot a stir. "One of Lorne's favorites."

Kenzie had a feeling that Lorne's favorite was anything Pat made. She would have put on a hundred pounds in short order if she lived in the same house as Patrick Parker.

They all sat down, dished up, and started to eat, taking the time to taste each dish and praise Pat's skilled preparation before the conversation was allowed to drift to other things.

"So, it's been a week for missing persons," Lorne commented, looking at Kenzie.

"First Elysse Allen, and then the discovery of Sharon Briggs, who had been missing for thirteen years," Kenzie agreed. "And then Elysse's reappearance... Oh, and Zachary had one this week too." Kenzie looked over at him. "A missing teenager that her parents hired Zachary to find."

"And at the end of the week, everyone has been found," Pat said. "That's a happy ending. Not for Sharon Briggs, of course, but at least... her family will know what happened to her."

Kenzie nodded. She didn't know how comforted Sharon's family would be to know that she might have been murdered. But maybe even for an estranged family, it was better to know and not to keep wondering.

Pat had continued speaking and Kenzie had lost the thread of the conversation. Kenzie looked at him, pretty sure he had just asked her a question.

"Sorry... I was thinking about the case."

"Is it different for you, working on a missing person case now, when you know what it's like to be on the other side?"

Kenzie swallowed, looking at him. Her mouth went dry. His eyebrows were raised curiously. Then a flush started to spread up his neck when she didn't answer.

Zachary looked at Kenzie, then back at Pat. "Because of Tyrrell?" he asked. "Is that what you mean?"

"I'm sorry, Kenzie," Pat said, shaking his head. The conversation could still have been rescued if he hadn't apologized. They could have talked about Tyrrell. Pretended that was who Pat had meant when he asked the question. But with Pat's apology, Kenzie could see the gears moving in Zachary's brain as he tried to figure out what was going on. Pat wouldn't apologize for mentioning Tyrrell had been missing.

Zachary's eyes turned to Kenzie, confused.

"Kenz...?"

36

Kenzie rubbed her forehead and tried to figure out the best way to talk to him about it. How to break it quickly, make it sound like it hadn't been that serious, and explain why she had not mentioned it to him before. She didn't see how she could accomplish all of her purposes at once. Zachary was going to be upset. There was no getting around it.

"Maybe we can talk about it later," Kenzie tried.

"What is Pat talking about? 'Now you know what it's like to be on the other side.' Since when? What is he talking about?"

"I just…" Zachary wasn't going to let her put it off until later. "It's… it was while you were in the hospital. After Christmas. Walter dropped out of sight for a few days, and I was worried about him. But he was fine. There wasn't actually any reason to be worried."

"Your dad was missing?"

"I didn't know where he was…" That wasn't quite the same as being missing, and Kenzie hoped he would leave it there and not ask for more details.

"And…?"

Kenzie shifted uncomfortably. She ate a forkful of her Chicken a la King but, for once, was not able to enjoy Pat's culinary skill.

"I called around. Some friends. To see if anyone knew where he

181

was, had seen him lately. I figured he was just... on a holiday. He could have been vacationing somewhere, out of contact. One of those places where you have to get a local phone."

"Your mom didn't know where he was?"

"No. But they're not together anymore." Zachary already knew that. And, unfortunately, also knew that they were still close and kept in contact with each other. "He didn't tell her where he was going."

"Don't they usually get together at Christmas? I thought you were going to go over to her house and maybe see him."

"I did, but he wasn't there. When he didn't return my calls, I was worried about it. But he eventually turned up..."

Zachary looked at Pat and Lorne, both with open, easily readable expressions. Stricken that Pat had revealed Kenzie's secret. She had asked them not to say anything to Zachary at the time because he had still been in the hospital. Of course they had assumed that she would tell him all about it once he was out of the hospital and feeling better again.

"You talked to Lorne and Pat about it, but not me."

"I... yes. You were in the hospital, just started on your new proto-col, and I didn't want to do anything to hamper your progress. I was afraid that if I told you about it, you would check yourself out to look for him. I talked to Pat and Lorne because... they'd been through what they had when Jose went missing. I wasn't sure what I should do, and they'd been through something similar. I needed someone to talk to."

"And you went to them, and everyone kept it a secret from me."

His voice was full of hurt and betrayal. She had gone to Lorne once before without telling him, and it had resulted in their breaking up. She hadn't been sure that they would ever be able to repair the rift and get back together, but they had managed to reconcile and had been going to couple's therapy since. But that time had been differ-ent. She had been asking Lorne about Zachary, about his history. Something that she should have gone to Zachary about, that was personal and private, and that she shouldn't have brought up with anyone else without his permission.

"It was about Walter," Kenzie explained. "Not anything to do with you. I knew you would be worried about me, and you didn't need that distraction when you were recovering. And everything turned out to be fine."

He stared at her for a minute, then turned his eyes to his meal, putting a barrier between them.

"Zachary…"

"I've told you not to do that. Not to keep things from me because you think I'm too fragile."

"I know." She swallowed. "And I've told you that it's something I have to judge for myself. If I think it's going to hamper your recovery, I'm not going to tell you. You might think that you can handle it and that it wouldn't have caused you any problems, but you don't know that. You were just in the first few days of your recovery. It was way too early."

"And since then…?"

"I wasn't sure how to bring it up. And especially since it didn't turn out to be anything. He was fine and just turned up on his own. It was silly."

"He was just on vacation?"

Kenzie prodded at her dinner, trying to figure out the right spin to put on it. "He said there was no need to worry about it and I should have just left it alone."

"Where was he?"

"I don't know. He didn't tell me that part."

Zachary was frowning, looking down at his plate. "So it was just a few missed phone calls? That's all it was?"

"Yes." Kenzie grimaced, unable to lie to him about it. "No. Do you remember me talking to you about the Russians?"

Zachary's brows lowered.

"About the tapeworm and the other parasites?" Kenzie prodded.

His expression brightened. "Yes, okay. I remember that." He nodded. "Right after Christmas."

"Right. So there was a bunch of stuff going on with these Russians… and we didn't really know what was going on, but figured it was something to do with organized crime. And I thought… that Dad being missing might have something to do with the Russians. So

I was worried that something might have happened to him, or he might be in danger."

"But it wasn't anything to do with the Russians."

Kenzie took in a deep breath and let it out again. She looked up at the ceiling. "He *was* involved with the Russians. They had hired him to lobby for them. But he wanted to think about it. Whether he was going to go ahead or not. Because he didn't want to be involved in anything to do with organized crime and didn't know where the money was coming from. So... he was hiding out from them."

She ventured a glance back at Zachary. He was blinking, processing this new information. Maybe he would focus on the Russians and what was happening with them rather than on Kenzie's failure to tell him about Walter's disappearance.

"You thought the Russian mob might have had something to do with his disappearance."

"Yes. Maybe. Or maybe he was just on vacation. I didn't have any way of knowing either way."

"You must have filed a police report."

"I... did. Not right away. The governor said to keep it quiet and let him make inquiries, and then said I should keep out of it."

"That guy is a piece of work. But you didn't stay out of it. You decided to file a report anyway."

"Eventually, yes. But then... Walter showed back up. So the case was closed. I knew he was okay. It was all over."

"Did he show up because he heard you were looking for him?"

"Partly, yes."

There was silence around the table. Neither Lorne nor Pat wanted to say anything and get in the middle of the discussion.

Zachary's fork clinked against his plate as he fidgeted, toying with his food.

"Is this why you've been having nightmares? Because you'd thought that you'd lost him or they might do something to him?"

"Sometimes I dream about that," Kenzie admitted. "But I know he's fine now. You've seen him. He's okay. I've met with him. Had dinner together. All of that. He and Mother and I even got together

184

for a sort of a late Christmas get-together." She shrugged. "I'm not traumatized by it. Like I said, it was silly to be so worried."

"It's not silly to be worried that he's involved with the Russian mob. Or that he didn't return your calls for...?"

"It was about a week. And I'm way past that now. You remember I was still pretty ticked off with him when he came to you about the theft case. But things have improved since then. I sort of... see him in a different light now. I can have a relationship with him whether or not I approve of his moral standards or political views. I'm not letting that stop me anymore."

"You should have told me."

"Not then. You would have checked yourself out of the hospital." Just like he would have if they'd told him that Tyrrell was on a bender. She'd had to manage the information flow, even if he didn't think she should.

"There's been plenty of time to bring it up since then."

"Yeah. And I should have. I meant to. It just... never seemed like the right time. And I didn't know how to bring it up. 'Oh, did you know that I thought my father was k—'" Kenzie's voice froze before she could get out the word "kidnapped." She cleared her throat and tried to finish the sentence, but couldn't. She just shrugged. She'd made her point. How difficult it was to bring it up out of the blue.

"You can't even finish your sentence," Zachary pointed out. "It *is* still bothering you."

"It's hard for me to talk about it," Kenzie admitted. Maybe if he saw that, he would see that she wasn't just being overprotective in not telling him. It was something she had trouble with. He could certainly understand an experience being too difficult to talk about yet. It would be hypocritical not to. There were plenty of things that he had kept from her that were still too difficult for him to talk to her about. Things that he *might* tell his therapist about in a private session, but some things were still buried too deep for him even to tell Dr. B. "It was nothing, but it's still hard for me to talk about it. I don't even discuss it with Walter."

"You're denying your own feelings when you say it was nothing. It wasn't."

Kenzie shrugged helplessly. She couldn't minimize it and convince him that it was too difficult to talk about simultaneously. Not without bringing the kidnapping into it, and she couldn't even say the word.

"You should talk to Dr. B about it. Or another therapist, if you don't want to see her."

"Yeah. I probably should. When I'm ready."

"Sometimes, you need to go before you're ready. Because otherwise, you'll never get there."

It was the voice of experience, and one that she should listen to.

37

The trip home to Roxboro was awkward. Kenzie was glad they had not gone to the Petersons' in separate vehicles, as they occasionally did. She didn't know whether Zachary would have made it back to the house. While he made an effort to keep the visit cordial, she could tell that he was upset about her failure to tell him about Walter's disappearance. They didn't address it on the drive back home or once they got there. Zachary did not go to bed with Kenzie, staying up to catch up on some computer work instead and falling asleep on the couch.

"Are we okay?" Kenzie asked as they prepared breakfast in silence the following day.

Zachary looked at her, then back at what he was doing. "I don't know. I have to think."

"Do you want to talk?"

"*Now* you're ready to talk about it?"

Kenzie swallowed. "I'll try, if you want to. But some stuff… is still kind of raw."

"But you didn't think you should tell me that."

"I would think you would understand that some stuff is really hard to bring up. Even just to say…"

"I've asked you if you were okay. What was bothering you. If

187

something was triggering the nightmares. You had a lot of opportunities."

"And I tried. I tried at our session this week, but…"

"But you said you weren't ready," Zachary remembered. "This is what you were referring to? Your father's disappearance?"

Kenzie tried to be as honest as possible. "In part."

"There's more?"

Kenzie swallowed and nodded. Zachary got the marmalade out of the fridge and put it on the table.

"I appreciate you telling me that," he said in a flat, neutral tone.

Kenzie didn't know if it was a tone that was carefully controlled to sound nonjudgmental, or if it was the unemotional tone he switched to when he was really hurt. She glanced at his face, but his expression was masked, giving nothing away.

"I am trying," she told him.

"It must be pretty bad."

Kenzie tried to answer, to agree or disagree, but she couldn't put the words together. Her knees wobbly, she sat down at the table, even though she hadn't yet put the bread in the toaster. Zachary noticed this and put a couple of slices in.

She couldn't find a way to reassure him or to tell him any of what had happened. When he eventually sat down at the table, she took his hand and squeezed it. He didn't pull away.

Breakfast was quiet, with little conversation.

Kenzie had thought that there had been a lot of email and voicemail messages when Elysse Allen had been missing and the remains had come to the morgue. There were dozens more than she would normally have. But that amount had been multiplied several times when she looked at the state of her email inbox when she got to the morgue. Not everyone had been convinced that Elysse was dead when they had initially found the remains. Some people doubted it or held out hope that the news was wrong.

But nobody could doubt that Sharon Briggs was dead, and the

fans seemed to have transferred all of their attention and enthusiasm from their fallen star to the poor Miss Briggs.

Kenzie performed several email searches to identify all the emails that referred to Sharon and moved them into a separate folder to declutter her inbox. She would need to comb through them carefully to ensure she hadn't missed any lab results or other legitimate ME emails. And maybe she would give the rest to Edwards. He would want to know what people were saying and if anyone who was emailing actually had information on Sharon, her death, or the other people who were part of her constellation.

The voicemails were the same. She would listen to the opening line, then press the button to save them and go on to the next one. It was unbelievable how many people had called to express their condolences, rage about the injustice, or encourage the medical examiner to do everything he could to find the killer. These people had never even met Sharon Briggs, probably never heard of her before her name was announced, and yet they acted as if they were close family members.

Dr. Wiltshire arrived at the office before Kenzie was finished going through everything. She liked to have her inbox cleaned and actioned and a stack of messages and reports ready for Dr. Wiltshire when he walked in the door. But that wasn't an option today. She raised her brows and rolled her eyes at him. He chuckled as he went by, and Kenzie thought she heard him murmur "good luck" as she listened to the beginning of the next voicemail message.

Eventually, she had control of all the legitimate email and voicemail traffic and took Dr. Wiltshire the messages he would need to respond to.

"Drowning out there today?" he asked her pleasantly.

"Yes. Thank goodness there are guards on the doors, or they would be down here pounding on my desk. Good grief. What makes people act so… *rabid* about a stranger?"

"People transfer their feelings about other situations onto this one. If they have lost someone tragically, before their time, or to some injustice, then Sharon Briggs becomes their surrogate to express those feelings."

"I suppose that makes sense," Kenzie admitted.

"That, or they're crazy," Dr. Wiltshire added.

She laughed. "Or that. I just can't believe the volume. It's more than it was for Elysse."

"She was probably not as relatable. She's a celebrity—rich, beautiful, living the life that many people would like to have. But Sharon is different. Someone who was struggling along in life, who had the few opportunities offered her snatched away."

"An everyman."

Wiltshire nodded. He paged through the stack of messages. "I'll take care of these. Thanks."

"It was a quiet weekend otherwise. So I guess I'll focus on filtering the rest of the emails. Seeing if there is anything that is actually pertinent to our investigation."

"There probably won't be, so don't be disappointed if there aren't any gems among the dross."

Kenzie nodded. "I won't," she agreed.

When she returned to her desk, the phone was ringing. She glanced at the display, and it was not the police department or one of the labs, so she let it go to voicemail. She sat down and started working her way through the folder of emails mentioning Sharon Briggs. It was going to take time to go through the hundreds of emails. For most of them, she only needed to read the first few words or the opening sentence. That, at least, helped it to go faster.

The phone started ringing again. Kenzie looked at it. Same number. Looked like a landline number. She hesitated, then let it go to voicemail again. If what the caller wanted to talk to her about was important, they would leave a message. If it was someone who just wanted to rant... Kenzie didn't feel like engaging with him.

A few more emails. There were patterns. A lot of people used the same phrases and expressed the same regrets. The public as a whole wasn't very creative. Some of the names popped up more than once. People who kept writing back after receiving no response. Expecting one person to be able to handle all of the traffic immediately.

38

The phone rang. Same number again. Kenzie sighed and picked it up.

"Medical Examiner's Office, Kenzie Kirsch speaking."

"It's about time!" the annoyed caller exploded. "I've been trying to reach you all morning."

Kenzie glanced at her phone. A lot of people wouldn't even start their office jobs for another hour.

"How can I help you?"

"I'm calling about Sharon Briggs."

"And what's your name? Did you know Miss Briggs?"

"Not *closely*."

Which probably meant she didn't know Sharon at all.

"Do you have information about her death? Anything that doesn't relate directly to her cause of death should be passed on to the police detectives investigating the case."

"There was always hanky panky going on at that house." Kenzie sat up straight. She hadn't expected the caller actually to have any knowledge of Sharon Briggs or her situation. "People coming and going at all hours of the day and night. You would have thought it was a hotel or an all-night diner."

"You lived near the house where Sharon lived?" Kenzie suggested.

"I'm not telling you anything about myself. I'll only tell you about that poor girl and the others she lived with."

"Okay. What did you want to tell me about her? Do you know anything about when or how she was killed?"

"It would have been one of them. Or one of the criminals that she consorted with. You wouldn't believe some of the types I saw going in there. Prostitutes and drug dealers. Terrible people. It's no wonder she died."

"Did you know any of the people going in and out? By name?"

"You think I'm just some crackpot old lady?" she demanded, her voice rising.

"No. I asked you if you knew any of them. It's pretty hard for us to follow up on people without some names."

"The big one who lived there, what was his name?"

Kenzie rolled her eyes. Now she was giving the woman information? "Charles Titon?" she suggested.

No one could fault Kenzie for revealing the name. His name was registered as the homeowner. He was dead and couldn't file a lawsuit for slander.

"Yes. Charles. He was the one who was there the most."

"He owned the house."

"But there were others."

"It would be helpful if you could provide names or descriptions we could follow up on."

"Most of them I don't have the foggiest. They came and went; it wasn't like Charles introduced them to me."

"Could you maybe describe them?"

"It was thirteen years ago! I don't have a photographic memory."

"No. I thought that you might remember something that would be helpful, though. I understand that you want to help get justice for Sharon... I was hoping you might be able to give us some clues about what happened."

"Is she still there? You still have her... remains? That poor, poor girl."

"Yes. Her remains are still here, for the time being. We're trying to find anything else that might be helpful to the police so that they can solve the case. Find out who killed her and bring him to justice."

"She needs to be buried so that she can be at peace. She can't be at peace when her body is in a refrigerator."

Kenzie wasn't sure how it made any difference whether Sharon was in the cold room or in the ground. It didn't make any difference to her. But she knew that it mattered to some people. She did her best to play to that desire.

"I want her to be at peace too. I want to bring this matter to a close so that she can rest easy."

"Yes." The woman's voice wavered. Kenzie wrote down the phone number as she waited to see if the caller could provide anything else. If nothing else, at least she could give Edwards the number. He could find out who the woman was and talk to her directly. Maybe he would be able to get something out of her. The woman gave a long sigh. "I never liked her much when she lived there. I feel bad about that. It was wrong of me to be so judgmental. She was obviously crying out for help, and instead of trying to do that… I just stood by and watched."

"How do you think she was crying out for help?"

"Those behaviors. Being promiscuous. Using drugs. All of the partying. It was a cry for help. For someone to notice her and to help her to escape that life. I've learned a lot more about those kinds of people since she lived there. I don't know what kind of a past she had, what kind of a family she was raised in, but I understand that people don't choose to be so unhappy. She was chasing the wrong things, trying to fill a void within herself that she didn't know how to fix."

"Mmm-hmm," Kenzie agreed.

"I should have befriended her. Let her know there was another way out. Then maybe it wouldn't have happened. She wouldn't have died like that."

"It was tragic." Kenzie waited to see if the woman had anything else to say about how Sharon had died. Did she really know anything? Or was she just surmising from what she'd seen on TV? She acted like she knew Sharon and the kind of life she had lived, but she might

P.D. WORKMAN

have just been good at reading between the lines. "Do you know who was there? Who was around when she died?"

"How could I? I don't know exactly when that was, and it was a lot of years ago."

"You know some of the people who were living there. You would recognize some of them now, wouldn't you? And maybe some of them still come around sometimes?"

"When she was gone, things changed. I was glad. I thought it meant that... she was the one who had instigated all of the trouble, and since she had moved on, the rest of the group had disbanded. I didn't know that it meant... she had died."

"How did things change?" Kenzie wanted to ask her about specifics but was afraid that she would be feeding the caller information that she would parrot back to the police and the court. What they needed was for her to tell them what she knew in her own way and not be tainted by anyone else. Kenzie chewed on her lip. She was not a trained interrogator and probably should not be the one asking the woman for details. She should have tried harder to pass her on to Edwards.

"Like I said. The partying stopped. Those people stopped coming around, so it was mostly just him. That Charles. He stayed there, didn't go out much. Sometimes he played loud music, but mostly he kept to himself."

"None of the others came around anymore?"

"Not often. Now and then, I would see one of the old faces there again."

Kenzie thought about the body on the bed. Had Charles just shut the door and entertained in the living room? Carefully policed everyone to ensure they went straight to the bathroom without sneaking a peek into the master bedroom? People often snooped around to satisfy their own curiosity about how someone lived. Check out the decorating. See if he made his bed. If he had a pile of reading material by the bed or unsavory kinds of entertainment. If Charles had been doing drugs, not just Sharon, people might have snooped to see if he had any drugs. Had anyone seen the body and not reported it? Was there anyone who knew what had happened to

194

Sharon but had kept quiet about it? Too often, when Kenzie watched true crime shows with Zachary, she learned of friends and family members who had known or guessed about a murder but had not gone to the authorities for some reason.

"Maybe you could work with a sketch artist on drawing some of those people who still come back to visit now and then?" Kenzie suggested. "Or maybe you can remember who was around a lot before Sharon died. Before the partying stopped. It would be really helpful."

"It was mostly another man and another woman. There were others… I think one of them was a drug dealer. And one of them… I remember talking to one man when I was working in my garden and he was lurking around the house. He said he was her brother and he was trying to find her."

"Is that around the time she disappeared?"

"Maybe… I suppose it probably was. I told him she didn't live there anymore. I didn't like the looks of him."

Hilda had said that Sharon had a brother. She should make sure that Edwards followed up on that. He probably already knew and had the man's name on his interview list. But in case no one had mentioned a brother, Kenzie should make sure.

"We'll certainly look into that. Do you know the identity of this drug dealer? What they called him? Was he well-known in the neighborhood? Is that why you knew he was a dealer?"

"Nobody introduced us," the lady said tartly.

Kenzie let her breath out slowly. She wasn't getting anywhere very fast.

"Okay. Well, call me if you think of anything else that might be helpful."

"No, wait, don't hang up!"

Kenzie paused, waiting.

"You need to find out who did it so that she can be buried," the woman told her.

"Yes. I'll do my best. It would help if I knew some of those other names."

She already knew two of them. Hilda and Ryder Phelps. They

might be the woman and the man who had hung around the most. But there were more that no one had named, and it frustrated Kenzie to know that so much time had passed and those names might never surface again.

"Did you know… there was a memorial?"

Kenzie's fingers tightened on the phone receiver. She found herself holding it in a death grip, unable to loosen up. "A memorial? What do you mean? There was a funeral for her?"

"No, not like that. Just that there was… a place where he put flowers. I didn't know… well, I didn't know she was still in the house. Nobody knew that."

She *hoped*.

"Where was this memorial?"

"In the yard. I always thought it was kind of weird. I thought he was bonkers, to tell the truth. Maybe brain damaged after doing all of those drugs."

"You thought Sharon had left, but he'd kept a memorial for her in the yard?"

"Yes… no… I thought maybe the flowers were for a pet. Something he had buried back there."

The thought flashed through Kenzie's mind that maybe they had been wrong. Maybe Sharon hadn't been left lying on the bed in the master bedroom. Maybe Charlie had buried her in the backyard at night when no one was around to see and, for some reason, he or Phelps had dug her back up before moving her remains to Petty Pond.

But there hadn't been any evidence of worms or underground insect activity. And the mummification suggested that she had been in a warm, arid place, not buried underground. Why would either of them bury her and then dig her up again? If she'd been buried for thirteen years without being discovered, neither of them really had any reason to fear discovery. Unless Phelps was planning to sell the house to someone with plans for a big garden or pool, and that seemed unlikely.

"Did he ever have a dog or another pet?"

DEATH OF A CORPSE

"Not a dog... I don't know about anything else. I wouldn't know if they had a guinea pig or hamster."

"No. But I don't know many grown men who would put flowers on a guinea pig grave, either."

The woman tittered. "That's something a child might do, but not a grown man," she agreed.

"Was there ever a child in the house?"

"No, it wasn't that kind of place. No one there had children. And I would certainly never bring a child into a place like that. This is a nice neighborhood, you know. But that was not a nice place. Not back then. I was glad when they settled down. I just didn't know that it was because Sharon had died."

It hadn't looked too bad when Kenzie had checked the street view online. Charlie Titon had cleaned up his act after Sharon had died. Because of guilt? Was he afraid he would be found out and blamed if he kept the same lifestyle? That someone else might get hurt or die? It was good that Sharon's death had sobered them all up and convinced them to fly straight. But too late for Sharon.

"It's very sad," Kenzie agreed. "I'm sure that things would have been very different if you had known what had happened at the time. You wouldn't have let him... leave her body exposed like that. You would have informed the authorities."

"Of course I would have," she agreed in an offended tone, as if Kenzie had suggested the opposite. "If I had known... things would have been very different. We would not have let it go on like that."

"We?" Kenzie repeated.

"The neighborhood. One of us would have done something about it. We cleaned this street up. If we had known about Sharon... we would have done something about it."

Confirmation that the caller was, indeed, one of Sharon's neighbors. Kenzie had figured that from the start. The fact that the caller could see Charlie laying flowers on a memorial in the backyard confirmed that she was quite close, maybe looking down on Charlie's backyard from the second story of a house beside or behind him.

Had anyone ever snooped further than that in their bid to clean up the neighborhood? Looked in through his windows? Talked to him from the front door and tried to get invited in or to see past him into the house? Neighbors often knew more than they should about each other.

"I'm glad you're trying to take care of Sharon now. I need to go. I have other calls and emails coming through and other people who have things to tell me about the case. And I will need to pass whatever information I can on to Detective Edwards so that he has a chance of solving exactly what it was that happened to Sharon."

"Charlie hit her over the head," the woman insisted. "What do you mean you need to know what happened? Everybody knows that's what happened. They said so on the news."

"Despite what they may or may not have said on the news, we haven't finished with the medical examiner's report yet. Unless there is an eyewitness or it was caught on camera, I don't see how anyone could know that for sure."

"It's what the man on TV said," she insisted.

"Okay. I guess I'll have to talk to him," Kenzie snapped, irritated. There was a moment of silence from her caller.

"Okay, then," the woman said meekly. "Thank you for your time."

39

I t wasn't until the end of Kenzie's workday that she was able to
call Detective Edwards. By that time, she felt like she had been
through a war. And all the exploded bomb shells were scattered
all over her desk in fragments. She tried to gather together all of the
threads of the conversations she'd had, the emails and messages she
had received, the lab work that had come back on Sharon Briggs's
remains, and any other thoughts or questions that had occurred to
her while she'd been fielding the inquiries and lectures she had
received from the public.

She stacked everything in a pile and tried to put them into some
order while waiting for Detective Edwards to answer the phone.

Of course he would be busy dealing with the investigation and
would not answer. He would be more tired than she was of random
helpfully unhelpful calls from the public, telling him things that he
already knew or wild theories that belonged in a TV thriller slush pile
rather than an actual homicide investigation.

"Hello?"

"Oh, Detective Edwards. Kenzie Kirsch."

"Ah, doctor. Do you have some more evidence for me?"

Kenzie thought of the remains still sitting in the cold room and in
sample jars and slides in various places. She'd received some lab

reports back, but nothing that enlightened them on the circumstances surrounding Sharon's death.

"Not physical evidence like you're hoping for, no," Kenzie admitted. "But I've been dealing with calls and emails from the public all day, and I don't know how much of what they have said to me is stuff that you know already and what is not. I don't want to withhold anything important, but I don't want to swamp you with irrelevant details or repeat what you've already heard."

"I'm sure most of it will be the same as what we've heard on the tip line today. You should just be referring people back to us."

"I've been trying but, for some reason, they want to talk to me and don't want to talk to the police. I guess they feel less threatened by me. I don't know. I've done my best."

"I'm sure you have, doctor. Well... do you want to hit the high points, and we'll see if there is anything we want to pursue further?"

"Okay. You know Sharon had a brother?"

"Stepbrother. Got someone looking into that."

"He was asking around for her after her death."

"Not surprising. The family must have noticed at some point that she wasn't around anymore. I would expect them to ask at least a few questions."

"It doesn't sound like they got along together very well."

"Step-siblings in an abusive home? Wouldn't expect them to."

"No. Me neither. Got a call from one lady who is some kind of neighbor. Said that he had a memorial or shrine in the backyard. Put flowers there. She thought maybe it was a pet's grave."

"Really. Who is this woman?"

"She wouldn't give me her name, but she is obviously in a house that looks into his backyard."

Edwards grunted. "We'll have canvassed her already, then. Why do people refuse to talk to the police when they're asked a direct question? It isn't like the neighbors are in trouble for not knowing that Sharon had been killed."

"I don't know. I have her phone number, if that helps. She said she felt guilty about judging Sharon by her lifestyle and being glad when she was gone. She has since decided that Sharon was just acting out due to her traumatic upbringing."

"More than likely."

"Hilda, the woman who reported Sharon missing, you talked to her already?"

"Of course. That's the first place to go."

"But she didn't tell you Sharon was fooling around with Ryder Phelps on the side."

Edwards chuckled. "No, she didn't. But I suspected as much. Phelps is carrying around a lot more guilt than a man who just happened to find a corpse in the house he inherited. Why do you think he was afraid to call the police?"

"I guess. I figured there was something going on there too."

"Anything else?"

"Not much... I have a bunch of little handwritten notes. You can look through them and ask me for details on anything that doesn't make sense or that you need more information on. I tried to write down anything that you might want to follow up on. Oh—what did you find at the house? I didn't see any more samples come through here for testing?"

"No pools of blood under the carpet, no. Bed linens all laundered or replaced. He did a pretty fair clean-up job on the house as well as disposing of the corpse. I suppose he didn't want any flesh-eating bugs crawling around the house."

"Maybe," Kenzie agreed. "Well... keep me informed if you find any more physical evidence. I'll have to finalize the medical examiner's report before too long. It would be nice if I could be more definitive and not have to say 'undetermined' for cause and manner of death. I hate it when I can't fill in those blanks."

"Throw your handwritten notes in an interdepartmental envelope. Mailroom should have them to me in the morning."

"Okay. Talk to you then, if you have any questions."

Kenzie felt some reluctance to go home. She knew she needed to face what was going on with her and Zachary, but she was worried she would return home and find that he had left, moving back into the apartment with Tyrrell. Would he decide he needed space to think things through? Or that he couldn't live with someone who apparently didn't trust him enough to tell him about things like her father going missing? It had been a long day, and Kenzie wasn't looking forward to going home and finding out what decision he had come to.

She forced herself to lock up her computer and drawer, shut off the lights and lock up the office for the night. All easy, automatic things that today felt like she was pushing through setting concrete to accomplish.

The walk back to the parking garage and her car seemed much longer than usual, two or three times its normal distance. She put her hand on her little red sports car, remembering the PI who had encouraged her to buy something that better expressed her personality. Way before she had ever met Zachary. That car had gotten her through some tough years. Throughout her medical schooling, she had looked forward to climbing into her baby at the end of shift to go home. It was like an old friend.

Hopefully, not her only friend. If Zachary were not home, she would feel very alone, and wasn't sure that calling anyone else would make her feel any better.

"Everything okay, Dr. Kirsch?"

Kenzie was startled and turned halfway to look at the security guard, watching her with some consternation.

"Oh. Yes, sorry, I was just lost in thought about something."

"Everything okay with the car? Nobody has been close to it, but if you'd like me to take a look before you get in…"

"No, no. It wasn't anything about the car. Just tired after a long day of work."

"If it was half as crazy in the morgue as it was on security detail today…"

Kenzie shook her head, forcing a laugh. "The phone never stopped ringing. I swear. Never. Stopped. Ringing."

He grinned at her. "I believe it. And after listening to these loonies..."

"I guess you've been getting it all day too."

"A love that survives death," the guard said in a reverent tone, then guffawed. "Do they really have any idea what it would be like to live with a corpse? They think that's *romantic?*"

"I know. I spend a lot of my day with corpses... I wouldn't want to go home to one too."

"Yeah, and if *you* wouldn't want to, what would it be like for a normal person?" He rolled his eyes and scratched the back of his head. "But I guess that guy wasn't normal."

"No. You do hear stories about this kind of thing now and then. And there is one culture in Indonesia that I know of where they sometimes keep the deceased with them for months or years, and it's seen as normal. They dress them, talk to them, move them around..."

"I'm all for respecting other cultures, but..." He shuddered. "I think that's just creepy. People know instinctively that the dead should be buried. That's what they do all over the world. You don't keep them laying around your house."

"Not all cultures bury their dead either."

"I know, some of them cremate them..."

"Or leave them on platforms in the trees," Kenzie offered. "Though I guess they're not allowed to do that anymore."

"Why would anyone want to do that?"

"Different strokes..."

He continued to shake his head, seemingly at a loss for words. Kenzie unlocked her car and opened the door.

"Thanks for keeping things safe around here. I feel a lot better knowing that you and the rest of the security staff are around."

"You bet." He grinned, showing a wide mouthful of teeth. "We're happy to do it."

40

Kenzie forced herself to go through the motions. Driving home, so distracted that she couldn't even remember if she'd had to stop at any traffic lights or had just blown through them. Driving into the garage. Getting out of the car was the hardest. She opened the door, grabbed her purse, and forced herself to put her feet out the door and onto the floor. Then walking to the connecting door into the house and arriving at the coat hooks and mud mat as she did every day.

She was almost afraid to look. The kitchen was still lit by the sun, though it was getting lower in the sky, and there was at least a lamp on in the living room. Kenzie pasted a smile on her face, knowing that her voice would reflect it if she were frowning, and called out.

"Hi, are you home?"

"Hey." There was the noise of Zachary getting up off the couch, and then he walked into view, rubbing his eyes with his palms. "I guess I drifted off," he said apologetically. "I guess I didn't get enough sleep last night."

It was very rare for him to sleep during the day. Unless he was sick or very stressed, like he'd been after the assault.

"Did you get any sleep at all last night?" Kenzie asked, taking off her shoes and entering the kitchen. She and Zachary came together in the doorway between the kitchen and living room. Zachary took Kenzie by the shoulders and kissed her briefly on the cheek. Quick and unemotional. Robotic. It didn't tell her everything she wanted to know, and it told her too much. He had not forgotten their troubles.

"No, not really," he admitted. "Maybe an hour on the couch at some point. I guess it was bound to catch up to me later, though I don't usually nod off, even if I'm short on sleep."

"Well, I'm glad you did. You obviously needed it."

She didn't say that she wouldn't mind taking a nap too. Without him in bed last night and all of the anger and anxiety whirling through her brain, she hadn't gotten much sleep either, and what she had gotten had been restless and not very satisfying.

"Can I help with dinner? Do you want to make something or order in?"

"I wish I could say I was up to making something. It would be healthier. Eating junk when you're stressed just makes your body more stressed."

"Unless it's ice cream."

Kenzie smiled. "Maybe there's a different rule for ice cream. What do you want to get? Italian? Chinese?"

"Chinese ice cream?"

"I don't think there is Chinese ice cream. What would that be? General Tso's ice cream?"

Zachary made a face. "You always choose the weirdest flavors."

"Chinese for dinner and ice cream for dessert, since you seem to be stuck on it?"

"Sounds good," Zachary agreed. "Anything particular? Are you feeling adventurous, other than the General Tso's ice cream?"

"No. Let's stick with our usual dishes. Spring rolls, some kind of noodles, rice, whatever you like for a meat dish."

He nodded and opened the kitchen drawer that housed a supply of menus for their favorite restaurants.

"You should go shower and change."

"That sounds heavenly," Kenzie agreed.

Kenzie was much more relaxed when the dinner arrived. Finding that Zachary was still at home and had not taken off was a big load off her mind. He must still believe that the relationship was salvageable, despite her keeping secrets from him. The hot shower helped relax the muscles she had been holding tense all day. She got out feeling mellow and looking forward to their evening together much more than she had to a night by herself, with only self-recriminations for company.

For the first few minutes, they just ate in silence, or murmured how much they were enjoying the food. They ordered in way too often, but Kenzie was often tired when she got home, and Zachary wasn't big on cooking, though he could pull together a semblance of a meal if he were motivated. It was just easier to order what they wanted most of the time.

Zachary glanced up from his meal and met Kenzie's gaze. He finished the bite he was chewing and licked his lips.

"We decided in couple's therapy that we don't have to tell each other everything," Zachary said without introduction. "There are some things that we might want to keep private or not be ready to talk about yet. If that's the rule for me, it has to apply to you as well. It wouldn't be fair otherwise."

Kenzie let her breath out slowly. "I didn't plan on keeping secrets," she said, a little apologetic, trying to explain it. "I didn't expect anything to happen that I wouldn't be able to talk to you about. And it isn't that I don't think you can handle it. I guess... *I* can't handle it yet, and there's nothing you can do or say that will change it, even though you want to."

"You don't have to explain. We agreed that saying that you don't want to talk about it or aren't ready to yet is enough. So it's enough."

She could see his jaw muscles clenching and knew that despite his calm, understanding tone, it took a lot for him to concede that the same rules had to apply to both of them.

"I guess the thing that bothers me the most is that you *could* go to Mr. Peterson and Pat about Walter's disappearance."

Kenzie nodded. She took a sip of her water, trying to wash down a lump in her throat that she knew wasn't going to go down.

"They're like parents to you, and in the last couple of years… I've come to see them that way too. I couldn't talk to my parents about it. They just weren't available. It wasn't something I could go to a casual friend about. Lorne and Pat had been through the experience of Jose going missing. They knew what it was like to wonder whether something had happened or whether they were overreacting. I needed to talk to someone who understood that."

He stared down at his plate, and Kenzie again felt that horrible feeling in the pit of her stomach that she had hurt him. Really hurt him by not being able to go to him, but taking it to Lorne and Pat instead.

"I'm sorry. I'm so sorry I did that."

"You shouldn't be. It should be okay. I want them to be your family. I want you to have someone that you can go to when you need to. I just thought it should be me."

She reached across the table and held his hand. At first, he pulled back, but then he enclosed her hand firmly in his, enfolding it gently. Kenzie stared into his eyes, her heart throbbing painfully hard. She knew she needed to tell him the rest, and she couldn't put it off any longer. She couldn't work it through with a therapist. He needed to know that she trusted him with the most painful stuff, that he wasn't just a comfortable friend to come home to and someone to place the dinner order or to cuddle with before bed.

"I need to tell you the rest."

He nodded and didn't say anything.

"Not here. I can't tell you while I'm looking into your eyes."

He raised his brows, unsure what she wanted from him.

"Just… on the couch. Cuddling."

"Okay." Zachary stood up. He didn't suggest they finish eating or put the food away before it got too cold or started growing salmonella. Without letting go of her hand, he walked her over to the couch and they sat down together. He put his arm around her protectively as they sat down. Kenzie snuggled into him, enjoying the warmth and closeness of his body even though it was already summer temperatures.

Was she really going to do this?

41

You were in the hospital. Walter was missing. I reported it to the police, to Campbell. I'd been told not to by the governor, but I was getting threats, and I knew I had to let someone know what was going on. Get help and figure out who was involved and where the threats were coming from. Campbell agreed that it had been too long to ignore Walter's absence, even if the governor had said to back off."

Zachary rubbed her back. She couldn't see the expression on his face and didn't want to. Worse was coming. He was going to be really upset.

"I got a call that his stuff was at a hotel. He had checked in and never checked out, so the charges were accruing on his credit card, but they didn't know what to do about his things. When the police saw the credit card charges, they went to the hotel and checked it out. Grabbed his computer and whatever else and told the hotel how to contact me to come get the rest."

Zachary made a noise of acknowledgment.

"So I did. I got his luggage, looked at the room he'd stayed in, talked to a few people to see if they knew where he had gone. Found his car in the parking lot and checked it out. Put his luggage in my car—your car, actually—and went home."

He nodded. "Okay."

"When I was in front of the house, walking around to the trunk to get his luggage out…"

Kenzie's voice seized up. Zachary gave her a squeeze and waited. Kenzie swallowed a couple of times and cleared her throat. The words still didn't come.

"You were walking around the car to get his luggage out of the trunk," Zachary repeated, prompting her to go forward, the same way as she would have tried to help him, giving his own words back to him and waiting for more.

"A white van came speeding down the street."

"Did they…" Zachary hesitated, trying to come up with the right question. "Did they hurt you? Did they take Walter's luggage?"

"I didn't get to the trunk. People got out of the van. Men with…"

Her heart raced, ramping up as if she were going through it all over again.

"Shh…" Zachary continued to rub her back. "You're safe. Anchor yourself. Five things you see?"

It was an exercise they used to help him through his flashbacks. Kenzie was surprised, somehow, that her reaction to the memory of the incident might be considered a flashback. She didn't actually see it happening in front of her. She wasn't stuck in a loop she couldn't get out of. But her body was reacting to the memory, and what else was a flashback?

"Okay…" She took a breath and felt like she wasn't getting enough oxygen. "The books, the kitchen, the carpet, the TV. Your socks." The tip of his big toe protruded from a hole in the sock on Zachary's right foot. She giggled a little.

Zachary wiggled his toes at her.

"Good. Things you hear?"

That was harder. Kenzie concentrated. "The traffic outside, your voice, a lawn mower, a birdcall, the AC."

"Are you okay? Do you want to do smells?"

Kenzie analyzed her body. Her heart rate had slowed. Her muscles were relaxing. "I think I'm okay."

"Tell me about the men in the van."

"They had masks." Kenzie swallowed, trying to keep the composure she had regained with the anchoring exercise. "They came out really fast. Grabbed me." She could feel Zachary tensing. She squeezed his knee. "I'm okay."

He nodded. "Yes. Then what?"

"They threw me in the van. I hit my head." Kenzie tried to recite the facts, keeping them short and unemotional. It was easier now. He anticipated what was coming. "They held me down."

"Did they...?"

"They drove me away. Put a hood over my head and took me out of the van and into a house."

She was in the home stretch now.

"I sat in a room. They gave me some stew to eat. I went to sleep."

His hand trembled slightly as he rubbed her back, wondering what horrors were still coming. What they had done to her. Kenzie took a deep breath in and let it out.

"When I woke up, Walter was there."

"Walter?" his voice went up, surprised.

"He talked to the Russians. And they let me go."

Zachary leaned forward slightly to look at her face, searching for more. For what had happened next and her reaction to the whole thing.

"That's it," Kenzie said. "That was the end of it. He took me home. Made sure I was safe. I sent him away."

Zachary leaned back into the couch. "What did he say to them?"

"I couldn't hear. According to him, he agreed that he would lobby for them as he'd originally promised. No more background checks. That was what they wanted."

"That was why they took you."

"Yeah. Leverage."

Zachary swore and pulled Kenzie to him, holding her against his chest like he could protect her from what had already happened. He swore again. "I'm so sorry that happened to you."

Kenzie nodded and tried to pull back and put some space between them. "Yeah. I know. I've been on the other side, when something has happened to you—more than once. I know how it feels. How angry and helpless you are."

Zachary nodded, looking slightly relieved at her putting his feelings into words.

"But it's over. It happened months ago. Nothing else has happened. I haven't so much as heard someone speak with a Russian accent since then. They're keeping their deal with Walter and staying away from me."

"How can you even talk to him? Knowing it was all because of what he did, trying to back out of their deal."

"He was trying to do the right thing and couldn't have foreseen that it would affect me. At first... it *was* really hard. I knew he'd acted immediately to protect me, that he had never intended anything to happen to me. He acted like everything was back to normal, but it wasn't so easy for me."

"But you've been talking with him in the months since then. Going out to dinner. Having visits."

"He got you involved in that burglary case, and things sort of got worked out between us. Between him and me. We had some long talks, and I decided... I don't want to lose either of my parents. I want to have a relationship with them. So I'm trying to do more with the foundation, and talking with them. Not just waiting for a short visit on Christmas Day."

Zachary shook his head.

"I know it's hard to believe," Kenzie said, "but we're actually closer than we have been in years. I don't blame him for what happened. And when we disagree on politics or ethics... we just leave it be. Talk about something else."

He breathed out several times, and Kenzie knew he was still fuming, wanting to take on Walter or the Russians or someone else for what they had done to her. But it hadn't been that bad. It could have been a lot worse.

"I survived," she told him. "You saw me the next day and I was just fine."

He frowned for a minute, trying to identify the day.

"I missed seeing you in the evening and came in the next day. I had a little cut on my head," Kenzie indicated the spot. "Where I bumped my head when they put me into the van." Her throat constricted when she thought about it, but she managed to get through it and smile at him as if it were perfectly okay. The only after-effect of the incident. A small cut on her head. She had disguised the cut and bruise as much as possible with makeup, but couldn't help the fact that it still needed an adhesive strip to hold it closed. He had still been able to see she'd gotten hurt.

"It was then?" Zachary thought back. "You didn't say anything. You said you slipped on the ice."

"I said I tripped and hit my head on a van." Kenzie remembered her words very well. "And that was the truth. I didn't lie to you. I just didn't tell you the full story. I couldn't then. It was way too soon."

"Yeah," Zachary said softly. Maybe thinking about one of his experiences. How he needed time to recover and think about what had happened and process it all before he could talk to someone about it. Kenzie had been trying to find the right time to bring it up since Zachary had gotten out of the hospital, but the weeks and months had slipped by without the time ever coming up. She should be grateful to Pat for his inadvertent slip-up. Without it, she might never have had the courage to bring it up herself.

Kenzie gazed into the kitchen, where their meal was still spread out on the table. "Do you want some more to eat?"

"We can just put it away and have it another time."

"You're not hungry? You can't eat anymore? You hardly had anything," Kenzie pressed.

"Are you going to eat?"

Kenzie evaluated her body. Was she hungry? Too upset to eat? "I'm not sure. I'll sit down at the table and see."

Zachary looked uncertain but, eventually, he nodded and stood up, offering Kenzie his hand and taking her over to the table as if he were afraid she wouldn't make it otherwise. They both sat down and looked at the food. Kenzie was suddenly ravenous. Getting the story off her chest and out into the open at long last had finally gotten rid of the tight knot in her stomach, at least for now. She felt like it was the first meal after a long fast.

42

Kenzie had to sift through another slew of emails and voicemail messages when she got into work the next morning. She had thought that they would slow down after the initial day. Everyone had wanted to be involved the first day, when there was so much hype, and they were so excited about the romantic "love that survives death" line that the media was using. But things did not seem to be slowing down at all. They might even be building, more people joining the movement, everyone writing, demanding answers, trying to explain what must have happened, even if they had no idea whatsoever. There were psychics, armchair detectives, researchers, writers, and people who were just plain speculating on what had happened to Sharon and who the guilty party was. They were calling for blood when there hadn't even been an arrest. There was no point in putting the cart before the horse. They needed a suspect before they could get a conviction and a fair sentence.

Eventually, she had worked her way through everything important or urgent, and she found herself back in the cold room, looking through the evidence that had been recovered from the remains. The clothing that had still been on the corpse. Anything from the pockets. Every little bit of trace that they'd been able to gather, from the mud that was caked to the legs of her jeans to every single hair and fiber, separated by color. Most of the hairs were blond, of course, Sharon's own hair, but there were some shorter strands that might not be hers and some darker hairs that clearly couldn't be. But did they belong to one of their suspects or an unknown? If Sharon had been seeing other men regularly, as well as her drug dealer and anyone she happened to brush up against on the bus or at work, there could be dozens of different contributors, none of whom actually had anything to do with her disappearance and death.

Kenzie spread out the robe that Sharon had been wearing. White terry cloth at one time, she assumed. But badly stained and broken down over the intervening years, soaking up fluids from the decomposition process and then immersed in the muddy water of Petty Pond. Parts of it were rotted completely away. Would they be able to identify any blood on it? Was there any point in trying with all of the other bodily fluids that had seeped into it? What would blood tell her that was new? They already knew that she had died violently. Maybe she'd had external injuries as well as the closed head injury, but it didn't really make any difference to the investigation if she did.

Contrasting with the terry cloth robe was a pair of skinny jeans. Sharon's waist had been narrow, unsurprising for a drug user. Using amphetamines would have kept her slim, and she probably hungered for drugs and alcohol more than food. Still, it was hard to believe that a grown woman had been that skinny. Kenzie tried to measure the waist with her hands. She could almost have encircled Sharon's waist with her hands, and Kenzie didn't have particularly large hands or long fingers.

She'd had on a bra, no socks, and one sandal.

It was a strange, disparate collection of clothes, as if someone had dressed her without understanding what actually went together in an outfit. Surely even one of the men could put a t-shirt with blue jeans.

Had Sharon been changing for bed when she had been killed? Maybe she'd gotten her feet tangled as she tried to remove her jeans without taking off her other sandal and had fallen over backward, hitting her head. If she were too drunk or high to undress, Kenzie

DEATH OF A CORPSE

could see something like that happening. An accident. Misadventure. No one's fault.

She couldn't think of many other reasons Sharon would be dressed as she was. She'd spilled something on her shirt and wanted to rinse it in the sink right away before the stain could set, so she had just pulled on a robe? She had been outside when it started to rain or someone turned on a sprinkler, and she'd taken it off because it had gotten soaked? The jeans had probably been wet too, and had simply air dried, the same way Sharon's body had begun to mummify.

The missing sandal was of no concern. It could have been lost any time between Sharon getting killed and Kenzie recovering it from the pond. It could be at the house, in Ryder Phelps's car trunk, or in the mud of the pond. Sharon might have lost it before she'd been killed. It might be completely irrelevant.

She wished she could find the one thing that would tell the story of what Sharon had been doing before she had died.

Several smears of particulates had been recovered from Sharon's clothes. Clay, silt, concrete dust, and what looked like cinders. They told their own little story, if anyone could interpret it. The silt would be from the bottom of the pond. The clay could be from the garden or backyard of the house, where maybe Charlie had tried to bury her. Or from the bottom of the trunk of the car she'd been transported in. It was all too common to tell her anything. On TV, it would be a different story. The experts would be able to identify exactly where each kind of dirt had come from. But the medical examiner's office did not have experts of that caliber or the money to contract them, even if they had thought that the dirt might be the key to unlocking Sharon's story, which it probably wasn't. They wouldn't even run DNA on the hair samples until they had a suspect to compare it to. In real life, departments had budgets and were expected to stick to them. To find the killer or the cause of death, but with the lowest price tag possible. Especially when it was someone like Sharon, a poor drug addict who didn't matter to anyone, except maybe the man who had given her a home and had kept her body for the past thirteen years.

215

Kenzie sighed and put the evidence away until it could be properly processed once there was a case to build. If Sharon had been killed by accident or by Charlie Titon, there would be no case to build, and they couldn't justify the expenses of testing every hair, fiber, or smear of dirt.

43

The file gave Cody Roundtree as Sharon Briggs's next of kin. Despite their different last names, Kenzie assumed this was the brother who had been looking for her at some point. Her mother must be dead. Her father was either dead or not a part of her life in the first place. The only person left to look after her remains was the stepbrother who she hadn't gotten along with.

Back at her desk, Kenzie tried the phone number, unsure whether it was current or the number he'd had at the time of Sharon's disappearance. Or if he still had the same one. It rang a few times and then was answered by a gruff male voice.

"Yeah?"

"I'm looking for Cody Roundtree."

"What for?"

Someone with debts, probably. Maybe even outstanding warrants. Or, perhaps just someone whose stepsister had been in the news recently. Maybe he was getting as many phone calls as Kenzie and Edwards.

"This is Kenzie Kirsch from the Medical Examiner's Office. I'm looking for Sharon Briggs's next of kin."

He swore.

"Is this Cody, then?" Kenzie asked.

"Yeah, this is Cody. But hell, what am I supposed to do? I haven't had anything to do with her. Not like she would want me to. Can't you call someone else? One of her friends? We're not even related."

"I realize you aren't related by blood, but you are legally. You're next on the list if she doesn't have any parents or natural siblings."

"What if I say I don't want to deal with it? I can't afford a funeral and all that crap. Do you know how much it cost when her mom died? It was thousands of dollars, and that was for the cheapest show we could manage. With the way everyone is behaving about her being found, and being murdered and all that, they're going to expect a big fancy funeral. Let them pay for it!"

"There are less expensive routes. Cremation is one possibility. And just because the public wants a big fancy memorial, that doesn't mean that you need to have one. You can just tell them that the family wants a small, private affair. Or that that's what Sharon would have wanted."

"Yeah. But like I said, she wasn't even my sister. I don't know why I should get saddled with this."

"Somebody needs to. And she doesn't have any other family, from what I understand."

"Too bad that boyfriend of hers died. I could have got him to do it."

"Charles Titon?"

"Yeah, he's the one, isn't he? Thought he could take care of Sharon, turn her around. Make her behave." He gave a sharp laugh. "That's a failing proposition. No one in the world could have made Sharon do what Sharon didn't want to."

"She was stubborn?"

"She wasn't going to do what anyone told her to. And if you told her to do something she wanted to do, she wouldn't, just to spite you. That's what kind of person she was."

Kenzie had known people like that. She tried to imagine Sharon as a teenager and young woman. She'd seen a few pictures of her now. Heard some of the stories. How other people saw her. What she had done, partying, promiscuous, not following the rules that polite society would have prescribed. From her time with Zachary and

Tyrrell, Kenzie understood that that stubborn, oppositional streak, the tendency to fight back and refuse to do whatever she was told, was probably rooted in a deep distrust of the people in authority around her. Her parents, guardians, or trusted adults in her life had not provided her with safety or the necessities of life, so she had learned to go her own way and not listen to the lies that the adults told her. It came from anxiety and self-defense. But it looked like rebellion and disobedience. Zachary's mother had told him that he was incorrigible. A child who had done his best to protect himself and his younger siblings, but who would always go off the rails, driven by the impulsivity of his ADHD and the anxiety of his PTSD.

"Did you stay in touch with her at all?" Kenzie asked Cody. "In the later years?"

"In the later years? She's been dead for thirteen, lady. What do you think?"

"No," Kenzie had to laugh. "I mean before that. Between the time that she left home and when she disappeared thirteen years ago. Were the two of you in contact much?"

There was a moment's hesitation while he considered the question. "We weren't close. We were never close. But after her mom died, I saw her a few times. Sometimes she lived on the streets or in some shelter. Later she was with Charlie."

"You went back there looking for her when she disappeared."

"Yeah, I did." He sounded surprised that she knew about that. "It wasn't like I expected to find her. I knew she'd disappeared, so why would she be there? But sometimes... people are hiding right where you expect to find them. They just don't want to be found. So maybe she just decided she wasn't going back to work anymore. That Hilda gal was always on her case about something. Maybe Sharon just didn't want anything to do with Hilda."

"I thought she and Hilda were friends."

"They were. In the beginning. She was real nice to Sharon, mothering her, getting her a job, all that. But she expected... gratitude, I guess. For Sharon to be beholden to her. And Sharon wasn't. She was out to get whatever she could from everyone around her, but she wasn't the kind to say thank you and send flowers. And Hilda didn't like how Sharon was with the guys."

"That she was seeing several men at once?"

"Yeah. Not just that, the way the men buzzed around her. Hilda's a nice girl, good-looking, and she never got attention like that. I think she was sweet on Ryder, but he only had eyes for Sharon."

"Hilda *liked* Ryder Phelps?" Kenzie was floored.

"Yeah. I think they were maybe an item before Sharon came into the picture? There were all kinds of connections between that bunch; I never understood all of the details. Friends and cousins and sleeping together, I never did sort it all out. But Hilda and Ryder, I understood that. She was always making cow eyes at him and, after Sharon was on the scene, he didn't care a bit for her. Looked right through her."

Poor Hilda.

Kenzie couldn't help wondering if Hilda had done anything about it. Had she tried to break the two of them up? Told Sharon to stay away from Ryder because she was already sleeping with Charlie? Tried to break the two of them up with lies or rumors?

"I didn't realize that there were problems between them. Hilda didn't mention that when I talked to her."

"Well, she wouldn't, would she?" Cody asked sensibly. "What *did* she tell you?" There was caution in his voice. If Cody could tell Kenzie about Hilda, then Hilda could probably tell her things about Cody too. More than just a passing reference to him.

"Not much," Kenzie said, hoping to allay any fears and, at the same time, running through what she had learned from Hilda. Had Hilda slipped out with anything that Kenzie should have paid more attention to? Hinted at something? "I know that she was the one who reported Sharon missing. I guess since they worked together, it makes sense that she would be one of the first ones to notice that Sharon wasn't where she should be. And Charles, of course. I'm a little surprised he wasn't the one to report her missing."

"He probably thought she would come back. She disappeared sometimes. And then she would show up again, just when you figured something must have happened to her."

"She had disappeared before?"

"I don't know if disappeared is the right word. Because... there wasn't really anywhere she was supposed to be. Yeah, Hilda got her that job, but she never stayed long at a job. Maybe long enough to get a paycheck or two, but not any more than that. Once she had money to spend..."

"I know she was a pretty heavy drug user."

"Yeah. And people like that don't hang on to money for long. Or jobs. Or friends. Sharon had been living like that for a few years. You never knew if she was on the street or dead in some alley somewhere. Or if she was shacked up with some guy or sleeping on someone's couch."

"Is that how it started with Charles Titon? She crashed on his couch one day?"

"Nah, she never had to sleep on Charlie's couch," Cody said with a knowing laugh. "They never had that kind of a relationship."

"How did they meet, do you know?"

"At some bar or party. I'm not sure. He thought he could straighten her out and she saw a good mark."

That sounded like quite the challenge. "How could he party with her *and* try to straighten her out?" Kenzie asked, trying to imagine how that would work.

"He couldn't," Cody laughed. "What's he going to do? Tell her to drink less? Do one less line of coke? Sure, he tried, told her when he thought she was going overboard, but he wasn't any boy scout himself. He could tell her it was time to go home if they weren't already home, but Sharon didn't take instruction well."

He'd already said that Sharon would do the opposite of what someone told her to. Charles, trying to step in as a parental figure in her life, while sleeping with her, would probably have done better to encourage her to drink and drug more. Then maybe she would cut back. But telling her that it was time to quit or to slow down or to go to bed... she probably drank more around him, rather than less.

"That must have been difficult for him. I'm surprised that they stayed together."

Cody made a noise in his throat. A snort of derision? Kenzie wasn't sure how to define it. They didn't stay together? Cody had already said that Sharon would disappear. Hilda had said that she was getting together with Ryder Phelps as well as with other men. Charles Titon's relationship with Sharon, being touted all over social media as *the love that survives death*, seemed very tenuous. Maybe keeping her body after her death was his way of proving to himself that he could hold on to her. The only way he'd ever been able to control her was to ensure that he knew where she was every night. Was that why she had died? So that he could control her?

"Do you think that Charles was responsible for Sharon's death?" Kenzie asked.

"I thought that was pretty obvious. I mean, she wasn't found in *my* house."

"I just mean that a determination of the manner and cause of death hasn't been made yet. It might have been accidental. Something that she did to herself because she was too impaired. Do you think that is a possibility?"

There were a few beats of silence while Cody considered this. "I suppose it's possible," he said eventually. "I just assumed that she and Charles had a fight."

"Did they fight a lot?"

"What do *you* think?"

"I thought that if he was trying to take care of her, and she wanted a place to live, they might both have reasons to avoid confrontation."

"Sharon never avoided a confrontation in her life. And whatever you're hearing in the media about this great love that Charlie had for her, it was never like that. It wasn't some big romance. They'll be making TV movies about the two of them the way that everyone is going on about it right now. The tragedy of it all, Charlie losing her right when things were starting to work out... but it wasn't like that. It wasn't like that at all."

"So you suspected from the start that he'd had something to do with her death."

"Well..." Cody took a few seconds to gather his thoughts. "When the news broke, I mean, that her body had been found. Before that...

I didn't know anything about what had happened. She might have OD'd and be a Jane Doe in a morgue somewhere. *No offense,*" he added, as if suggesting that a body might remain unidentified despite their best efforts was disparaging what Kenzie did.

"It does happen," Kenzie admitted. "If we don't have enough information to identify someone, there's not much we can do about it. It helps if there is a missing person report out so that we can match them up, but even then, sometimes there is not enough identifying information to make a positive match."

"It isn't like on TV," Cody said helpfully.

"That's what I try to tell people," Kenzie agreed. "We don't run DNA on every set of remains that comes through here. It's expensive, and you have to have something to compare it to. If you don't have DNA for the missing person, and you can't make a match to a missing person by dental, skeletal, or fingerprint evidence…"

"I guess we were lucky you were able to identify Sharon."

Though his tone said otherwise. Maybe he would have been happier if they had never identified her. Let her just be interred as a Jane Doe, like he had thought at the time.

44

Kenzie hadn't expected to be called to Charles Titon's—or now Ryder Phelps's—house for the police search of the yard. Edwards had been fine with just using his police officers and a couple of crime scene techs to search the inside of the house for any blood evidence or other forensic samples that might help to move the case forward. Maybe he wasn't satisfied with the fact that they hadn't found any usable evidence inside the house, so he wanted Kenzie in attendance for the outside scene. Maybe it was just a courtesy because she had been passing as much information as possible on to him from the people who had continued to call and email her, and her conversations with Hilda, the anonymous neighbor, and Cody Roundtree. People seemed to feel freer to talk to her than with Edwards, the tough homicide detective who could either put them in jail or think that their testimony was useless. People didn't have the best opinion of cops.

The police started with a grid search of the backyard. It wasn't a huge property, luckily. The backyard of an old house, on a lot just wider than the house. Nothing that would require a riding mower to cut the grass. The police marked off a grid and each square was examined and logged in a binder. Kenzie moved from one square to another to make any additional observations. Anything that might relate to the case was carefully documented, a picture taken with a numbered marker and a scale. A button. A handily sized rock that could be used to bash someone in the back of the head. Gardening implements. The remains of crushed beer cans that looked like they had been forgotten there years earlier. Edwards had called the previously anonymous neighbor who had said that Charles had put flowers on a memorial in the back-yard to identify the location of the memorial. Maria Smith apparently had nothing better to do than to complain about loud parties and watch out her window to see what her neighbors were doing.

"Memorial was in this area," Edwards said, his pen hovering over the squares on the map in the binder, and then pointing to the identi-fied area in the yard. "So we will probably excavate those squares once we finish the surface search." He wiped his forehead with the back of his hand, looking at the work currently being done. "With my luck, we'll find the remains of his dead dog."

"The neighbor—Miss Smith—said he didn't have a dog."

"Not that she knew about. She didn't know he had a corpse in the bedroom either."

"Well... fair enough. I would think that he would have to take the dog out for walks, at least to the yard. Which he wouldn't likely do with a corpse."

Edwards grinned, showing teeth. "Not as likely," he agreed. "But maybe a cat or a rabbit. It doesn't have to be a dog."

Kenzie nodded her agreement. One of the cops doing the grid search waved to her, and she went over to see what he had found.

"Do you think this is anything?"

Kenzie looked down at the hook of a coat hanger that was mostly buried in the dirt. Not something she would have wanted to mow over accidentally. It would either wreck the mower or launch a newly cut hook of metal across the yard. Maybe both. She shook her head. "Document it, but I don't think it's relevant to the case. She was hit on the head, not..." Kenzie tried to think of how a coat hanger might be used to harm someone, but was at a loss. "I don't think it's relevant."

The cop nodded philosophically and placed a numbered marker next to the hook.

A few probes into the area that Maria Smith had identified as where the memorial flowers had been placed showed that the soil was only loosely packed, as if it had been dug more recently than the rest of the yard, which was pretty hard-packed and sun-baked. On the one hand, this might be significant. But Kenzie feared that it would be, as Edwards had suggested, a buried pet rather than anything to do with Sharon Briggs's death. What would anyone have buried that related to her death? They already had her remains. If Charles Titon had initially tried to dig a grave to dispose of Sharon's body, he had given up and decided not to. And then why would he put flowers there, when Sharon's body was inside the house with him? Had he dissociated himself that much from what had happened to Sharon and the fact that it was her body in repose on his bed?

The work required to dig a hole like a grave was significant, and people who sat in their cars or in front of computers all day were not well-equipped to do it. Kenzie would have suggested that they use a backhoe instead of trying to dig it by hand. Still, she knew that if they did so, there was a significant danger of destroying evidence, if there was anything of significance in that plot of ground.

So even though someone else had already loosened the soil, it still took time. Enough time had passed that grass and weeds had grown over the patch, and they had to be removed first, taking with them as little dirt as possible in case there was any evidence tangled in the roots. Then they began to dig, taking turns with the shovel as each cop thought he would be more efficient than the previous in digging the area up.

It was easy to identify the area that had previously been dug, round rather than rectangular, by how loose the soil was. They didn't try to dig wider than that, since it was unlikely anything had been buried there before without loosening the dirt. How long would it take for the ground to become hard-packed like the rest of the yard? It probably depended on how many people were walking over it, pressing it down. From the looks of the yard, it was not used recreationally. The grass and weeds were not awful, so it was mown every week or two, but that was probably the only time Titon had bothered to walk through the yard.

That and to lay his flowers down on the spot. The fact that it was treated as a memorial probably prevented any foot traffic across it. How long had Titon continued to put flowers there? Just for a few day or weeks? Did he place flowers there on the anniversary of Sharon's death each year? If he did, and Maria Smith could tell them what day that was, maybe they could pinpoint exactly what day she had died, instead of estimating it from the date Hilda had reported her missing. It would be good to have confirmation that she had died on the date that Hilda said she had disappeared, since Hilda could, of course, be lying and setting up an alibi for herself. Kenzie didn't seriously believe that Hilda had killed Sharon, but she wouldn't be the first woman to strike out in a jealous rage. According to Cody, Sharon had been messing around with the man that Hilda wanted for her own. And by Hilda's own mouth, she had been aware of it. She had aimed the jealousy motive back at Charles Titon, who would not have been happy about his girlfriend being involved with his cousin. Maybe she was trying to hide her own motive. She certainly hadn't been forthcoming about being attracted to Ryder.

"Dr. Kirsch?"

Kenzie shook off her musings and looked at the man who had spoken to her, one of the crime techs. "Sorry, yes?"

"Do you want to look at this soil?"

"What did you find?"

He motioned to her without explaining. Kenzie approached the area, trying to keep her feet, protected by paper booties, away from the upturned earth and anything that might turn out to be evidence. She and the tech knelt at the edge of the shallow, circular hole and looked down at the dirt.

She immediately saw what had attracted the tech's attention. There were a number of pieces of charcoal, most of them quite small, mixed in with the soil, and grayish sand. There were a couple of larger chunks of wood that Kenzie could still see the burn pattern on. Kenzie looked at the wood for a moment and then at the circular area.

"It was a fire pit."

"I would agree," the tech agreed.

He looked at her, and Kenzie turned and looked for Edwards to see if he could find any significance in this. "Sharon wasn't burned," she said. "And this is definitely wood, not bone, so it isn't from other remains that were cremated and buried here. I don't think it's a burial site at all. Just... reclaiming the area where the fire pit once was."

Edwards shrugged. "There's no indication that someone tried to burn the body, right?" he said. "He may have tried to dig a hole first and found it too difficult, but there isn't any evidence that he then tried to burn the body, is there?"

Kenzie shook her head. "I was just looking at her clothes. There wasn't any indication that anything was burned. Some missing pieces of cloth had rotted away, but I didn't see anything suggesting that they had been burned."

"Do we bother any more with this?"

"How deep does the disturbed soil go?"

They brought back the probes and pushed them down into the soil, seeing how far they could get before hitting hard-packed earth or clay.

"Another four to six inches," Edwards said, shaking his head. "There's nothing buried here. He just mixed the ashes in with the soil and let the grass grow over it. Maybe spread a bit of grass seed to help it along."

Kenzie agreed. It was a letdown; she had been hoping that finding a dug-up area where Charles had placed his memorial flowers, they would find something significant.

But maybe it was just the location of some particularly good memories. Cuddling in front of the fire with Sharon on a warm summer night. Gathering there with friends to share stories and camaraderie. And when Sharon had died, he didn't want to use it anymore. So he dug it in and placed flowers there from time to time, thinking about those pleasant summer nights with wood smoke wafting through the air.

45

Kenzie was startled abruptly from her dream with a clonic jerk, one of those whole-body muscle clenches that she sometimes experienced when she dreamed she was falling or something else made her try to protect herself from damage in the midst of a vivid dream or when just drifting off to sleep.

Zachary's hand found her back and he rested it there, warm and soothing, for a few seconds. "Are you okay?"

"Yeah." Kenzie stretched and shifted, but didn't pull away from the warmth of his touch. "Just a dream. Scared myself awake."

He rubbed in a slow, firm circle. "A dream about the kidnapping?"

"No." She was happy to be able to say that it was not, and for it to be the truth. It was good that he knew what had happened now, and he could help her through those times when her body decided to take her back through the experience, but that wasn't it this time. "No... I think it was my case." She lay there, mind drifting, trying to take hold of what exactly had happened in the dream. There were disjointed images, and that feeling that something was just beyond her reach that would pull it all together, if she could just catch it. "Something about the fire," she murmured.

His hand was quickly withdrawn, before Kenzie realized what she

229

had said. Zachary's worst trauma trigger, rather than a kidnapping like Kenzie's, was the fire that had burned his house down when he was ten. A fire that he had unintentionally set, and the blame had followed him all the way through his life. He had been trapped in that fire and would have burned to death if it hadn't been for the fire-fighters who had arrived and rescued him.

Kenzie rolled over and put her arms around Zachary to comfort him, flip-flopping their roles.

"No, I'm sorry. It was a campfire. Outside in a fire pit, contained and controlled, perfectly safe."

He shuddered in her arms. He was much better about fire than he used to be. He had faced his fear and overcome his reaction to seeing a fire, even just a candle flame, in real life. But his memories of the house fire were still there, and could still be triggered by other things, especially if he didn't see the trigger coming.

"Anchoring," Kenzie prompted him. "What do you see? It's pretty dark; maybe we should start with one of the other senses."

"The window. The streetlight outside."

The window was mostly covered by the blind, but it did let some of the light from the street outside into the bedroom.

"Yes."

"You." His cheek was pressed against hers, so Kenzie wasn't sure how much of herself Zachary could actually see, but she would accept it.

"Anything else?"

He drew in a shaky breath. "I can't..."

She knew he was still seeing the fire. "Do you want me to turn on the lamp? Or do another sense?"

"Your voice. Keep talking to me."

"What else do you hear?"

"A train in the distance." Kenzie had to strain her ears to hear the far-away horn of the train passing by the outskirts of town. He must be able to hear well over the crackling and roar of the fire in his memories if he was able to differentiate that. "The house creaking. Tires on pavement."

"That's only four. Anything else?"

He ran his fingers through her tangled, curly hair. "I smell you," he whispered. "Your shampoo."

He wasn't shaking anymore. Kenzie let him lie there, recovering. He had said to keep talking, so she murmured to him.

"They were all friends. They did things together. Or maybe not *friends*; I don't think they all liked each other that well. But they liked to get together to party. Alcohol, drugs, music, teasing and flirting, maybe some making out."

"Who?" Zachary asked.

Kenzie didn't bother telling him. She wanted to talk it through, but couldn't tell him too much. Edwards had warned her about pillow talk and, even though she knew that Zachary would never leak anything to the press or online, she did her best to comply with his directions.

"They stopped getting together after she died. Like she was the glue that held them together. All of these different parts, these different relationships. Even his cousin stopped coming over, as far as I can tell. He might be lying, but I can't see anyone being invited over after that."

Zachary made a noncommittal noise. Fine with being treated as a sounding board even if he didn't know exactly what it was about. Or just happy to have her talking.

"Did he kill her?" Kenzie mused. "Was it an accident? Did anyone know?"

"Sometimes people know things," Zachary whispered, "but they keep quiet."

Kenzie had found that to be much more accurate than she ever would have thought when she was younger. Her parents had always taught her to talk to them about things, to make good decisions. To right wrongs and "fess up" if she had made a mistake. But she found that much of the rest of the world lived by a different code. Don't snitch. Never admit you are in the wrong. Keep the authorities out of it. Protect yourself and your loved ones from any undue interest. So many people she heard interviewed on true crime shows or had talked to in her role in the Medical Examiner's Office admitted to having known about abuse, murder, or other terrible crimes but had never come forward. They didn't want to be in the spotlight. They didn't want to reveal their own part in the crime. They didn't want a loved one to be arrested, even if he had done terrible things.

"Are they *all* lying?"

Zachary didn't know exactly what she was talking about, but she felt him shrug one shoulder. "Probably."

Kenzie couldn't help chuckling at that.

"Everybody lies," Zachary said. "Especially to protect themselves."

"If one of them killed her, would they all protect him? They didn't all get along together. Wouldn't they turn on each other?"

"If they were all from the culture where you don't talk to the cops."

"Hmm." He had a point there. They might not like each other or have complex relationships that she didn't understand, but they didn't come from the same background and upbringing as Kenzie. She had never been one to test whether her parents would use their money or influence to protect her from the reach of the law, but plenty of people in her parents' society did. They had enough money and influence to smooth things over and ensure their wayward children did not have to face the consequences of their actions. In the culture that Sharon and her friends had come from, they didn't have that privilege. The police and courts would be quick to bring the full extent of the law down on them if they were believed to have killed someone or committed some other heinous act. They had to pull back, to put a wall of silence between themselves and the law, even if they weren't real friends. Because that was what they had to do to protect themselves.

"I need to remember this."

"What?" Zachary turned toward her slightly to ask the question. His body was relaxed now, the flashback and its effects past.

"I need to remember this in the morning. This stuff."

"Okay."

The two of them drifted back to sleep, cuddling in each other's arms.

46

Kenzie remembered more the next day than she would have expected to, which was good, because Zachary could remember nothing of the night before and couldn't remind her of what she had wanted to remember. If she'd even told him details in the first place, which she hadn't.

She called Edwards, but he didn't answer. She left a message for him to call her, though she wasn't sure she had anything that he could use. It wasn't even a fully formed thought.

"Do you have anything going on this morning?" she asked Zachary as they tidied up after breakfast. "I would like to go talk to a witness... but maybe I shouldn't go alone, and Edwards hasn't returned my call."

He nodded, but was frowning. "What kind of a witness? Is this person dangerous?"

Kenzie shook her head. "I'm pretty sure she's not. She's just a nosy neighbor, you know? Had some insights into a case because she overlooks the backyard of the suspects. But she herself didn't have any reason to do something violent. She's not a suspect at all." Kenzie shrugged. "Little old ladies, you know? I'm not afraid she's going to do something. I just think I should have someone there in case she says something that needs to be verified later."

"Sure. I can come along." He put the plates into the dishwasher. "You could just record her, you know."

"She might not agree to it. She hasn't wanted anything to do with the police, so... I don't know how she would respond to that suggestion." Kenzie turned the plates in the dishwasher around to face the sprayer and closed the door. "She'll like you, I bet. You're always charming to the grandma types."

He made a face. "I'm not sure how I feel about that."

"If you shave, anyway. You should shave first."

He liked his stubble. It helped him to hide in plain sight. People didn't want to pay too much attention to some scruffy guy hanging around. Make eye contact, and he could be a homeless person who would start to harass you or ask for money. Or be schizophrenic and blast you with paranoid religious ramblings. But she would prefer that Zachary was clean cut and presentable for a talk with Mrs. Smith.

Zachary grumbled, but headed toward the bathroom to comply. "If you want me to shave, you just have to ask. You don't need to set up a whole scenario," he teased.

Kenzie laughed and finished tidying up and getting her things in order.

Kenzie knew which house was Maria Smith's from Edwards. And even if she didn't, it wouldn't have taken her long to knock on doors that had a sight line into Charles Titon's backyard before she found her. As it was, she knew which house it was, and she and Zachary presented themselves on the doorstep.

The door was answered by a woman in her thirties. Kenzie looked behind her, confused, looking for the older woman. "Oh, hi. I'm looking for Maria Smith?"

She had assumed that Maria lived alone, but no one had said so. Kenzie had just pictured her as a little old lady looking out her windows because she didn't have anything else to do to occupy her time. There was no reason she couldn't be living with a daughter or granddaughter. Or some kind of companion.

"Yes, that's me."

Kenzie couldn't find the appropriate words. She caught a look from Zachary, one eyebrow raised questioningly. *This* was her little old lady?

"Oh. I'm sorry. I thought…" Kenzie trailed off. She thought what? She had made some assumptions that had clearly been wrong. Very wrong. Maria Smith was not much older than Sharon and the people in her circle. They were contemporaries. She felt the first vague misgivings stirring in her gut. Everything that Maria had said now had to be considered in a different light. Had she known any of them personally? Did she have an ax to grind? Did she know more than she had let on because she wanted one particular person to be implicated by her testimony?

Kenzie forced a smile. "Well, it's good to meet you. I'm… Dr. Kirsch. From the Medical Examiner's Office."

"Oh!" The brunette stepped back, looking Kenzie over. Her eyes went to Zachary. "And…"

"My associate. I was wondering if I could ask you a few more questions?"

"Well, yes, of course." She opened the door farther to allow Kenzie in. "You didn't have to come over, you could have just called me." She shrugged, looking a little bit embarrassed. "I guess there was no point in trying to make a report anonymously without blocking my caller ID first. I don't know why I didn't think about it. That detective on the case called me back, asked me for my name and address, asked more questions about Sharon and everyone." Maria made a twirly gesture in the direction of Charlie's house. Ryder's house. "That's why I'm surprised to see you. I would have thought… he had everything he needed."

"Well, we work together. Two different prongs of the same investigation. Sometimes the questions will be from the police perspective, sometimes from the forensics."

"So you're here about the forensics."

Kenzie nodded.

"I saw them over in the yard," Maria said. "Did you find anything?"

"I can't really talk about that. But I did want to know a little bit more about your perspective on the yard here, and what you may have seen before and after Sharon disappeared."

Maria led them to the living room and sat down. Kenzie and Zachary sat on the couch. "Well...?" Maria shook her head. "I'm not sure how I can help you. I already told you everything I know and answered your questions. And the detective's."

"Did he come here or talk to you on the phone?"

"Just on the phone."

Had Edwards made the same mistake as Kenzie had, assuming that Maria was much older than Sharon and her friends? Kenzie wasn't sure why it made such a difference to her. It wasn't like she had lied about her age; Maria had just not said how old she was and Kenzie had made assumptions. But now, Kenzie had to wonder if she were jealous of Sharon and her escapades. Maybe Maria was tired of being boring and predictable and wished that she could be carefree and party with friends whenever she wanted to.

Maybe she was the one who had been jealous of Sharon's attentions to Ryder. She could have met him in the neighborhood and thought she had a chance with him until Sharon had entered the picture. Maria might have been working up to talking to Ryder, seeing if he would go out with her, and then that door had been slammed shut with Sharon's appearance. Or she could have liked Charles rather than Ryder. Exchanged pleasantries with him over the months leading up to Sharon moving in and thought they were getting closer, that they had something in common, only to have it all ruined by Sharon.

"So, how much did you know about Sharon and her friends?" Kenzie asked. "Did you have much contact with them?"

"No, no. I didn't know them at all. Just saw them in the yard sometimes."

"You often saw Sharon with Charles or Ryder," Kenzie said, trying to shortcut what they had already established on the phone call. "And you said that sometimes there was another woman, and that would be

Hilda. And her brother. You said that there were other people over there too. Drug dealers and prostitutes."

Kenzie was watching Maria's face. Her expression wavered when Kenzie mentioned drug dealers and prostitutes.

"I don't know. I meant... I don't know that's what they were. I know Sharon was using drugs, and she looked like... I mean, she could have been turning tricks."

"You saw her drug dealer? I think that's what you said."

"I don't know. Someone who might have been a drug dealer."

"Not one of her usual guests."

"No. Yes. He didn't spend much time with her. Usually just showed up, exchanged packages, and he was gone again. What would you think?"

"I'm sure I would think the same thing. And were there other women who came by? Prostitutes? Or were you talking about Sharon and her friend?"

"Yes... I guess I don't *know*, but sometimes you get a feel for these things, you know? The way people act around each other. People who only come for a little while, and when they come out again later..." Another shrug, and Maria's face got pinker. "I just think they were. Sharon and that friend of hers. I think they were both... seeing men."

"Acting as prostitutes."

"Yes."

Kenzie hadn't picked up any clues that Hilda was prostituting herself. It didn't sound out of character for Sharon, but she wasn't sure about Hilda. She was the one with the honest job, who was trying to help Sharon get straightened out.

According to her.

The services Hilda said she was performing and what she was actually doing to earn money might be two very different things.

"Out of this house?" Kenzie motioned toward the house. "Charles's house?"

"Yes. Well, I don't know," Maria quickly took it back. "I don't really know anything about it. What went on behind closed doors over there. Obviously." She rolled her eyes over the fact that there had been a body lying there dead for thirteen years without her realizing it. She had never been inside the house and couldn't swear to anything that had happened there.

"You think that Charles knew what was going on? Maybe that he was acting as her pimp?"

"Charlie? No, no, I never said that. I'm sure he didn't have any idea what was going on while he was out of the house. He worked during the day. He was very responsible."

"And Ryder? The other man who was there the most? Charlie's cousin?"

"I don't know. No, I don't think he was pimping her out." Maria made a face. "Do we have to talk about this? I wasn't there. I didn't see exactly what happened."

"You talked to Charles?"

"Talked to him? What do you mean?"

"He was your neighbor. Maybe you said good morning when you saw each other on the street. Helped shovel each other's walks. Exchanged cards at Christmas. You saw each other, knew who each person in Charles's house was."

"We talked occasionally," Maria agreed grudgingly.

"You were both young people. Not that different in age. Did you ever want to go over there and join them?"

"No."

"When they were gathered around the fire, laughing and having a good time together, you didn't wish that you were part of that circle?"

"Around the fire?"

"That's where the fire pit was, isn't it? Where he used to lay the flowers after Sharon was gone?"

"Yes."

"You knew there wasn't a dog or a pet. There was a fire pit. That's what used to be there."

She nodded. "I wasn't lying. I just didn't think…"

"Did you feel left out? Not being a part of their circle?"

"I said no," Maria growled.

"Did you call the cops on them? Threaten to send them over if they didn't quiet down so that you could sleep? Only you weren't really sleeping, were you?"

Kenzie had seen it enough times before. Neighbors who got on each other's nerves, invaded each other's privacy, yelled and made threats.

Maria looked away. "Sometimes."

"Because you didn't like them having fun when you couldn't join in."

"It wasn't like that. I could see all the illegal stuff going on over there. If neighbors look the other way and let stuff like that go on, the neighborhood goes to the dogs. You have to stay on top of these things. Make sure that people are responsible, that they follow the rules. To preserve the value of the other houses."

"But they weren't doing anything illegal when they just sat and visited around the fire."

"They drank. Used drugs."

"You couldn't tell that."

"I could see. I could smell the smoke. I could see what they were doing."

"Was her brother there too? Sharon's brother?"

Maria thought about it, frowning. "I don't know who everyone was that got together with them. I think I remember her mentioning her brother once, but I'm not sure. There were a few of them that came and went; I couldn't keep all of them straight."

"But they never invited you."

Her mouth was a hard, thin line. "No. I didn't say I wanted them to. I could have asked to join them, you know. But I wasn't in their circles. I didn't do the kind of stuff that they did. I wasn't into the party scene. I'm a responsible person." She made a gesture to encompass the area around her. "I'm a good homeowner and neighbor. I have a good job. Show up for work every day. I don't drink or smoke or use drugs. I don't sleep around. I'm a good, responsible person and *I* show my neighbors respect."

"But they didn't."

"No," Maria agreed in a tight voice. "They did all of those things

239

and just… laughed and partied, acted like they didn't have a care in the world."

That was how it looked from the outside. Kenzie was sure that the members of the party had plenty of troubles of their own. They might seem happy and carefree, but they were using to hide from the problems they had. The parties were not satisfying on any spiritual level. They were just a way of coping with the problems they had.

Zachary looked at his wrist in a deliberate gesture, though Kenzie knew he didn't wear a watch. "We should go," he prompted Kenzie.

She looked at him, surprised at the interruption. She looked at Maria, the other questions that she had planned dissolving. She had what she needed from Maria, and Zachary was right. They should be getting on their way. Maria was not the nosy old lady Kenzie had thought she was, and that needed some rethinking and maybe a report back to Edwards.

"You're right," she acknowledged. "We have some other things we need to look at."

Maria raised her brows. "Are you going to arrest them?"

"I don't have the authority to arrest anyone. Who do you think should be arrested?"

"All of them."

"For Sharon's death?"

"I don't know which one of them killed her. For sure one of them did. And the others were all involved with drugs and everything else. Why won't the police ever arrest anyone?"

"Because they didn't arrest them when you called about the noisy parties, drugs, and prostitution you thought were going on there?"

"Yeah. Never made one move to arrest them or even give them a fine. Now you *know* what they did. So you have to."

"We still don't have an eyewitness," Kenzie said. "Unless you actually saw it happen."

Zachary stood up and, with one hand on her arm, had Kenzie standing a second later. "Time to go."

Kenzie gave Maria one more look, waiting for her to admit or deny that she had seen something. Zachary gave her a little tug.

"You know how to reach me," Kenzie said finally. "If you have anything else you want to tell me."

She and Zachary left. The door clicked shut behind them, and Kenzie turned to him.

"What was that all about?"

"She's probably watching through the peephole or window. Wait until we're out of sight."

They walked to Zachary's car, a little way down the street, and got inside.

"Well?" Kenzie asked.

"I didn't think you were safe."

"What, did you think she was going to pull a gun on me?" she demanded sarcastically.

"Maybe. I don't know. You were winding her up. And she doesn't seem real stable."

Kenzie was taken aback. "You don't think she would really have done anything violent?"

"She could have. Neither of us had any way to protect ourselves if she did have a gun or another weapon. You should leave the questioning to the police."

"I am. I called Edwards before we came over."

"Let him do the questioning," Zachary repeated. "Get her on video. In a secure setting."

"You're one to talk," Kenzie grumbled. "Where is all of this great advice when it's one of *your* investigations?"

"Well, that's different." Zachary grinned.

"Because it's you? Because you're a man?"

"Because I do it on impulse. This isn't my investigation, so I'm not drawn into it that way." He shrugged. "I got us *out* on impulse instead. You're right. There's probably no danger. But she hasn't been cleared as a suspect, has she?"

"I don't think any of us considered her one. Until I saw her. I just thought…"

"She was a little old lady."

"Yeah."

"So let Detective Edwards look into her background. The

complaints she made back then. Whether she has an alibi. But putting her on the spot and pointing out how jealous she was of them... She's a suspect, and if she did something to Sharon and you push her, she could decide you need to be dealt with too."

"Don't expect people to react logically," Kenzie repeated the advice she and Zachary had each given the other from time to time during their investigations. People reacted emotionally, not logically, and it could happen much faster than expected.

"Yeah."

"Okay. Good advice, even if I don't want to hear it." Kenzie looked at Maria Smith's house and wondered if she were still peering through the window, watching to see what they would do. She pulled out her phone and tried Edwards again.

47

This time, Edwards answered. "Hello? Oh, Dr. Kirsch. I was going to call you. You're on my list of phone calls to make."

"I'm sure I am," Kenzie said dryly. Right at the bottom of it.

"What can I do for you?"

"First of all—and this isn't why I called you to start with—what do you know about Maria Smith? The woman who called with the tips about the memorial flowers in the backyard?"

"Nothing, really. Haven't checked into her. Why? She hasn't really provided anything that's been of much help."

"When she called and talked to me, I thought she was some crackpot nosy old lady."

"Yup."

"But she's not."

"Not what?"

"She's not *old*. She's the age of Sharon and her friends."

Edwards considered that. "Really."

"Yeah. I don't know if she witnessed anything or not. She might have. She was definitely jealous of Sharon and her lifestyle. Or had a crush on one of the men in the group. She was on the outside, looking in."

"Well, that might warrant some more investigation."

"Yeah. I was just over there talking to her."

"Why? You shouldn't be conducting interviews."

"It was part of my investigation. And I didn't know... that she might be a suspect."

"What did you want to know from her? That is relevant to your postmortem on the remains?"

"Well, I did call you first, but... did your people find any roasting sticks?"

"Roasting sticks?" Edwards echoed.

"They had this fire pit. Sat around it drinking and partying. Maria confirms that they would drink and do drugs and get a little rowdy. But I'm thinking... what about food? Did they just drink? Some of them must have gotten hungry, even if Sharon didn't. Did they order in? Bring in food from the grocery store? I'm thinking that they might have roasted wieners. Or marshmallows."

"Well, maybe."

"There was at least one coat hanger partially buried in the yard. I saw it. So were they using bent—or unbent—coat hangers for roasting sticks?"

"Uhh..." Kenzie could hear pages turning in the background and didn't know if he were looking up something to answer her question or if she had interrupted some other activity and he didn't want to be talking to her. "Yes, there were some roasting sticks inside the garden shed. And some folding lawn chairs. All for gathering around the fire pit, I assume."

"Can you have the techs check the roasting sticks for blood?"

There were a few beats of silence. "Of course. But if they were used for fresh meat, they might all have blood on them. What do you know? What did Maria Smith tell you, exactly?"

"This didn't come from Maria. Just something I was thinking about myself. Trying to find something that fits the circumstances. And also... where are the blocks?"

"What?"

"The fire pit was a perfect circle."

"More or less, yes, that would appear to be the case."

"Then it was probably constructed with one of those kits. The curved, interlocking blocks that make a circle to enclose the fire."

"It could have been. Or they might have used rocks for the edging. Or nothing at all; sometimes people just have a space that they have cleared where they burn stuff."

"But it seemed like a perfect circle. If they had just cut away some sod or laid down some rocks, it would have been oval. Lopsided. Unless they used a compass or other tool to mark it out and dig it."

"And where are the blocks used to build the enclosure?" Edwards said. "Or the rocks used to edge it? Or even the shovel used to dig out the sod in the center?"

"There wasn't a shovel in the shed?"

"No. Though if Phelps tried to dig a hole to bury Sharon's body somewhere, he might have abandoned it or thrown it out."

"Too bad. Would have been good to test it for blood too. Maybe he'll tell you where he left it?"

"I wouldn't count on it. But you never know, I might be able to get something from him."

"Could you get the whole group together? Everyone that was there regularly? Ryder and Hilda and the brother, Cody?"

"We don't usually recommend interviewing people together. They are more likely to reveal cracks in their stories if they are interviewed separately. And then we can feed them different information, too, say that one had revealed an important piece of information…"

"I think in this case… they weren't all friends. I don't think they'll cover for each other. I'm hoping that the opposite is true, that they would turn on each other."

"I don't know. I'll talk it over with my team and see what we can agree on. Maybe we can do something."

"Okay."

"But first, we'll test whether there is blood on the roasting sticks, and you can tell me how you think it all fits together."

Kenzie nodded. "Okay. Are you going to send someone over right now? Because I'm just down the street. I've got my death kit with me. I could do a quick field test."

"Even if it is today, it won't likely be for a few hours. You may as well go back to the office. I'll let you know what I find out. But I don't want you hanging around there, making people suspicious. It's not a good idea to spook suspects before you're in a position to make an arrest. They'll just run."

Kenzie looked toward Maria's house. "Okay. We'll get out of here," she agreed.

48

It took a while for Edwards to get everyone to come to the police station at the same time for an interview. Kenzie was trying to remain inconspicuous in a corner of the room, there to give Edwards any input he needed on the forensic evidence. She wasn't exactly inconspicuous, though; everyone looked at her as soon as they walked into the room.

But they were soon distracted by seeing each other. Kenzie got the feeling that the three "friends" had not been together since Sharon had died. It was awkward for them to all be in the same room together. They didn't know how to greet each other, whether to be happy to see each other, if they should talk about Sharon, and where they should sit. There were no social guidelines for the situation.

Edwards was brusque, directing everyone to seats and then shutting the door. He turned on a recorder, announced to the room what day it was and who was present, and sat down, opening a file folder in front of him and looking around at his guests.

"You all know each other pretty well, I think?"

"What is this about?" Hilda asked, looking anxiously at Ryder and Cody. "I thought you wanted to talk to me alone."

"Thought it would be easier to kill two birds with one stone," Edwards advised. He sported a five o'clock shadow even though it was morning, and when he scratched his jaw, the rasping sound made Kenzie cringe. She could only imagine how it would have pained Zachary, with his recently developed sound sensitivity. "Three birds," he corrected himself, and wrote something down in the file.

The impression he gave was that of an overworked cop who didn't really care how anyone felt about being jammed in the same room. As long as he could check off all the boxes to show that he'd investigated the case thoroughly and go home to get some much-needed sleep.

"That won't be a problem, will it?" Edwards asked, making it sound more like an order than a question. "We'll get all of you out of here twice as fast. Maybe faster."

"I really..." Hilda trailed off, looking at the men. She clearly didn't want to talk in front of them. It was easier to throw the blame on someone else if they weren't right there in front of her. The men saw this as well and stared at her stone-faced, jaws clenched.

"Let's just get this over with, Hilda," Cody told her. "Then we can get back to our lives."

Our *individual* lives was his obvious meaning. They wouldn't ever have to talk to each other again.

"Get what over with? I've already answered questions. Why did we have to come here?"

"Because I have more questions." Edwards stared at her with bloodshot eyes.

Hilda swallowed and thought better of complaining further. It would go faster if she just cooperated the best she could. Or let him ask his questions and stayed silent. She looked toward the door, and Kenzie wondered whether she would just get up and leave. She could, of course. Edwards didn't have enough evidence to detain any of them.

Not yet.

"When was the last day you each saw Sharon?"

They exchanged glances.

"I'm not sure," Cody offered. "She hadn't been home in a long time. I might have seen her at a club or something a few months before she disappeared, but I don't know. It was thirteen years ago. I don't keep a diary."

"I didn't know her," Ryder said flatly, sticking with the fiction he'd already told the police.

Hilda and Cody gave him surprised looks, then looked at each other, evaluating this. Was it better for them to support his story or to give him up?

"And you?" Edwards asked Hilda.

"I already told you. Two days before I filed the missing person report. My statement is on that file. Nothing has changed. That's how it happened."

"Really." Edwards wrote a few notes in his notebook. "The five of you partied together," he said without looking up. "So there's no point in acting like you didn't."

No one said anything.

"Including you," Edwards raised his head to fix his glare on Ryder. "We know that you knew Sharon well and were at the house often. Maybe even living there part of the time."

Ryder swallowed. He looked around, but Edwards hadn't provided them with beverages. He searched for a way to protest this claim but, when he looked at Hilda and Cody, he knew there was no point. He looked down at his hands, resting on top of the table. "Okay," he admitted. "I knew her."

"You knew her *well*."

"Yes."

"Don't lie to me. It puts everything else that you've said into question. *Everything*." He gave Ryder another glare, hinting at the very serious crimes he was willing to charge Ryder with, knowing what he did now.

Ryder made a noise that sounded like a whimper.

"When was the last day that the five of you were together? Charles Titon, Sharon Briggs, and the three of you?"

There were simultaneous protests from all of them.

"We didn't—"

"We never—"

"I don't know—"

"I told you—"

They looked at each other, their words getting tangled up with each other.

"There are witnesses, and you know there are," Edwards said. "Every person who lies in this room is going to get caught. I will personally verify every word that you say, and if you tell me a single lie, I will know it. And I will assume that if you're lying to me, there's a reason for it, and that reason is that you're guilty of the murder of Sharon Briggs. In at least an accessory role. So think before you speak. When was the last time you were together?"

They looked at each other. The two men looked blank, as if they had no idea when it had been. Maybe they would have been able to provide month and year, but date? How could they be expected to remember the details of what had happened more than a dozen years before? Exact dates?

Hilda looked at each of them in turn, then gave the date. Not the day that she'd said she'd last talked to Sharon. So was it the truth? Had she talked to Sharon after that? Or had she been attempting to fudge the date to provide herself an alibi?

"Does that sound about right?" Edwards asked the men.

"Something like that," Ryder agreed. "I don't know the exact date, but that feels about right."

Cody nodded his agreement. His face was red. Maybe embarrassed at being caught out in a lie. Maybe just getting too warm in the room. The temperature was rising with the number of people sitting or standing around. Interview rooms were only meant to hold two or three people. Each body made it harder for the air conditioning to keep up.

"At a party?" Edwards asked.

"Not a party, just... hanging out together," Ryder insisted.

"Was there drinking?"

"Yes," Ryder admitted.

"Drugs?"

He scratched his head. When Edwards waited, staring at him, he eventually nodded. "Maybe," he conceded.

"Then it was a party."

"But I don't think—"

Edwards gave him a *don't mess with me* look, and Ryder shut his mouth.

"Around the fire pit in the backyard?"

There were even more surprised looks at this detail. They pretended that they weren't looking at each other, but were obviously concerned that Edwards was getting too close to the truth. Who had talked to him?

"Did you get together around the fire pit?"

Grudging nods.

"Yeah, so?" Cody asked, deciding to be confrontational about it.

"Why don't you start? Tell me what happened."

Cody swallowed and looked at the others. They didn't appear to have any intention of rescuing him so that he didn't have to tell Edwards the story.

"Uh... just like you said. We were having a fire in the back. It was hot during the day, but nice at night. Good for a fire and just sitting around talking to each other."

"Because you were all such great friends."

"We weren't all buddy-buddy," Hilda said. "Just... some of us were friends with each other, like me and Sharon. I didn't really know any of the others well."

They didn't jump in to agree or disagree.

"Didn't I tell you what would happen if you lied to me?" Edwards demanded.

Hilda looked down immediately, looking guilty.

"The five of you were in and out of there all the time."

"It's been years since I even saw them," the woman protested. "We weren't friends."

"Not like you *wanted* to be," Cody said with a leer.

"I never wanted anything to do with you. Eww." Hilda made a face.

"Not me, him," Cody gave a nod toward Ryder.

Hilda flushed. Ryder gave a short laugh and looked at Hilda, then raised his brows and stared off, thoughtful. Hilda continued to get redder.

P.D. WORKMAN

"I don't care who liked who," Edwards said. "You were all there. Tell me what happened."

Ryder wiped his face. He was started to sweat. Just the heat of the room? Or something else?

"We had some drinks," Cody said, shrugging one shoulder. "A smoke. Hung out around the fire. Just like other days. It was a warm summer. We liked to go outside when it started to cool off, give the house a chance to cool down while we enjoyed a beer."

"And went home."

"Exactly." He nodded.

The others looked a little relieved at the telling of the story. Maybe that was all that Edwards wanted to know, and he would let them go home now.

"You didn't eat?"

Cody shrugged. "I don't know. Maybe."

"Maybe you roasted wieners. Did you use the wiener roasting sticks?"

They avoided looking at each other now. Maybe afraid of seeing or telegraphing their alarm at the mention of the roasting sticks. But it was obvious in their body language.

"Maybe," Cody croaked.

"You're supposed to be telling me the truth. Did you cook wieners or not?"

"Yeah, probably. Some nights we did."

"But no one has used those roasting sticks since Sharon disappeared, have they?"

Hilda swallowed. "Why do you say that?"

"Because there is still blood on one of the sticks."

There was actually blood on more than one of the roasting sticks. But one of them had been bloodied and wiped off, while the others had only tiny specks of blood on them. Contaminated by the first.

All of them were sweating now. Edwards flipped over a page in the folder and thumped his finger down on the page.

"There were also cinders on Sharon's clothing. Ashes."

He looked around at each of them. No one dared speak.

"And then there were the preformed blocks used to build the fire pit."

"What blocks?" Ryder asked.

"Where did they go?"

"How would I know? I haven't been to the house in years. Not until after Charlie died. When I took possession, there was no sign of the bricks or the fire pit."

"Why would Charlie get rid of it? Why dispose of the bricks and dig the ashes into the ground?"

"I guess…" Ryder cleared his throat and coughed. "I guess he wanted his lawn back."

Edwards stared at him. Ryder looked away, tapping his fingers nervously on the table.

"He never said anything to me about the fire pit. That's the truth. I don't know what he did with the bricks."

"Took them to the dump, maybe? Or washed them off and sold to some unsuspecting dupe?"

"Why not? He could do what he wanted with them, couldn't he?"

"They were evidence."

"Evidence of what?" Cody broke in. "Why don't you explain what you're trying to say, Detective Edwards? This sounds like a witch hunt to me."

"Evidence that the four of you killed her."

Jaws dropped around the room. Faces that had been red turned white, drained of all color. They were all looking at each other now, eyeing the door, the only means of escape, trying to decide who to throw to the wolves. In the end, Kenzie supposed she could have guessed the answer.

"We didn't have anything to do with it," Cody said, swallowing hard and looking back and forth at the other two before returning his gaze to Edwards. "It was Charlie."

"Oh, it was Charlie. And that's why all three of you reported him when it happened. Only… oh yeah, you didn't, did you? And when I approached each of you after Sharon's body was found, you didn't say anything about it being Charlie. And when I brought you all here together and asked you what had happened, you didn't say it was Charlie."

"But it was," Cody insisted.

"How? Tell me what happened. You're Sharon's brother. Why would you be covering up for someone else? The only reason for you to be quiet is if you were involved."

"I wasn't, I swear. It wasn't anything to do with any of us." He included the other two with a gesture, inviting them to stand together with him, united. Kenzie was still hopeful that they would all turn on each other.

Edwards folded his arms across his chest and waited for an explanation.

"Okay," Cody said. "Here's how it happened…"

49

They had been drinking for a while. It was getting dark, the flames glowing and dancing in the middle of the yard while they swapped stories, told bawdy jokes, and discussed what was happening in their favorite TV shows.

Sharon was the only one who had been using. Everyone else had work the next day, and they weren't hardcore drug users like Sharon. A little weed now and then. On a weekend when they didn't have to be at work the next day.

"You should slow down," Hilda warned Sharon. "You're supposed to be on tomorrow. You're going to be wrecked in the morning."

"I'm not on until the afternoon," Sharon said, waving away her concern. "Besides, I'm just fine in the mornings. This is nothing. I won't feel it."

"You've had too much," Hilda told her, concerned about the amount she had been using all afternoon and evening. Sharon didn't normally use right in front of her, and she was alarmed to see how much product Sharon was going through. That couldn't be her normal. She would be dead on the street.

But Sharon had been in a mood all day. Angry at the world. Defiant. Not willing to put on a "show" for anyone. She was who she was, and she did what she did and if anybody didn't freaking like it, then that was just too bad. They could all just—

"You can do whatever you want," Hilda told her, trying to stop the vitriol. "I'm just concerned, that's all. I'm not telling you what to do."

"You'd better not," Sharon growled. Everyone else was mellow and relaxed, sitting in front of the crackling fire.

"Just leave her alone," Ryder told Hilda. "She can take care of herself."

"I know. I said that. It's up to her; I'm not trying to force her to do anything."

"You're trying to talk her into it. Same thing."

"It's not the same thing. I'm just telling her. You should be too. You should want what's best for her, and you've seen how much she's taken tonight. It's way too much. She's going to be completely wasted tomorrow."

"I don't tell her what to do," Ryder told Hilda. But he was looking at Sharon, reassuring her that he wasn't going to push her. *He* would let her do whatever she wanted. His eyes were big and dark, making stupid cow eyes at Sharon again. And Sharon didn't even seem to notice. She was always so indifferent toward the men around her, ignoring or pretending to ignore their flirting. And it always drove them mad, making them want to impress her that much more.

"*You* just keep your eyes to yourself," Charlie warned, scowling at Ryder. He was usually oblivious to whatever was going on between the two of them. Hilda swore he could walk right by them making out and not even notice. Ryder's eyes moved to Charlie, evaluating him.

"My eyes? I should keep my eyes to myself? How about you take care of yourself? You're not my boss."

"This is my house," Charlie warned. "I could kick you out any time. Sharon is *my* girl, and if you're going to keep acting like you're free to do whatever you like with her, I'm going to—"

"You're going to what?" Sharon challenged. "You aren't in charge of me, and you don't own me. Ryder can do what he likes. *I'll* be the judge of whether I like it or not."

"Just tell him to take a hike," Charlie told her.

"I'll do what I like."

Charlie jumped to his feet. Cody didn't know whether they'd had a fight earlier in the day, or what was going on. But Charlie, usually so laid back and calm about everything, was itching for a fight.

"This is my house," he repeated, no longer threatening Ryder about turfing him, but talking to Sharon, towering over her as she sat in her chair, uncaring, unimpressed by his anger. Probably too far gone to care about much of anything anymore. "And while you're living in my house, you—"

Sharon's fist shot out, beer bottle still in hand, hitting Charlie so hard in the chest that he gagged and stumbled backward and couldn't get his breath back right away. She sprang to her feet and was feinting at him while he tried to breathe, hands held up protectively.

"It's your house and I have to obey your rules?" Sharon challenged. "That line didn't work when my mother tried it on me either! I don't have to obey anyone's rules. If you want me around here, then you let me do what I like. Otherwise, I am out of here!"

"No," Charlie said, holding his hand up, trying to stop her.

"I'll do whatever I please. I'll drink, and I'll smoke, and I'll shoot up. And you'll like it, or I'm gone. And I'll look at whoever I like, and I'll—" She grabbed Ryder by the front of his shirt and hauled him to his feet with no apparent effort despite her skinny build. She pulled Ryder to herself, wrapped her other arm around the back of his neck, and pasted her mouth to his. Ryder was too startled to react at first, then kissed her back, then pulled away, his face suffused with blood. He held up his hands to prevent an attack from Charlie. But Charlie was standing there, too stunned to do anything.

"Whoever I want," Sharon repeated, looking around at them. Her eyes landed on Cody, and she plopped herself in his lap and wrapped her arms around his neck, kissing him next. He flushed warm with pleasure but didn't let her stay for long. He had his reputation to uphold. He pulled his face back from hers. Charlie grabbed Sharon, wrenched her up from Cody's lap, and threw her away from himself.

Sharon was strong, but she wasn't heavy, and she flew away from him like a tossed rag doll. Sharon crashed to the ground and, for an instant, Cody laughed at her awkward landing. There was a comedic quality to it. And Charlie never reacted physically like that. It was so out of character that Cody didn't know what to do other than laugh.

But Sharon's head thunked back against the wall of the fire pit with a noise like a melon and she cried out sharply. She was frozen for a minute, all spindly arms and legs sticking out in every direction. Then she scrambled to her feet again.

"Leave her alone," Cody shouted at Charlie. Getting to his feet and grabbing one of the split pieces of wood, he brandished it like a bludgeon. "You got no right to tell her what to do. She can do whatever she wants. You can't manhandle her like that!"

Charlie shoved Cody and shouted something back at him. Cody couldn't even remember what he said. He swung the piece of the log and landed a blow on Charlie's arm so hard that Cody's own arm vibrated from the blow.

Cody had probably broken Charlie's arm but, with the rage inside him or the amount he had drunk, Charlie hardly seemed to know that he was hurt. He couldn't reach the split wood in the pile to defend himself. He reached down, grabbed one of the wiener sticks, and brandished it like a foil, one of those skinny swords they used for fencing. Cody laughed. There was no way that Charlie could do any damage with that skinny little skewer. It wasn't even sharp. Charlie lunged forward, intent to do some harm. Cody calmly stepped to the side to avoid it.

It was a moment before he realized what had happened. Sharon had been behind him, and Charlie had stabbed the wiener stick at her instead of Cody. He opened his mouth to belittle Charlie. He was such a little—

Charlie's eyes were wide in horror. Cody turned his head to look at Sharon, the coat hanger sticking out of her chest or stomach. She had such a short torso that it was hard to tell exactly where it had hit. Sharon grabbed the stick and wrenched it out. She threw it to the side.

"Don't be an idiot!" she slurred at Charlie. "Don't be—" She degenerated to a series of colorful curses.

She always had been inventive. Cody admired her for her creativity, whether she was mocking her mother or apologizing to a cop. She always seemed to know what to say and could get herself out of the stickiest of spots.

"Are you okay?" Hilda asked, the last one to get to her feet. She went to Sharon, hugged her, and looked at her as if trying to figure out the solution to a problem. "Shar, you should sit down. You really hit your head hard. And someone should look at that." She poked clumsily at Sharon's stomach, trying to identify the place that the roasting stick had punctured.

"If I can talk, I'm just fine," Sharon pointed out. She stretched out her t-shirt so that she could see the hole the stick had made, and then she lifted the shirt to look at herself, giving them all a peep show. Sharon had never been shy about her body.

The blood dribbling out of the puncture was black in the low light of the fire.

"Oh, you're bleeding," Hilda said. She swayed on her feet. Obviously not the best person to call on in a medical emergency.

Sharon rolled her eyes, swore, and pushed Hilda back into her chair before she could faint. She looked again at the leaking hole. "It's not anything."

"You need to go to a doctor!" Hilda insisted, her voice rising like a siren. "You could be bleeding inside. They need to stitch it up and give you a tetanus shot!"

Sharon lowered her shirt and pressed it against the hole, wincing. "Yeah? Who is going to drive me?" she demanded. "Oh, that's right, *no one*, because you're all drunk! I'll drive myself."

"You can't drive. You're hurt," Cody told her. Never mind that she was also drunk and high as a kite. It was a wonder she could even feel the wound. "We could call a doctor. Call an ambulance." It took him a few seconds to find the right words, which just showed how much he'd had to drink. He was usually pretty articulate.

"Forget that," Sharon said, knocking at Cody's phone with the bottle she still held in her hand. She had apparently managed to hold on to it despite her fall and being stabbed. That was commitment. It was too bad she couldn't commit to a man like that. "I don't want any cops here. Don't call."

"But you need help. You need medical care."

"I'll go to the clinic tomorrow. It's not that bad. It will probably stop bleeding before then."

"You need to lay down," Charlie told her firmly. "Come on. Inside."

"I'm not going," Sharon protested, but she let him pull her inside. Everyone followed, wanting to see what was going to happen and make sure that Sharon was okay. Cody grabbed Hilda by the arm as she staggered, too drunk or too woozy from the sight of blood to walk a straight line. He deposited her on the couch in the living room once they were inside and told her to stay put.

50

I n the master bedroom, Charlie and Ryder were fighting over caring for Sharon and what needed to be done.

"We need to put pressure on the wound," Ryder insisted. "Direct pressure until it stops bleeding. If it doesn't stop bleeding, then someone has to take her to the hospital."

"We will," Charlie agreed. "We just have to wait a bit until one of us is sober enough. You know what will happen if we show up drunk in the ER with her."

"We don't have to go in. We can just leave her there."

"Dump her?"

"I didn't say *dump* her," Ryder growled. But he didn't come up with a better word for what he intended.

"Just leave me alone," Sharon protested, but her voice didn't seem as loud as before. Maybe it was because they were inside instead of outside. Maybe she had been shouting outside because of the adrenaline of the fight.

"Get her shirt off," Ryder suggested and, between the two of them, they wrestled off her t-shirt. Ryder handed it behind him to Cody, who held it, staring at Sharon lying there in her bra, blood pulsing out of the wound.

Pulsing.

At first, Cody agreed with the others. It was only a small wound, not bleeding that heavily. It probably hadn't hit anything vital. How much damage could you do with a coat hanger?

Sharon moaned and put her hand to the back of her head, distracting all of them from the stomach wound for a moment.

"She hit her head really hard," Cody told them.

Ryder leaned on the bed and put his hand behind Sharon's head, feeling it and turning it around so that he could see the back where she had sustained the blow.

"Just a little cut," he reported. "Hardly broke the skin. And there's no bump. Just a little swelling in the skin around the cut. She'll be fine."

"It hurts," Sharon complained. She coughed and groaned.

"Where does it hurt?"

"My head."

"On the back where you hit it?" Charlie asked.

"Everywhere." Sharon brought both hands up to her head and held it between them. She groaned again.

"It's probably the drugs more than anything," Charlie deduced. "Coke does that sometimes. It's just the coke, baby. That's all."

He turned his attention back to the blood on Sharon's belly.

"I can't really see how deep it is. Can you…" Charlie made a wiping motion to Cody. He looked down at the shirt in his hands and wiped the blood off. They both bent in for a look.

It was still pulsing. Heavy dread settled in Cody's stomach.

"You see how it's pulsing?" he pointed it out. "That means that it hit an artery, doesn't it?"

"No, if it was an artery, it would be *spurting*," Ryder said, pushing Cody back and looking at it. "All over the place. Like, spraying. That's just oozing. It's not bad."

Cody folded the shirt into a square and pushed it back into place over the bloody wound. He pressed down on it, wondering how much pressure would be needed to stop the flow of blood. And how long would it take?

"Is that okay, Shar?" He asked uncertainly. "Does that hurt?"

She moaned softly but didn't seem to be in any extra pain from the pressure on the wound. Cody held the t-shirt down firmly, counting in his head. It would take more than just seconds. Five minutes? Ten? How long until it stopped bleeding? Hopefully, Ryder was right, and it was just minor.

"Who woulda guessed that Sharon would be the one to break up the party?" Ryder joked.

Sharon was always the last one standing. Insisting on one more drink or one more song, reluctant to let the night end even when everyone else was leaving, passed out, or going to sleep. Wanting to squeeze every last minute of fun out of it before she had to go to bed.

Cody looked up from the makeshift bandage he was holding over her belly into her face. She was very pale. But it might have just been the poor lighting. Or the blow to the head.

"Are you still with us, Sharon? Hang in there."

He waited for a response but didn't get one.

"Sharon?" Keeping the pressure with one hand, he shook her with the other. "Sharon, you okay?"

"It hurts," she told him hoarsely. "Just want to sleep."

"I know. It's all going to be okay."

How many times had he told her before that everything was going to be okay when he knew it wasn't? He was the older sibling and should have protected her from the abuse instead of causing her more pain and trauma. He should have been the good guy. The helpful older brother. Stepping in as a surrogate parent and making sure that she didn't get hurt, didn't get into drinking and drugs, that she ate properly and got to school. Instead, he'd just sunk lower and lower, tangled up in a dysfunctional relationship with her, alternately hating her and hating himself for what he did to her.

It was better now that she was out of the house, but he hadn't been able to stay away from her. He still made these little trips to Charlie's house to see how she was doing, hang out with everyone, and pretend that he was part of her circle of friends.

Her breaths were getting longer, with more time in between. She was relaxing now that the adrenaline was wearing off. Maybe some of the drugs were wearing off too and, in a few minutes, she'd fall asleep. She'd feel better in the morning. She would be the only one without a hangover, laughing at the rest of them for being such wusses. She could drink any one of them under the table and still get up before them in the morning. Maybe from all those mornings at home, getting up and sneaking out of the house before any of them were up, to escape the abuse that would start again as soon as Cody's father was awake.

"She's going to sleep," Ryder told Charlie.

"Yeah."

Everything would be peaceful for the night. One of them could take her to the clinic in the morning for a tetanus shot and antibiotics or whatever follow-up treatment she needed.

Sharon's body convulsed and, at first, he thought it was a seizure, then realized she was throwing up. "Roll her over!" he shouted. For a moment, they were fighting each other, Charlie and Ryder trying to roll her in opposite directions, then they all got coordinated and rolled her onto her right side.

"Hit her limit tonight," Cody observed. It didn't happen very often, but Sharon's body was obviously trying to get rid of all the poison she had been pouring into it. She coughed and gagged and vomited out whatever was left in her stomach. There was no blood in what she expelled. Cody breathed a sigh of relief.

Then her body was convulsing again, and this time it *was* a seizure. They all held on to her. Cody tried to keep the wadded-up shirt pressed tightly into the wound, but it was difficult to keep it in place with her bucking around. Charlie and Ryder tried to hold her still.

It lasted a minute or two—the longest minutes of Cody's life. Then the convulsions eased and they rolled her onto her back. Cody lifted the shirt a little to peek at the wound underneath. It was no longer pulsing. That was good. It was slowing. A few more minutes of pressure and she would be as good as new. A bruise on her head and a new scar to show how tough she was. She would tell stories about it, making up more and more dramatic explanations for whatever guys she was entertaining.

"Is she asleep?" Ryder asked.

"Yeah." That was pretty normal after a seizure, wasn't it? Cody shook her arm, but she didn't stir. He watched for the rise and fall of her chest, but her breathing was so shallow he couldn't detect it. "Sharon?" He shook her again and swore. "Is she breathing? I can't see her breathing!"

Charlie shook his head irritably. "She's fine. She's just sleeping. Why don't you guys knock off for the night? Party's obviously over."

Ryder had a room. Cody could drive home, but he was probably too impaired and would crash on the couch instead. Hilda was close by and could walk home if she wanted to, or crash there with them if she didn't want to walk by herself at night.

Cody watched Sharon's chest, waiting for her to take a breath. He didn't believe she'd stopped breathing, but he needed the reassurance. To actually see it. He caught her wrist and felt for a pulse, but couldn't find it. He put his fingers on her throat and felt for the stronger pulse. The carotid. He waited, but could feel nothing.

"We gotta do CPR," he told the others urgently. "She's not breathing. There's no pulse."

"Call an ambulance," Hilda said from the couch, where she was apparently still awake. "I'll call them."

"No. No ambulance," Charlie ordered. "They'll bring the cops. They can't see her like this. And who knows how many drugs are around? I don't feel like getting arrested, do you?"

"CPR!" Cody repeated. On TV, they would have started it already. Someone would be doing the 30 compressions and someone else the two quick breaths. And they *would* be calling an ambulance no matter what the danger of one of them getting hit with drug charges.

"I'll do it," Ryder offered. He sprang onto the bed and nearly did a face plant off the other side. He got up, positioned himself over Sharon, and started pressing down on her chest. Cody wasn't sure Ryder's hands were in the right place or that he was compressing hard enough. Sharon's chest wasn't going down like that of the CPR dummies Cody had trained on at work when they did their first aid training.

He expected Sharon to object. To push Ryder off and tell him to

265

leave her alone. But she just lay there, flat as a pancake, no tone in her muscles.

What had happened? How could it have happened so fast?

Ryder wiped Sharon's mouth and blew breaths into her, but her chest did not rise as it should.

"Cut it out," Charlie growled, giving Ryder a shove. "Just leave her alone. Just let her sleep it off. She'll be fine in the morning."

"She's not breathing!"

"She'll be fine." He pushed Ryder again. "Just get your hands off of her. You can never keep your hands off of her, can you? She just needs to sleep."

Slowly, Ryder stopped and drew back. He looked at Cody. Cody shook his head. There was no point anyway. Ryder wasn't moving any air into her. None of them could drive her to emergency or call an ambulance. In the morning, Charlie would be forced to admit what had happened and deal with it.

Ryder climbed off the bed. "This is messed up," he murmured to Cody. "This is so messed up!"

"I know." They walked out of the room and left Charlie to have Sharon to himself. The last night they would spend together.

There were looks exchanged among the three of them. Kenzie was not a trained police interrogator and wasn't sure what their expressions and the interplay meant. Maybe Edwards would understand the dynamic between the three of them better. Whether Cody was telling the truth or whether he had made up a story and was hoping they would back him up on it. And would they? He hadn't made any of them look particularly good.

But the story fell together well and fit the facts that Kenzie knew. All of the pieces were there. The ashes on her jeans and in the soil, the blow to the head and missing fireplace bricks, the blood on the roasting stick. Sharon's missing shirt.

A lot of the details could not be checked. The scene had been cleaned and contaminated and cleaned again since Sharon had died.

No traces of her blood or vomit in the bedroom. The symptoms Cody described fit with the epidural hematoma and a small stab wound that had managed to nick an artery—maybe the aorta—and bleed mostly into the abdomen or chest, allowing only a little blood to escape to the surface.

Of course, Cody had had thirteen years to refine his story to make it believable. It showed him as concerned and engaged, not getting involved in the fight or panicking, doing his best to give medical aid to Sharon. CPR sometimes broke bones, but Sharon's remains had no sternal or rib fractures. Then again, from Cody's description, Ryder hadn't been doing the compressions with enough force to break bones and hadn't moved her to a firm surface.

"You knew she was dead then," Edwards said.

Cody shrugged. "What were we supposed to do? It was just a freak accident. Charlie didn't want anyone calling for help, and what would it matter? There wasn't anything they could do for her. I didn't think it would make any difference whether they came then or in the morning. And in the morning, Charlie would be sober and call someone himself. It was his house. His girlfriend."

There were nods of agreement from Ryder and Hilda. What difference would it make whether or not they waited? Sharon would be dead either way. They would have to answer the same awkward questions either way. But sober, instead of drunk, which was probably better.

"So you all just went to bed."

"We were all wasted anyway. It was late and we'd all had a few. Not like Sharon, but we were all… a little impaired. And with everything that had just happened, we wanted to sleep. I did, anyway. I didn't want to have to think about it. I wanted to crash and figure it out the next day."

"What happened the next day? None of you reported it. What exactly was said between you?"

Cody looked at the others.

"I got up and Charlie was sleeping on the bed with… her. She had on a bathrobe, like she'd gotten up for a shower and then laid down again. For a minute, I thought maybe I was wrong the night before because I was drunk, and she was okay after all. Everything was fine. But I got a closer look at her, and her skin was all… waxy. She didn't look like something alive. She looked like a mannequin. A doll. I don't know. I woke Charlie up and told him he had to call 9-1-1 so that someone would come and take her away. He told me she'd been cold, so he put the bathrobe on her. That I wasn't allowed to wake her up."

"What did you say to that?"

"I said she was dead. Straight out like that. I wasn't going to play games with him, pretend that she wasn't or that there was any hope. I wanted to shock him, I guess. Bring him back to reality."

"What did he say to that?"

"He said I was wrong. To just leave her alone. To leave them both alone and get out."

Cody looked at the other two. They both nodded.

"He didn't want anyone else around," Ryder said. "I paid rent. I had a room there. And he kicked me out. He said I couldn't stay. Get my stuff and go. We all discussed it for a few minutes. None of us *wanted* to stay there and have to talk to the paramedic and police and everything. So we said we would go… and wouldn't tell anyone. We wouldn't say that we had been there, and Charlie could deal with it however he was going to deal with it." Cody paused. He swallowed. "Of course… we didn't know then…"

"That he would just keep Sharon there and not tell anyone for the next thirteen years," Edwards finished.

"Yeah. Well… it wasn't really obvious, was it? You wouldn't expect us to guess that he'd do that?"

"No," Edwards agreed. "But you still had a responsibility. Both the night it happened and in the morning. To see if you could do anything for her after it happened and to report it to the authorities. You don't just walk away from something like that."

"Well, we didn't think we were," Cody said stubbornly. "We thought that Charlie was going to take care of it."

"And when he didn't? You must have figured out pretty quickly that he hadn't reported it."

"I called it in," Hilda spoke up self-righteously. "I'm the only one who tried to do anything about it."

"But you didn't tell the police that you knew she was dead and what had happened to her."

"I couldn't because we weren't saying that we had been there that night," Hilda said, missing Edwards's point completely. "But I told them that she was missing. Filed a report and everything, saying that the last time I had seen her, she had been at Charlie's house and gave you the address and everything. Why didn't the cops check it out? Why didn't they go in there and see her?"

It was Edwards's turn on the hot seat and, though he wasn't required to explain anything to anyone, he did.

"Charlie told them that Sharon had left him in the lurch. She had been unable to pay her rent and had taken off a few days before. He said they should talk to her family and friends to ask them where she might be. It was a perfectly reasonable explanation. Without her family and friends being honest and telling us what had happened, how could we have been expected to get into his house? If he won't invite law enforcement officers into the house, they can't force themselves in without a warrant or exigent circumstances. To get a warrant, we need reasonable suspicion that he's killed her and still has her in the house. With all of you lying, how were we supposed to know that?"

They looked down at their hands or the table, not taking responsibility for it.

"If one of you had hinted that she was dead, that you believed she was still in the house, we would have been able to get men in there. If any of you had said that you thought Charlie had done something to her and there might be evidence in the house, we would have had someone in there checking it out. But you all decided you'd rather keep it quiet and say nothing. You would just let her body rot at Charlie's house."

"We didn't know he was going to do that," Ryder protested. "Or that he *had* done it. None of us had been back in the house since she died. You think we would have just ignored her rotting corpse in the bedroom? Pretending it wasn't there or that she was still alive, like

Charlie was doing? The guy is family, but he was *cracked*. Who does something like that?"

"You had never been back at the house again."

"No."

Edwards looked around at each of them. "None of you?"

They shook their heads. Edwards stopped, staring at Cody. He shifted uncomfortably. "Okay, I went back there. Talked to Charlie at the door. Asked him what was going on. Asked around the neighborhood after Sharon, hoping it would trigger some interest in what had happened to her. I tried to see through the blinds on the window to see if she was still there. I honestly didn't think that she still would be. I thought he must have taken her out somewhere... to bury her. Something."

"Burying a person isn't nearly as easy as you would think."

Ryder shook his head in agreement. "You have no idea! They make it look easy on TV, like all you have to do is move a few shovels full of earth, and presto, you have a grave deep enough to bury a person. No one tells you that it takes hours, and that's just for a rough, shallow grave. The ground is hard and if you're not used to handling a shovel or other tools..."

The others were staring at him. He stopped.

"Why didn't you tell me when you moved back in there?" Hilda demanded.

Ryder looked around as if the answer might be written on the walls. "After that long... I didn't want to have to answer all the questions. I thought it would be a lot worse, that I might be thrown in jail for not reporting it when it happened. That someone from her family would come after me." He looked over at Cody, but clearly didn't mean that he was worried Cody would hurt him. But there might be other people in the family.

"She's got nobody," Cody said. "I'm all that's left, and I never was any good for her."

51

Kenzie looked up from her desk at the approaching footsteps from the direction of the elevator. She expected it to be a law enforcement officer. They were still posting guards at the entrances until Sharon's remains were released and they could tell the public that she was no longer there.

But rather than the familiar uniform, she saw someone she hadn't been expecting. Cody Roundtree. She composed her face to give him a friendly, concerned smile.

"Cody. Err—Mr. Roundtree. I didn't expect you to come here in person."

She had left more than one message for him, letting him know that he just had to get his funeral home to give her a call, and they would arrange for the transportation of her remains to the appropriate location. She had not expected—or wanted—him to come to the morgue in person.

"Sorry. Yeah, it's probably sort of a faux pas to just come over here," Cody said, shrugging and looking away from her.

"Well, no. It's perfectly okay. It's just not usually done."

"I wanted to see you."

She had been afraid he was going to say, "I wanted to see her," and Kenzie would have to explain to him the condition that Sharon's remains were in. To tell him that he really didn't want to see her like that, so... unhuman. Kenzie knew, or at least could guess, that Sharon and Cody had been through a lot together. They were only stepsiblings, and she didn't know how many years they had spent together, but it was clear from his description of what had happened to Sharon on that fateful night that he regretted how he had treated her earlier in life. The media had romanticized Charlie keeping Sharon's remains so much that Cody might well imagine her as a Snow White, perfectly preserved, just waiting for someone to come and rescue her at long last.

But he *hadn't* said that he wanted to see Sharon, luckily.

He had said that he wanted to see Kenzie. She felt immediately awkward. It wasn't inappropriate for him to come to the morgue to make arrangements to transport her remains, but alarm bells went off when he said he wanted to see her. This was a man who had clearly crossed more than one moral boundary in the past, whether it was because he had low self-control or it was a conscious choice.

She moved her knee and pressed the security call button on the bottom of her desk.

"You wanted to see me?" she repeated.

"You were kind to me on the phone," Cody said. "And I know you brought Sharon back from where Ryder dumped her. And you've been with her all the way through this. Detective Edwards speaks very highly of you, says you're the one who broke the case."

Kenzie rolled her eyes at that. "It isn't like we *needed* to break the case. You already knew what happened."

"Well... yes. But without you and him, it wouldn't have gotten out in the open. And I think... it was right that it did. It was better for Sharon. Now... she'll be able to rest."

The elevator dinged and footsteps sounded in the hall. Cody glanced back over his shoulder and continued.

"So, I just wanted to thank you," he said. "For taking care of her."

It was such a different reaction from what Kenzie had received from other family members who had confronted her at the office that her eyes welled with tears for a moment. She smiled at him and tried to swallow the lump in her throat.

"Well, that's very kind of you. You're welcome. I was just doing my job. But I'm happy if that is a comfort to you."

He nodded. "It is."

The security guard came into sight. He slowed from his fast walk once he could see both of them. Kenzie couldn't exactly wave him off now that he was there, and she didn't try to explain.

"The funeral home that will be taking care of things," Cody said, sliding a note card across the desk to Kenzie. "I'm doing what you suggested... having her cremated."

Kenzie nodded. "I think that's the best choice when the remains are so..." She grimaced. "Advanced."

The security guard nodded to Kenzie and slowed to a stop, standing a few feet to Cody's right and watching him carefully.

"Okay. I'll make sure that she's ready for transport when the funeral home guy gets here," Kenzie promised.

"Thanks. I'm glad that... she'll finally be at rest."

It had been a long wait for Sharon. It was time for her to reach her final destination.

Cody turned and headed back the way he had come. The security guard raised his brows at Kenzie and waited until Cody was down the hall. "Everything okay?"

"Yeah. I just wasn't sure how that was going to come out."

"He seemed all right when I let him into the elevator. And had all of the right paperwork."

Kenzie had emailed Cody instructions and a copy of the death certificate earlier, allowing the funeral home to deal with him and getting him past security.

"Thanks for coming down anyway."

"Of course," he agreed. "We'll always look after you, doctor."

52

When they got settled in for their therapy session with Dr. Boyle, Kenzie looked at Zachary, signaling him to lead off. Zachary looked at her for a moment longer, making sure that was really what she wanted, then turned to Dr. B.

"I think Kenzie would like to talk about some problems that she's been having lately," he said. "So we can talk about how I can... deal with it."

Kenzie shifted uncomfortably. Maybe not the clearest introduction of the topic, but it would have to do.

"Of course," the doctor agreed. "Kenzie, do you want to talk about it?"

Kenzie swallowed. She nodded her head slightly to approve the topic.

"We talked before about the Elysse Allen case and the fans being at the building and attacking Kenzie's car," Zachary reminded Dr. Boyle.

"Touching it," Kenzie corrected. "They didn't damage it."

"No, but the cops came and rescued you."

"Yes."

"And she said there *was* something else going on," Zachary

continued. "Something was bothering her, but she wasn't ready to talk about it."

Dr. B nodded. "Yes. And if she isn't ready to talk about it, that's okay."

"I didn't push it," Zachary assured her. "I just let her be."

Kenzie nodded to confirm this.

"But then it came up by accident when we were visiting my—Mr. Peterson—my foster father and Pat."

The doctor smiled. "I know by now who Mr. Peterson is," she said with a soft chuckle.

Zachary flushed a little. "I guess you do. Anyway… Kenzie had talked to them while I was in the hospital. Back in December. And she had told *them* about it." Even though he had accepted that it was natural for Kenzie to go to Lorne and Pat because they understood what it was like for someone they knew to be missing, and that she hadn't been able to go to Zachary about it when they were trying to stabilize him on the new medications, it still came out like an accusation.

Kenzie took a deep breath and released it. If Zachary felt betrayed about it, that was how he felt. She couldn't stop him from feeling that way.

"Or at least, part of it," Zachary added.

The therapist looked at Kenzie, evaluating her. Kenzie wondered if she was flushed and if Dr. B could tell she was sweating due to the conversation. She would be good at assessing people's physical responses to emotional triggers. She probably saw much more than Kenzie would ever give her credit for.

"Are you okay with this, Kenzie?" the doctor probed. "If you are not ready to discuss this, you can put the brakes on at any point."

"No. It's okay."

"Okay." She nodded to Zachary. "And what had she discussed with Mr. Peterson and Pat?"

"About her father being missing. He didn't show up at Christmas and didn't return any phone calls, and she was worried that something might have happened to him. That he could be dead. Because he always returned her calls."

Dr. B's eyes widened. "Oh, dear. Yes, I can see how that would be worrisome."

"And she didn't talk to me about it," Zachary explained. "She didn't want me to check myself out of psych to help her. And she never brought it up after that. In all of the months since then."

"Is he still missing?"

"No," Kenzie shook her head. "He reappeared shortly after that. In January, after New Year's."

"Okay. That's good to hear. He's okay?"

"He... says he is. I don't know. I don't think he's telling me the whole truth about it. I think... he was—he might have been..."

The words were still too difficult for her to reach. Dr. Boyle and Zachary waited patiently for her to finish the sentence, but Kenzie couldn't get there yet. She looked at Zachary for help.

"He might have been kidnapped," Zachary finished.

Kenzie nodded. "Maybe. He says not, but I think he was."

"Why wouldn't he tell you that, do you think?"

"Because... he doesn't want me to worry about it. He doesn't want me to bring it up or make a big deal of it. He thinks it will change our relationship and I won't see him as... indestructible or infallible or something. That I'll think less of him because something bad happened to him."

A slow nod from the therapist. "Do you think that's his concern, or do you think you might be feeling that way yourself? That because this happened to him, he's not the person you once thought he was."

"He won't tell me. So it's *his* issue, not mine."

"But you are assuming that something did happen to him and he is lying to you. You are assuming you know his rationale for not telling you. Those are *your* thoughts and judgments."

"Okay... yes."

None of them said anything for a few moments.

"That's not the end of it," Zachary said eventually.

Kenzie and Dr. B looked at him.

"Go on," Dr. Boyle encouraged, tapping her pen lightly on her desk while she watched the two of them, analyzing every movement, every expression.

"She couldn't talk about it at Mr. Peterson's, but she said she would. That she wanted to."

"And has that happened? Or is that what we're hoping to do here today?"

"She told me." Zachary looked at Kenzie again, ensuring she was still okay with this. Kenzie had told him that he would need to do it. She had managed to tell the story once, to him, and wasn't sure she would be able to again.

Kenzie nodded.

"While she was looking for Walter, *she* was kidnapped."

He squeezed her hand. Kenzie had been preparing, breathing carefully and trying her best to stay present and anchored so that the flashbacks wouldn't be triggered. She held Zachary's hand tightly.

Dr. Boyle's eyes got even bigger. "Well... I can see why this was such a big deal."

Kenzie nodded.

"Have you talked to anyone about this?" the therapist asked, her eyes penetrating and concerned. "I don't just mean Zachary, but anyone else? A professional?"

Kenzie shook her head.

"Did you report it to the police?"

"No."

Zachary looked at Kenzie, thinking about this. Maybe surprised that he hadn't thought to ask earlier.

"Can you talk about what happened while you were kidnapped? That must have been very traumatic."

Kenzie shook her head. "No... nothing happened. When they... *took* me... that was very scary, and I hit my head and..." She shook her head, unable to provide any other details. "Then... we went to a house. And I sat in a room, alone. No one touched me or threatened me. They fed me and I went to sleep."

Dr. Boyle nodded.

"And... Walter—my dad—came and got them to let me go, and he took me home. It was only a few hours. Then everything was fine."

"And you feel like it was a personal failing," the therapist suggested.

"No. I couldn't help it. I couldn't have done anything to prevent it."

"But you thought that you were safe. That you were indestructible. And now… you know that you're not."

Kenzie recognized her own words reflected back to her and knew that even though she would never have been able to put it into words, it was true. She did feel like she should have been able to prevent the kidnapping or at least see it coming. That she should have been able to get away. That she should have been able to negotiate with them. That she should have escaped or at least looked for some way to escape. But she had tried to do everything they told her to. She tried to be a good hostage and not take a single step out of line. To anticipate what they wanted her to do and be the perfect captive so they wouldn't hurt her and would eventually see that they should let her go. That she wouldn't be a danger to them.

And she had been true to that. She hadn't told the police what had happened. Hadn't tried to get them arrested or even to have Walter talk to them and tell them to stay away from his daughter from now on. She went on being the perfect kidnap victim, keeping everything to herself.

"I think Zachary's right and you need to work this through with a professional."

Kenzie shrugged. She knew it was true, even if her heart and brain rebelled against the idea. It was like being at war with her own body.

"Do you want to set up individual sessions with me? Or would you like me to give you some recommendations? I can refer you to someone."

Kenzie nodded. "Recommendations," she agreed. "I don't want… I think it's too much if you're Zachary's personal therapist and mine and doing couple's therapy. Things will get confused."

Dr. B did not seem offended by this and didn't argue that she could keep everyone's secrets and not be biased toward one of them over the other. She was Zachary's doctor, and Kenzie wanted to talk to someone who didn't know him. So she could focus on her issues and not his.

"I'll give you some names," Dr. Boyle agreed. "And if you like, I'll call and give the therapist you choose a heads-up, so he knows what's going on and you don't have to break the ice."

"Okay. Thanks."

She wasn't sure she would take that step. She would have to think about it. She might not want Dr. B telling the story from her perspective, passing her own bias and evaluation on to the new doctor.

Zachary squeezed her hand again. Kenzie pulled it from his grip, wiped sweat onto her pants, and then took his hand again. He gave her a solemn nod.

She had done it. She had taken the first step. After that, it would be easier.

53

Kenzie's phone rang and she grabbed it off the dresser to see who it was. Dr. Wiltshire sometimes called if he wanted her to attend a death scene early before going into the office. But it was Lisa's name on the face of the phone. Kenzie rolled her eyes. Her mother liked to call her before she was at the office since Kenzie often worked late and Lisa wasn't sure when it was safe to call her at home in the evening. And Lisa often had evening functions to attend, raising money, cutting ribbons, speaking to women's groups, or opening a wing at the hospital. But early mornings before work were not a great time for Kenzie to talk. She had never been an early riser and didn't leave much extra time in the morning between getting up and going to work.

But she could give Lisa a few minutes. Family was important and Kenzie was trying to build a better relationship with her parents. Lisa might just want to tell her to check her email and make sure that she signed some documents that needed to be filed today.

She swiped the slider on the phone. "Morning, Mother."

"Good morning, MacKenzie. I didn't get you up, did I?"

"No, I'm up. What—" She cut herself off before asking brusquely what Lisa wanted. "How are you this morning?"

"I'm well. And... how are you?" Lisa's voice was more tentative than usual. "How are you feeling?"

"Good. Can't complain."

"You sound good. I worry about you, you know. That you work too hard, take too much on. And with Zachary's issues and your couple's therapy..."

"No, no. I'm fine." Kenzie wondered if her mother had sensed some of the anxiety that she'd been having since the kidnapping. Maybe that was why Lisa had seemed so stressed the past few months. "I really am."

Should she try to tell Lisa about the abduction? Sooner or later, she would probably have to, but Kenzie wasn't sure she was ready yet. It had been difficult with Zachary and Dr. Boyle. Telling Lisa would probably be even harder. And Lisa would know that it was something to do with Walter, even if Kenzie didn't tell her that part, and Lisa would not be pleased with him. Or with Kenzie for not telling her months ago.

It could wait. It was not an early-morning, on-the-way-to-work type of discussion.

"You don't sound as stressed as you have lately," Lisa admitted.

"No. Really, I'm good. How about Dad? Have you heard from him lately?"

"He was here over the weekend. Had some business to attend to in town."

When he was in Burlington, Walter usually chose to stay at the family home, where he still had a bedroom and study, rather than at a hotel. Kenzie was glad that her parents were still on good terms with each other, even if it was sometimes confusing. She was never quite sure how to expect them to behave toward each other. They were divorced but still acted like a married couple when they were together. Kenzie had not even been aware of it when they had separated and divorced. Granted, she'd no longer been living at home and had been in her own little social bubble at the time, trying to figure out her life and where she was going. But they had also kept it very quiet.

"So he's good?" Kenzie asked.

There was a pause, longer than Kenzie thought necessary for her mother to consider the answer to the question. "Yes. He seems fine."

Kenzie considered that for a moment, wondering if Lisa were being completely truthful. She couldn't help being concerned about her father's weight loss and whether he had shed the pounds because he had not been fed well during the week he had disappeared or if he was sick. Maybe he was trying to improve his lifestyle, eating less and exercising more.

"And Zachary?" Lisa asked dutifully, her voice sounding far away. "How is he?"

"He's doing really well right now. His meds are good, with not a lot of side effects. He's been getting out walking and taking pictures more. Actually has a bit of a tan."

"Good for him. It's important to take care of your mental health."

"It is," Kenzie agreed. "Tyrrell still seems to be enjoying his job at the foundation. He's doing good work?"

"He seems to have taken to it very well," Lisa agreed. "He gets done his assignments and puts in the time needed. He is in regular contact and we haven't noticed any problems."

"Good to hear."

"Hillary keeps a close eye on him. If there are any problems, we'll know about it and act immediately."

"He said he was helping out with grant applications."

"Yes. He's a great help. He's also brought a number of mental health and addiction organizations to our attention. We are, as you know, trying to focus more on those issues."

Because of Zachary. Kenzie had been shocked when her parents had told her that because of Zachary's open dialogue about his mental health issues, they had decided it was something that the foundation needed to focus on more. Not just kidneys and other physical health issues, but emotional wellness and resiliency as well.

"That's great."

"I have been thinking of you with all of this business that has been in the media," Lisa said, segueing to another topic. "That poor girl."

"Sharon Briggs? Yes. It's quite the story. I can't really talk about it, but… it was an interesting case."

"Actually, I was thinking of that other girl. The social media one, on that platform…"

"Elysse Allen?" Kenzie was surprised.

"Yes. That's the one. I do feel bad for Sharon Briggs, of course, but nothing more can be done for her. But Elysse… she will have to rebuild her life. It's impossible to tell what really happened during that time that she was away. It will probably be years before the full truth comes out. And now… she has to rebuild her life. She will have lost a lot of friends."

"Fans, anyway," Kenzie agreed. "I would hope that her family and friends would stick behind her."

"Yes… you would hope. But sometimes, those are the most difficult relationships to maintain. They will feel betrayed by her, and a lot of those relationships will probably never recover."

Was she sending a signal to Kenzie? About how she was still waiting to hear exactly what had happened to Walter during the time he had been missing? Or that she had some inkling of what had happened to Kenzie and was hoping it wouldn't take her years to tell her story?

"I guess you're right," Kenzie said uncomfortably. "It can be… pretty hard to talk about something like that. Her family will have to be patient until she gets to that point."

"It will be interesting," Lisa said, "to find out what *really* happened."

Did you enjoy this book? Reviews and recommendations are vital to making a book successful.

Please leave a review at your favorite book store or review site and share it with your friends.

Don't miss the following bonus material:
Sign up for mailing list to get a free ebook
Read a sneak preview chapter
Other books by P.D. Workman
Learn more about the author

PREVIEW OF THEY SOUGHT VENGEANCE

They Sought Vengeance is book #14 in the
Zachary Goldman Mysteries series

CHAPTER 1

T he *No Grounds for Alarm* cafe was quiet. The morning rush was over and most of the staff were wiping down counters and chatting idly with each other, taking the time to restock and get ready for the lunch rush. Sun streamed in the front window. A few customers trickled in, ordered their beverages, and either wandered back out of the cafe with blank expressions on their faces or sought out a table and sat down with a computer or other device to work on something important. Or to check out their social media feeds.

Zachary had arrived before the appointed time to check out the location and ensure he wasn't late for the appointment. If there was one way to lose a new client, it was by being late. It didn't matter what the reason was; it could be perfectly legitimate. The client would go somewhere else.

So he sipped his coffee and watched the customers trickle in, speculating which would be Karen Camden. He had a picture in his mind after hearing her voice, but had not run any background on her. He wanted his first impressions to be of her in person, not on social media, news articles, or wherever else he might find records of her life.

She hadn't had a lot to say on the phone. She hadn't been referred by a friend, but had heard his name in the media on one of his other cases, though she didn't specify which one. A few of them had made the news. Zachary was always a little leery of the potential clients who had seen him in the media. They tended to have unrealistic expectations of what he could or would do. And somehow, those people didn't seem to understand that they would be expected to pay an upfront deposit and that he would be paid for all of his work, whether he came to the resolution they wanted or not. People who approached him because of a business listing or as a referral from another client were much more realistic and likely to pay their bills.

A woman stepped in the door and looked around the coffee shop rather than immediately going to the service counter. She was slim, probably in her mid-twenties to early thirties. Dark brown hair and blue or gray eyes. She had an attractive face but was made up in a very plain style, her hair pulled back in a no-fuss ponytail that made her seem severe. The woman wore a dark green skirt, a white short-sleeved blouse, and black flats.

Zachary smiled and raised his hand slightly. She walked over to his table.

"Mr. Goldman?"

"Zachary." He stood up and offered his hand, which she shook firmly. She had long tapered fingers and dry, warm hands. Her perfume was a combination of light florals with a hint of citrus. "Nice to meet you, Miss Camden."

"That's missus. But you can call me Karen."

She wore no wedding ring. No jewelry, except a gold chain around her neck that disappeared into her blouse and might have had a locket, stone, or charm on it. Zachary ran his hand over his own very short black hair, aware that she was also evaluating him. He had shaved for the meeting, but usually had a few days of stubble, which tended to make people look away and discount him. For once, he didn't look too gaunt. The cocktail of medications he was on no longer included drugs that made him nauseated. Kenzie didn't let him forget to eat, and they indulged in a few too many restaurant meals, leading to her working hard to keep from putting the pounds on and Zachary filling out and reaching what his doctor considered a healthy weight for once.

Introductions and initial evaluations out of the way, Zachary suggested, "Why don't you grab a coffee, and then we can get down to it?"

She nodded her agreement and went over to the counter. She glanced at the densely-written blackboard only briefly, and had either been there before and knew the menu, or already knew what she wanted. What she brought back to the table looked like the cafe noir —plain black coffee. Not one of the fancy, calorie-laden varieties that covered the board.

Karen pulled out a chair for herself and sat down. She wrapped both hands around the coffee mug as if she were warming her hands and stared down at the black, shimmering surface. Zachary waited, having a sip of his own cafe noir. It was often difficult for a client to bring their troubles to a stranger. Jumping right in and explaining what they needed was a big step. There might be small talk first. Questions about Zachary's background and references. Fishing to find out his knowledge on various topics or situations while they weighed his words to see whether he was really the right man for the job or if they even wanted to hire anyone. Sometimes it was just too much, but usually, given a period of silence, each would speak up and tell him a bit of their story.

"My father recently passed away," Karen said eventually, not yet looking up from her coffee. "It was unexpected. The police looked into it but said it was a natural death. He had some health conditions." Her shoulders rose and fell. "The coroner said it was heart failure. He had cardiovascular disease. But it wasn't expected," she reiterated. "And... we think that there's more to the story. It was too sudden. There was no warning."

Zachary nodded. "It can be difficult when someone passes away so suddenly."

Karen grimaced. She took a drink of her coffee and put the cup down again. "You think that we're just imagining things because it was unexpected. But there's more to it than that."

"We? Who else is concerned about it?"

"My brothers and I. There are four of us altogether. Three boys and a girl. And the others think that something is wrong too; it isn't just me. We kept going back and forth on it, and we finally decided to... hire someone independent to look into it.

"So the four of you think... what?"

Karen sighed. She looked out the window at the people walking by on the sidewalk. "We think... he was poisoned."

That seemed oddly specific. But maybe something about his death had led them to think that it was poisoning.

"You think he was murdered."

"Yes." She nodded, one jerk of her head. "I guess... yes. That's what we think. Or what we are hoping that you can prove or disprove."

"It might be hard to disprove. There are hundreds of poisons that could have been used. Who do you think killed him? You have a suspect in mind?"

Maybe her mother or a business partner or rival of her father. When people came to Zachary, they had often already built up the story in their minds. And despite the preponderance of murder mysteries on TV and in books, murders were usually obvious and the killer easy to identify. If they thought they knew who the killer was, they were probably right. Maybe the mother, since they had all met together to discuss it and agreed to hire someone.

"Well, one of us, probably," Karen said. A blush started at the base of her throat and chest.

"You or your brothers?" Zachary wasn't sure he had understood her correctly.

"Yes. We're clearly the ones who benefit from his death. None of us were... *close* to him. I know it's probably weird, but we're all... looking at each other, wondering which one of us did it."

"So you decided to hire a private investigator? To investigate *you?*"

"Yes. The four of us." She shrugged. "I mean, we're not going to figure it out by arguing with each other. If one of us did it... then that person should go to prison. We might not have been that close to him... but it's still not right. We can't just divide up the inheritance and give a quarter of it to the killer."

Better that a third of it should go to each of the non-killers.

"Is the estate... significant?"

She nodded, jaw clenched tight. "It's millions."

CHAPTER 2

Zachary tried not to react to this declaration. "The estate is worth millions?" he asked, pulling out his notepad and pencil to start jotting the pertinent information down.

"Yes. Even just the house is a couple million. When you figure in all of his accounts, what his company is worth, and the art and furnishings and vacation property... Yeah. It's enough to make all of us very comfortable." She took another sip of the coffee. "It doesn't matter to me whether I get fifteen or twenty million. My motive for finding out if one of the others killed our father is not to get his share. It's just... justice. Because the person who did this shouldn't be allowed to profit from it."

"Right," Zachary agreed. His mind boggled at the very idea of inheriting fifteen or twenty million dollars. Why had they chosen *him* to investigate it? There had to be other private investigators out there who were used to dealing with a bigger fish. Hiring a small one-man—well, two-person—operation instead of one of the big security firms with a whole fleet of investigators seemed like an odd choice. "I am willing to take on the case and have the time for it in my schedule right now. I'll need an up-front retainer." He had his usual rates on a card that he handed out to people, but in light of how large the estate was and their expectations, he might have to increase his rates. "I'll email you the details. And if I need to contract other investigators, I'll let you know first so you can control costs."

"We want you," Karen said firmly, looking Zachary in the face for the first time. "Not anyone else. We don't want word of this getting out. One person can stay unobtrusive, and we can explain why you're there, but we don't want strangers running around the neighborhood asking questions."

"Well... okay, then. Just be warned that it may take longer to get to the bottom of this with only one person. And my full-time admin, of course. She won't be on site, all of her activities will be remote, and her fees are built into my rates."

Heather, Zachary's older sister helped him with some of the computer investigations and kept him organized. She would be amused at his calling her a full-time admin, but he didn't want Karen to think she could nix Heather's involvement too.

"But I need to make sure that you understand... I won't necessarily be able to prove that it was murder or who the culprit was. I know that on TV, the private investigator always figures everything out and brings the murderer to justice, but real life doesn't always work out that way. Some cases remain unsolved for years, even decades. You can tell me if you want me to stop investigating at some point. Or I may come to you and tell you that I've exhausted all of my leads. And it might not have happened the way that you imagine."

Karen nodded. "I know it's a long shot. The coroner already said it was natural causes, so that's a big obstacle. But he could be wrong. Sometimes they are."

"I know." Zachary had experienced that before. Getting the medical examiner to reverse his position was difficult, but it could be done. And Kenzie working in the medical examiner's office gave him a bit of an "in." He'd been able to convince Dr. Wiltshire to change his mind and reopen a file before. "I've succeeded in getting to the truth in other cases. It's just a warning... sometimes things are not as they seem. Or we can figure out what happened, but still not be able to prove it and put the culprit behind bars."

"I'll take that risk."

. . .

"Okay. Why don't I get the details from you? Your father's and brothers' names. Where or who I should start with. Interviewing you, I assume. And you haven't mentioned your mother...?"

"She died five years ago." Karen's lips compressed into a thin line.

"Oh, I'm sorry. So it's just you and your brothers now? And was anyone living in the same household as your father? Or was he alone?"

"Logan is living there. And household staff. We all come and go as we please; we have our own keys. And we were all home for a family dinner the night he died. Mom had always insisted on having a dinner once every month or so, and we've tried to keep that up, even if it's just the five of us." She sighed and looked away from him. "It's a little suspicious that he would die suddenly right after having dinner with us."

"Right after? While you were there?"

"That night. When everyone had gone home. He died... in his sleep, I guess. In his own bed."

Zachary nodded. He wrote down Karen's name and Logan's, trying to keep his printing tidy enough that he would be able to read it later, but not take so long that she grew impatient with him.

"So there is you, and Logan; tell me something about each of you. And your birth order."

Karen sat back, her posture relaxing. This was more familiar ground. She had talked about herself and her brothers many times before.

"Alex is the oldest, then Eddie, then me, and Logan is the baby."

"Which is why he is the only one still at home."

"He wasn't. He moved out when he went to college. But... things didn't work out. He ended up dropping out and going back home again. If it had been me..." Karen trailed off, thinking about it. "I would have found a job so I could afford my own apartment instead of going back there. I think it was a bad choice."

"What is Logan like?"

"Well, he's the baby of the family, so a little bit spoiled. Actually, maybe a lot spoiled by my mom, but not by Dad. Unless it was because Mom insisted on something. You know, if she told him he had to let Logan do something. But he would only do it grudgingly, under protest. Loud protests, so that everyone knew it was not his idea."

"Was he verbally abusive?"

"I suppose. We never really thought about it that way. Or I didn't, anyway. I just thought of it as Dad being right, because he was always right. If he got after me for something... then I knew that I was in the wrong, because there was no way *he* was. Now that I'm older, I have more perspective, I guess... yes. He was."

"Was there physical abuse as well?"

"No, I don't think so. I mean... he would grab one of the boys and force them to do what he wanted them to. But that's just part of parenting. I don't remember him ever causing any kind of injuries. Not that I knew about. I don't remember any hitting or anything that might have done permanent damage. Just... being rough and forceful."

"Was there any other reason that Logan was spoiled, other than being the youngest in the family?"

"What do you mean?"

"Was he sick a lot? Your mom had a hard time getting pregnant again and knew he would be the last baby? He looked more like her side of the family?"

"Oh." Karen was nodding, thinking about it but already sure of her answer. "Yeah... I guess it was a hard birth, and he was born early. He had learning disabilities. I remember he was in speech therapy before he was five. He was awkward physically, just the kind of kid that gets bullied at school for being different. A dweeb or a baby. So there were a lot of reasons for Mom to want to protect him and make things easier on him."

"Right." Zachary nodded, reflecting on his own learning disabilities and behavioral problems when he had been in school. His mother had not been the nurturing type and he had not gotten therapy in the earlier years that might have set him on the right course. And when the family had dissolved and he had landed in foster care, group homes, and institutions, there had been no one to spoil or protect him. He'd already been identified as a bad kid, and the foster parents and other adults responsible for his care or education had not gone easy on him.

"I guess I didn't understand that as a kid," Karen said with an embarrassed smile, "I never understood why he got out of responsibilities and was allowed to get away with stuff that I never would have. And why he got all of the attention and help when I was told to work harder."

"Even if she had explained, you probably would have been too young to understand." Zachary hoped this would let her off the hook as far as her guilt toward her brother went. "And they were probably of the school of thought that he should look and act like everyone else as much as possible so you didn't see all of the differences."

"Maybe. I expect more of myself now, but I still catch myself thinking of him as a spoiled brat. That he just needs to quit messing around and work harder, like I was told to."

"What was he going to college for?"

"I don't think he had decided. Just some kind of general upgrading to start with. But he couldn't handle it. I should be more sympathetic about it than I am."

"And then there are... Alex and Eddie," Zachary prompted.

"Right. Alex and Eddie." Karen closed her eyes for a moment, gathering her thoughts. "Alex is the eldest, always the perfect one. The good son who got straight A's and followed all of the rules and did what was expected of him without question. He was the one who got all of the attention and praise from Dad... but I'm starting to wonder if he was treated differently in private. If things were said that none of us the rest of us knew about."

Zachary nodded.

Karen went on, "Eddie was a wild card. He was always a bit of a rebel. Always trying to get away with things." She looked up at Zachary, her blue eyes wide with worry. "I don't see how it could be any of us. I know it must have been, but it just doesn't make any sense. I can't see any of my brothers doing anything to hurt Dad.

Even if they were just trying to make him sick and not kill him. I can't wrap my mind around it."

———

They Sought Vengeance, Book #14 of the *Zachary Goldman Mysteries* series by P.D. Workman can be purchased at pdworkman.com

ABOUT THE AUTHOR

P.D. Workman is a USA Today Bestselling author, winner of several awards from Library Services for Youth in Custody and the InD'tale Magazine's Crowned Heart award, and has published over 90 mystery/suspense/thriller and young adult books, including stand alones and these series: Auntie Clem's Bakery cozy mysteries, Reg Rawlins Psychic Investigator paranormal mysteries, Zachary Goldman Mysteries (PI), Kenzie Kirsch Medical Thrillers, Parks Pat Mysteries (police procedural), and YA series: Tamara's Teardrops, Between the Cracks, and Breaking the Pattern.

Workman loves writing about the underdog, who the reader may love or hate. She has been praised for her realistic details, deep characterization, and sensitive handling of the serious social issues that appear in all of her stories, from light cozy mysteries through to darker, grittier young adult and mystery/suspense books.

P. D. Workman, does not shy from probing the deep psychological scars of childhood trauma, mental illness, and addiction. Also characteristic of this author, these extremely sensitive issues are explored with extensive empathy, described with incredible clarity, and portrayed with profound insight.

— —KIM, GOODREADS REVIEWER

Some of Workman's titles have been translated into Spanish, French, Portuguese, German, and Italian.

Workman began writing at an early age and is a prolific reader as well as writer. She is also passionate about teaching and learning, expresses her creativity through art and cooking, and loves exploring the Calgary parks and green spaces where the Parks Pat Mysteries are set. She was a legal assistant for many years and has done extensive charitable work.

Workman was born and raised in Alberta, Canada, and is married with one adult son.

———

Please visit P.D. Workman at pdworkman.com to see what else she is working on, to join her mailing list, and to link to her social networks.

———

If you enjoyed this book, please take the time to recommend it to other purchasers with a review or star rating and share it with your friends!

- tiktok.com/@pdworkmanauthor
- facebook.com/pdworkmanauthor
- twitter.com/pdworkmanauthor
- instagram.com/pdworkmanauthor
- amazon.com/author/pdworkman
- bookbub.com/authors/p-d-workman
- goodreads.com/pdworkman
- linkedin.com/in/pdworkman
- pinterest.com/pdworkmanauthor
- youtube.com/pdworkman

Find P.D. Workman's books at

PDWORKMAN.COM

Scan the QR code below